Doris Grumbach is one of this country's most distinguished novelists and critics. Her novels include *Chamber Music*, *The Missing Person*, *The Ladies*, and *The Magician's Girl*, all of which are soon to be available in Norton paperback editions, as is her memoir *Coming into the End Zone.* She was previously the literary editor of *The New Republic* and has been a regular book reviewer for National Public Radio. She lives in Sargentville, Maine.

The Missing Person

By Doris Grumbach
in Norton Paperback

Chamber Music
Coming into the End Zone
The Missing Person

The Missing Person

Doris Grumbach

W. W. Norton & Company
New York • London

Printed in the United States of America

First published as a Norton paperback 1993

Library of Congress Cataloging-in-Publication Data
Grumbach, Doris.
The missing person / Doris Grumbach.
p. cm.
ISBN 0-393-30946-0 (pbk.)
I. Title.
PS3557.R83M5 1993 813'.54—dc20 92-39865
CIP

ISBN 0-393-30946-0

W. W. Norton & Company, Inc.
500 Fifth Avenue, New York, N.Y. 10110
W. W. Norton & Company Ltd
10 Coptic Street, London WC1A 1PU

1 2 3 4 5 6 7 8 9 0

For Elizabeth Cale
who liked Franny Fuller from the first

NOTE: This novel is a portrait, not of a single life but of many lives melded into one, typical of the women America often glorifies and elevates, and then leaves suspended in their lonely and destructive fame.

1

The Columnist

For one small chapter in the twentieth-century American epic, Mary Maguire, movie gossip columnist for the *Los Angeles Star,* served as bard and meistersinger, recorder, reporter, and, on occasion, inventor. Out of the tattle of her daily reporting Stars were born, raised, celebrated—and burned out. She was the Good Fairy who followed Franny Fuller happily into her extraordinary stardom; she was the Fury who hovered around Willis Lord's silent head as he went down into cinematic oblivion. In the chronicles of movie time hers was to be the endurance record, the level, continuing line against which meteoric rises and catastrophic descents were graphed. She outlasted them all while she wrote their histories. She was moviedom's Milton, Hollywood's Homer.

What she wrote about Franny Fuller expanded into the poetry of a million dreams and fantasies. Her own life was more prosaic. An Irish-American virgin at the age of thirty, she took care of her senile father until he died, and then her cancer-ridden mother until her death. The priest put it gracefully: "She has gone to God," he said.

Two days after the requiem mass Mary Maguire took the streetcar into Los Angeles where her uncle Sam, still hale after thirty years of riotous Southern California living, was managing editor of a newspaper. Sam Maguire said he was very sorry about the death of her mother. He explained that, regrettably, he had not been able to get to his sister-in-law's funeral because a big story, about an arsonist who had been caught setting fire to the draperies in a department store, had broken the day before. He asked if it seemed, well, *odd* to Mary not to have anyone to take care of. "You must be feeling at loose ends. Is there anything I can do for you?"

Mary was prepared for this stock question. "Yes," she said. She *was* at loose ends, she needed and wanted a job, something to do, and she knew what it was she wanted to do. She had lived in Hollywood all her life, she loved the crazy old place and everyone and everything in it. She had read *Screen Romances* and *Silver Screen* and *Photoplay* since she was a girl. From them she had learned the life histories of every Star and Starlet, vamp and Latin Lover, what picture had been made at which studio, how much it had cost to produce, how it had done at the box office, and who was in danger of being dropped by the Studio because of what erotic adventure or artistic failure.

Her idea was to report for her uncle's paper the Doings, as she said, of the Stars and the Studios, of the Film Folk. She told him she knew she could do it. The traditional, excited rhythms of movie gossip were firmly established in her head. All she needed to do was move about a little, visit the studios on occasion, leave her telephone number at publicity offices, get to know the key people: publicity agents, press representatives, that sort of thing.

It so happened that Sam's editor had been talking to him about pepping up the paper a bit, bridging the short distance between Los Angeles and the suburb of the Stars. Mary's suggestion appealed to Sam. He liked the idea of helping his niece and his newspaper in one stroke. He told her he would talk it over with the chief. Two days later he called her to say the job was hers: "Send us a thousand words every other day, and twelve hundred for the Sunday paper. And Mary, keep the items short and sweet."

Mary Maguire went to work, bringing to her column, which Sam had named "The Doings of the Stars," the same dedicated service she had once devoted to caring for her parents. Her mornings were spent on her "rounds," as she called them, she lunched on the expense accounts of agents and publicity people anxious for her attention to their clients, and in the afternoons she read her mail, usually full of letters sent to her by angry bit players and employees of Paramount Pictures, Famous Players, First National, and the other studios who knew some "dirt" about a Star or the head of a studio, perhaps both together in one "item." Many of the letters were anonymous, so Mary was able to quote freely from them while denying any personal knowledge of the subject herself. In the late afternoons she wrote her column.

Never has a prose style been more perfectly suited to its subject. It combined profuse, amazed, exclamatory words and phrases with delicate suggestions of firm morality. Her religion contributed to the tone of her prose. She began her day by walking the few blocks from her house to Saint Mary's Church where she read her missal in the pew before the Mass began, and for a short time afterward. The stern, italicized style of instructions and prayers in the missal infected the sentences she wrote in the afternoon. The missal's admonitory tone, forgiving and compassionate yet subtly reproachful, was audible in her short paragraphs about the wrongdoings and missteps of the Czars of the studios and their Stars. Occupied in early morning with the parables of Eve, the Virgin Mary, Mary Magdalen, and Saint Therese of Lisieux, her subjects were, not surprisingly, usually women.

While Mary Maguire celebrated the success of great stars, like the glamorous and mysterious Delphine Lacy, she much preferred to write about unhappy women, like Juanita Hansen who drank and was photographed in Tijuana sitting on the lap of a young Negro jazz drummer, staring at herself in his drugged eyes. Mary was fond of writing about leading men who took drugs, caught by the enterprising camera of a night-court reporter in a police station "on their way down," as she put it. She relished the distressing sagas of once-beautiful and famous women now grown sick and miserable, or fat and flabby, and shiny-haired, sloe-eyed men who declined, under the pressures of success and money, into corpulence and delirium tremens. Her regrets were honest, but she never failed to encompass them with full historical detail, about when the declining Stars had lovely figures, fine homes in Beverly Hills and Malibu, and stalwart, devoted husbands, before, as she wrote, "the glow had dimmed," and before they had been used cruelly by mercenary admirers.

Her column was successful. She followed the fortunes of the Great with somewhat insincere pity and avidity, telling what became of the Fallen Stars, how they had lost everything, or entered a convent or a shelter operated by the Salvation Army, a drying-out place near Palm Springs or a "haven" for the mentally collapsed. Eminence interested her far less than decadence; she understood that her readers felt an obscure, understandable pleasure reading about degradation but resented, in a perfectly human way, too long a tenure by the Famous on the pinnacles of success.

Mary Maguire, and then her readers, reserved their Christian compassion for the Stars who had declined into drink, drugs, divorce. These endings had their commercial value. They represented the last drop of pleasure the fans got from the Star who had nothing left, no looks, no talent, nothing but notoriety. It might happen that she would be picked up for shoplifting a silk scarf from a Sunset Boulevard department store. The studio make-up man came out fast and fixed her face before she was booked and photographed. She looked very good at the hearing, better than she had in years. So the studio would find a small part for her in a new Rex Ingram film, and those who belonged to the next generation of avid moviegoers remembered her name from the shoplifting story in the newspaper and paid admission to see what the old doll looked like *now* on the screen.

After several years of this success (Sam saw to it that her column was syndicated in fifty-six papers) Mary Maguire began to be regarded as the leading purveyor of Hollywood news and gossip. In 1927 the *Reader's Digest* reprinted for its millions of readers her heartrending account of the funeral of a Great Leading Man who had died tragically young. Her digested story came upon the heels of a piece in which she had rued the preeminence at the box office of a canine hero with the resonant name of Rin Tin Tin. She criticized the plots of dog stories, the well-loved tales in which virtue was embodied in a member of the animal kingdom and vice in black-haired, black-hatted, darting-eyed canine haters.

So "at the peak of his great career," when the Sheik died, Mary Maguire was ready to laud *human* bereavement on a generous scale. She went to New York for the funeral of the thirty-one-year-old, soft-eyed hero, the plastic-haired, hypnotic lover who had obsessed the daydreams of millions of American women: young girls, wives, grandmothers. Her newspaper story rehearsed for her mesmerized readers a vision of passion made melodramatically apparent in every gesture of this seductive man, a vision which enslaved women to his image.

She reported that thousands lined both sides of Broadway in New York City for forty blocks from the funeral home where their beloved Star lay in state in a satin-lined mahogany casket. When the procession, the hearse, twelve cars filled with floral tributes, and an interminable line of black Packards filled with bereaved Hollywood greats, began its slow journey toward the Brooklyn Bridge, women screamed and cried and tore their clothes, throwing pieces of blouse and skirt at the passing cortege. Her story was intended for her column, but newspapers all over the country transferred it to the front page, with Mary Maguire's byline prominently displayed.

Early yesterday morning I watched as ten thousand women pushed their way into the Broadway Funeral

Chapel to view the remains. At least seven persons fainted and were taken away in ambulances. I saw one who fell to the floor and others stumbled over her to get to the casket.

The crowds outside were colossal. I was standing near the Rialto Theater when the coffin passed. Women on the sidewalk in front of me shoved toward the street. They were moved back behind the barriers by lines of New York's Finest. The crush was so great that the plateglass windows of the haberdasher's store near me were shattered as women fell in against them. I was lucky not to be cut by the flying glass. I saw a woman whose tears were red from a cut on her head and another holding her glove over a gash on her arm to stop the blood.

But they all stayed on to see the end of the procession, crying and screaming, "Rudi! Rudi!" I mourned with them for the Great Lover who died so young. Only the good, as they say . . .

It was a year of other American greats. The word, in its ugly plural, was heard everywhere. Stories about the greats of the Silver Screen—silently comic, mutely glamorous—were accompanied by reports of a great swimmer, a woman of power and determination, who fought the frigid waters of the English Channel for fourteen hours and thirty-one minutes to engrave her name and achievement on the imaginations of athletic teen-aged girls. An aviator called Lucky Lindy, after the folk song that celebrated his feat, traveled across a hostile ocean from one hemisphere to another, a shaggy-haired Lone Eagle (as Mary Maguire called him, thus bestowing upon him an enduring epithet) in a one-engine plane, America's Great Flying Hero.

Mary Maguire's importance to the world of the movies was established when, despite an inexplicable silence in the Hollywood press about the developing phenomenon of talking pictures, she wrote a single sentence at the end of one of her 1927 columns: *"Would not surprise this reporter one bit if Warner's Vitaphone or Fox's Movietone—SOUND coming out of long-silent lips and music from instruments—will make a real difference at the box office next year."*

She was there to record the revolution: a black-faced Jewish actor whose song could be heard, followed by a line of history-making speech: "Wait a minute. You ain't heard nothin' yet, folks. Listen to this."

The talkies provided Mary Maguire with a new, rich theme: the loss of Greatness through inadequate vocal cords of silent Stars. She celebrated the fallen idol, Willis Lord, who had been struck down from his screen heights by a high-pitched, almost effeminate voice. Made a sad laughingstock of in the first scene of his first talking picture, his tense, castrato tones accompanied his passionate glances and wide, fevered gestures. Embarrassed laughter was filling balconies and boxes of Roxies and Rivolis in every city in the United States, Mary Maguire reported. No longer could he hide behind the italics of amorous titles. The squawks of unperfected sound machinery and his own frightened voice had betrayed him, and rendered the Great Favorite foolish. His career was ended, his contract (said to be the largest in Culver City) threatened: *"Have heard nasty rumors that Joe Pinsky and the other lions at MGM are trying to buy back the Lord's contract which still has three years to run. But the Great Lover refuses to be silenced,"* wrote Mary Maguire. *"Washed up . . . ?"*

The moguls had their ways. Lord's strong, evocative name was dropped from publicity announcements of new pictures, the face known to millions as the apogee of the Latin Lover's—the tight, black mustache, the triangular black brows, the patent-leather hair parted perfectly in the middle of the high white forehead, the glowing, ardent eyes, and the sudden, bewitching smile—vanished from the adulatory pages of *Modern Screen.*

"Where has WL gone?" asked Mary Maguire in a question that could only be called rhetorical. *"No one sees him in his old*

haunts. Was not at the jam-packed Pickford birthday party. Can it be he is taking voice lessons from the impeccable Coleman?" No one knew. In one cruel sonic stroke, the brilliant Star had disappeared into silent outer darkness and was seen no more.

"Sad," wrote Mary Maguire.

But, it must be said, Mary Maguire could, on occasion, report on success. Delphine Lacy: in her vast hunger for gossip Mary Maguire was single-handedly responsible for the creation of her legend. She became, under the columnist's skilled hand, an introspective solitary, the lover of classical music played on her mammoth Capehart phonograph in the deep privacy of her windowless tower study. A close reader of Schopenhauer and Freud, living alone in her house that resembled a fortress rather than a California mansion, a building decorated by four towers with crenelated tops, an escarpment running from the elevated first floor almost to the high gates: so Mary Maguire described her and her place. The French star became a symbol of all Hollywood was not: secret affections, existing only in rumor, the possessor of an inner life rich in European culture, it was said, the inhospitable owner of a vast and protected estate, three Great Danes that roamed the lawns without her, and a 265-horsepower Duesenberg in which only the chauffeur was even seen. She became the perfect movie paradox: famous yet private, beautiful and single, celebrated but never seen in public. It was let out from studio publicity sources that her heart had been broken by the cinematic failure of her longtime costar Willis Lord, but no one ever caught a glimpse of them together.

The heated rumors of their affair slowly died away; her legend grew and prospered.

And what of Mary Maguire herself? Did the sad stories she wrote for her millions of readers affect her? She had to acknowledge, in the few moments before and after daily mass she allowed for introspection, that she had become hardened to human misery, that her youthful mercy, nurtured by the daily sight of her declining parents, had given way before avalanches of glittering star-histories. She cared, not for personal fates but for sticks of copy.

Was she lonely in her emotional sclerosis? If she was she did not notice it, for her name, her byline everywhere, made it easier to be a single woman in the capital of couples. She moved through dinner-dances, supper parties, lavish lunches and dinners, cocktail parties—broad, full-bosomed, aging, her tightly curled still-red hair perfectly matched to her red lips—without any companion except her knowledge of Who She Was and the instant recognition granted her by the people whose careers she chronicled.

The prolific celebrator of failure began to "do" books, full-length biographies. She was especially skillful when she was able to inject inspiration into her "lives." The down-and-out Star who has lost her looks and her way gets religion, or AA, or Faith in Herself. Fans appreciated this kind of glamorous, elevated inspiration. They were lifted up by the vision of how far the Star could fall. It confirmed their belief that salvation is possible only by means of simple, self-administered spiritual strength. Because they themselves had some connection, no matter how tenuous and sentimental, with a church, they enjoyed the spectacle of the Great One finding the Path, ever since the time that Mary Pickford, full of dimples, wrote a book urging her huge following to Try God.

Mary Maguire's most successful book was *The Fabulous Franny Fuller* (As Told to Mary Maguire), written at the height of the Star's career. When she could be persuaded to sit down for any period of time and talk, Franny Fuller had told Mary Maguire something of her life story. Mary took her monologues down in shorthand, about her childhood and adolescence, about her first marriage to Dempsey Butts, the football player. Franny told why she had let the photographer take that famous picture of her naked to the waist, posed as the figurehead of a yacht, the one that was made into postcards the year before she signed her first contract. She told about Eddie Puritan, who "found" and named her, about her great friend and stand-in, Dolores Jenkins. She spoke (reluctantly) of Arnold Franklin, the poet she had married after her divorce from Butts. In passing, as if it was no real part of her existence, she mentioned her habit of disappearing, her "escapes," as she called them.

Mary Maguire took Franny's flat details and made them exciting. She showed Franny sitting on the fifty-yard line Sunday after Sunday watching Demp play, even attending afternoon practice sessions at his training camp. But Mary Maguire was too intelligent not to guess the truth (which she wisely suppressed), that football was a complete mystery to Franny Fuller, as much a mystery to her as were Iowa-born Demp and his family. Franny never understood why they all cared so much about the game and about each other. She had sat in the stadium worrying about her hair tangling in the wind, about the cold, about chilblains, and her good clothing being ruined on rough, dirty seats.

Mary Maguire understood, indeed knew, more than she wrote. She realized (but never put in the book) that Franny Fuller had no idea why she was there, or who she *was* as she sat in the stadium with the other players' wives, or after the game in the restaurant, with all the Buttses who came from Iowa for a game every year, pounding each others' shoulders and buttocks and asking her, "Wasn't he *great?*"

Franny told Mary Maguire that the better everyone seemed to feel when they were together at summer training camp or on those Sunday evenings after games in the fall, the worse she felt, as if maybe the sun had gotten to her. While they all talked at once to each other, Franny was silent, remembering things like how Jean Harlow had died from sun-poisoning. She was afraid to watch games played outdoors. But all Mary Maguire wrote was about how Franny went to the games, watched Dempsey quarterback his team, sat with the other wives, and cheered.

Franny told her about the nun, the Parish Visitor, who came to the door the evening Franny took too many sleeping pills. As Mary put it for Franny, "That holy woman saved my life." Franny mentioned Ira Rorie the Negro, and his Cadillac. But Mary didn't go on to tell about how Franny stayed with him for more than a week. She decided Franny's fans weren't ready for that kind of fact. Premium Studios, which had asked to have a last look at Mary's manuscript in return for providing all the still shots for illustrations that she wanted, would have hated it. Mary explained to Franny that to men she was a princess: pure, in a spiritual way. In the book Mary made Ira Rorie out to be Franny's chauffeur. *If he ever sees that book,* Franny thought, *it will give him a laugh.*

At the end of the biography, Mary Maguire wrote about what acting in the movies meant to Franny Fuller. Nothing of what she wrote came from the interviews. Franny could never have voiced those elevated sentiments. She didn't know they existed. Mary wrote that Franny prepared herself for weeks for her parts. She went to the library, her book reported, to look up details about the character she was preparing to play. She read four historical books before she played Madame Pompadour in that musical. She studied up on the twenties when she was going to play the girlfriend of one of Al Capone's mob.

In the book Mary Maguire attributed this cerebral approach to Franny's having married a poet like Arnold Franklin. *That's a joke,* Franny thought when she read it. *Arnie did that kind of thing, not me.* Franny once told Keith, Arnie's agent, that Arnie couldn't move his bowels without reading about it first and then checking in another book to be sure he was doing it right.

Mary Maguire managed to mythologize almost everything there was to tell about Franny Fuller. She wrote that Franny believed she was an actress, that she was *acting* in her pictures. *But she is wrong,* Franny thought. That shadow was really Franny Fuller up there, or more accurately, Fanny Marker, finally getting a chance to show herself, much larger than reality would permit, on the screen, the shadow she'd been since she was fourteen, the dumb, beautiful, desirable blonde elevated into flat immortality on celluloid, with blue ponds for eyes and a pool of blood for a mouth. The Real Thing, not an actress, a silhouette named Fanny Marker, now changed to Franny Fuller.

The terrible thing was (and only Fanny Marker knew this at first) was that it was all there was, *all* of her. Even bringing to bear the ambitious zeal of a conquistador's search for gold, nothing more of her could be discovered. Her admirers, indeed her lovers and husbands, should have known. But they were all deluded by the glow of her face into believing that behind it was a person. It was only a surface, a front, a face as empty of structure and furnishing as the back side of a movie set. Everyone thought that under that face painted on by make-up artists, those twin peaks pushed out toward the customer in the theater and legs photographed from under the floor level to make them look eight feet long, there was a real woman. But all there was (and Franny Fuller knew it too well) was a surface created by Cinemascope, a filmed penumbra shot flat out of a projector onto a mammoth and hospitable screen.

Fanny Marker looked very much like all the girls Hollywood attracted, the ones who paraded in beauty contests in their home states, high-kicked in chorus lines in Broadway musicals, danced with customers in the big, dimly lit bars and dance halls in every large city in the country. Franny recognized herself as one of them. She suspected they were all related, sisters in passivity, girls who could never resolve anything for themselves because they had never been told it was possible. They differed from men who were able to think things up for themselves and then make them work. The world paid attention when men chose to be something, strove toward a goal they had set. Franny believed that all women were like her, waiting for the Great Something they had dreamed about all their lives to happen to them, to be done to them, to arrive.

True to her credo, events came to Franny as she waited for them, her drifting, dazed self biding its time. She had known this self since her girlhood. But everyone kept telling her she really was Someone because she looked the way she did. There were times when she was able to forget her secret knowledge that there was no direction to her days, no meaning to her beautiful face, that in the long catalogue of human beings she was a missing person.

Realizing this, when no one else did, neither Demp nor Arnie nor Dolores nor even Mary Maguire, Franny felt black despair spread through her, like night coming down through Coldwater Canyon. She was filled with the stifling fear that someone would find out about her, and realize her absence. There was no Franny Fuller, no FF as the columnists and the advertisements called her, making her seem important, as if people could recognize her by her initials alone. When she was fourteen she had dreamed about having just one name, like Garbo: Laverne or Melinda. But the Studio thought it had a great thing going when Mary Maguire in her column first called her FF. *Well, at least,* Franny thought, *it's better than Fanny Marker.*

2

The Movie Actress

Fanny Marker grew up in Utica where she was born. Most of her girlhood was spent dreaming. The dream started when she understood that she was beautiful . She was born that way, had been beautiful, her mother said, from the moment she laid eyes on her in the hospital. Once, on request, she gave *Photoplay* a baby picture of herself. (It has been reprinted many times since.) Sitting on a gilt throne in front of a fake palm tree, Fanny is pressing a pudgy finger into a fat cheek. The baby-faced little girl smiles charmingly. Her other hand is playing with a golden ringlet that has escaped the pile on her head.

Fanny didn't remember the day the picture was taken. But she remembered Jerryboy who was living with her mother years later. He would take his finger with its black, squared-off nail and push it hard into her cheek. It hurt, but he would laugh and say, "You won't get far with that one dimple."

Fanny moved through her childhood in a daze of visions of beauty. She worked at the other cheek with a sharpened pencil point until it cut the skin, but another dimple never developed. Later she learned from the beauty-hints column in *Silver Screen* to draw on a black beauty spot there. Perc Westmore said it was good, the magazine reported. It worked fine, drawing attention to the one she already had, making it more interesting. But in Jerryboy's time, when Fanny was fourteen, her beauty began to be more than a baby picture on the dresser. Her mother looked at her hard, sometimes, when Jerryboy fooled around with her and poked at her like that. It was fear, not pleasure, that Jerryboy's look made her feel.

She remembered his feet. He was a sheet-metal worker at the time he lived with them. He wore a hard silver hat and huge heavy gloves and a stiff, sweaty jacket to work. After he got home he took off his high boots and left them in the front room of their flat. Fanny could smell them when she passed them going to the john; they smelled like old vomit. His socks were stiff and black on the bottom. He'd leave them hanging off the tops of his boots and walk away, and then she saw his feet, always dirty. But the worse thing was, he had little pads of black hair on his toes, and the first and second toes on each foot were grown together with a yellow skin between them. She was terrified of those feet, and of him. He walked around the apartment barefoot, following her mother into the bedroom, leaving his boots there near Fanny's daybed in the front room, like a movie stand-in for him.

The way he behaved toward her convinced Fanny she was what he kept telling her she was—beautiful. She could never find anything to say to him when he called her that. Even then, she realized, she never knew what she was going to say until she said it—so it was hard for her to begin. Jerryboy talked mostly to her mother, about the men at work and his union. Her mother would tell him about the girls at the beauty parlor and the customers they "worked on."

Jerryboy and her mother went out a lot together nights after work. Fanny would then have the flat to herself. She would lie on their bed with her knees pulled up to her chin, her arms clasping her legs, and stare, dreaming, at the ceiling. She would think about the Stars on the Silver Screen, about plucking her eyebrows and her widow's peak and whitening her hair like Harlow. In her daze she put on her mother's stockings with spider clocks and high heels like Carole Lombard wore and walked around like Joan

Crawford, her hips swaying, into the lights of the Premiere, curvaceously (a word she had learned from the gossip columns) leaning toward a curly-haired young man on one side of her, and a slick-haired older man on the other. Both would gaze fondly down at her (they were both very, very tall) as they advanced through the cheering crowd into the theater. But she would smile brightly into a camera hidden in a velvet curtain.

The fantasy would spread. She saw herself, not Carole, not Joan, but *her* face, the side with the dimple, hers, Fanny Marker's. Then she would seem to cry out, "No, not that name, for Christ's sake! Laverne Lucienne! Melinda Courtney!" A beautiful name was what she was searching for, to go with the beautiful face she had and the Star she was going to be.

The dream went on and on. She forgot her mother, the beauty operator who gave marcels, shampoos, and perms, encased in her all-in-one, her large bosom flattened under a white uniform with short, pink-cuffed sleeves. Gone was Jerryboy at night or the somebody before him but just like him: "My roommates," her mother called them. No webbed feet in the bedroom, no groans and grunts, no sounds like the bed straining and giving way, no more mysterious scuffling noises.

Fanny would walk, bathed in light that came down in pointed beams from the sky. The soft, black night would be shot through with those lights and where they came together, like in geometry, there she'd be, Melinda Lucienne, the vamp of all the Jerryboys' dreams. But way out of reach, untouchable, her dimple shining and shadowy like a crater on the moon. Silver, glowing: "Look at her up there!" the Jerryboys would scream.

She lived in her daze most of the time she did not have to go to school. It made her mother angry. Her mother was a big woman, with a face that had once been pretty but was now round and somewhat flat. She looked friendly. Her eyes creased when she smiled; she had what Perc was to call "laugh lines." But Fanny knew they meant nothing. Her mother's face changed fast, and then she looked as though she were sizing Fanny up and would never come to any good opinion of her. She seemed always to be judging her and disliking what she saw. Fanny never noticed her using that look with Jerryboy or the other men she knew. But with Fanny it was always there. Jerryboy would say, "Leave the kid be." Then her mother would look away from Fanny, and the laugh lines would appear again as she looked at Jerryboy. She'd throw her head back so her neck would seem thinner. But when she looked back at Fanny she'd be estimating again, like when the butcher held up a piece of lamb for her to see over the glass counter. She gave Fanny the same look.

Fanny had been named for her. Her father, whoever he was, left before she was born, so she was given her mother's whole name, like a boy gets with junior tacked on to his father's whole name. She became Fanny Marker, the daughter of Fanny Marker the mother. Mary Maguire liked this fact and put it into her book. She asked Franny if she missed not having a father. Franny said she didn't: "Hell, who is a father? Someone like Jerryboy but older, maybe?"

Franny told Mary Maguire that her mother always reminded her that she was both mother and father to her. Once, in the year before Fanny left home, her mother told her that again: "I am your mother and your father and you'd better not forget it." Fanny laughed and said, "Sure, Pop," and her mother, her eyes cold with fury, had slapped her face hard.

"Call me Daddy, Bubbles," Jerryboy said to her once, and laughed.

"Are you a daddy, Jerryboy?"

"Somebody's, I'll bet," her mother said in her low man's voice, almost like a growl.

"You can be damn sure," he said and laughed again.

Jerryboy didn't like two Fannys in one flat, he said, so he

called her Bubbles after a stripper he once knew. She hated the name, she hated him.

Arnie once told Franny he could remember every place he had ever lived growing up in Brooklyn, the beach at Far Rockaway he went to in the summer, even all the movie theaters he had gone to with his sister Saturday afternoons before the prices changed. He said that growing up had only one thing wrong with it. It had a way of dimming all those good memories, weakening all the happy rituals of going away and coming back and moving, all the relationships to places and neighborhoods of one's childhood.

Fanny could not remember one of the places she had lived in. They were all the same. She always had to sleep in the front room that had some kind of orangey or green wallpaper or flowers or something, and rotogravure photos of the Grand Canyon or New York at sunset thumbtacked up over the chesterfield. Once she had slept in the hall when the front room was too small for a daybed. For her, summers were no different from any other season, only hotter. But she did remember the men who had lived with them, a man named Fry who her mother called Frenchy, and someone called Benjamin something or other who her mother called Benjyboy. She seemed to like that kind of nickname, as though she were a mother to them all. She was older than most of them. After a while they'd leave, like sons do when they grow up. One she threw out when she heard the cops were after him for something he'd done in Syracuse.

But Jerryboy. He was the one Fanny remembered best. He picked on her whenever her mother stopped doing it, especially when she was daydreaming and not answering him. While she dreamed, she sucked on the ends of her hair. Jerryboy would sweep his hand across Fanny's face and pull the hair out of her mouth.

"Stop that, damn it."

She would look at him and say nothing.

"Why do you do that, for chrissake?"

"Do what?" She moved away, thinking he was going to hit her, not knowing she was doing it.

"Eating your hair like that."

"Oh that. I dunno. Do I do that?"

Then he'd laugh and suddenly come toward her and poke at her cheek with his thick black nail. Her mother was changing her uniform in the bedroom and putting on her pink wrapper, sighing as she unhooked her all-in-one. As she performed this ritual she had a habit of singing in a low monotone, especially when she was annoyed or angry, the song that was her favorite: *"It cost me a lot, but there's one thing I've got / It's my ma-a-an."* Fanny could hear her in the bedroom singing it aloud to herself, and sometimes, with a stagy smile and her hands holding her breasts, she'd sing the lines to Jerryboy.

She looked out the door, the weighing look on her unsmiling fat face. Jerryboy stopped laughing and went into the kitchen for a beer. Fanny returned to her dreams. It was Mary Maguire who wrote about it as Frances Fuller's "Grimm childhood."

Until Fanny was fourteen she didn't think too much about how bad it was. Utica really wasn't there for her, or school for that matter. When Mary Maguire asked her, she couldn't remember the names of the schools she had gone to, or the addresses of the flats they had lived in. They were just a series of places to lie down in and dream. She lived there, reading movie magazines and thinking about her face, and about the other beautiful people and the Great Things that had happened to them. She believed that these things would happen to her. She waited, her eyes shut against countless wallpaper patterns, curling linoleums, and the sounds from her mother's bedroom, for the events of her dreams to occur: *A sunburned jewboy in white flannels and saddle shoes comes into Schwab's Drugstore at Hollywood and Vine. She is there on a stool sipping iced tea. He looks at her and his black eyes widen and he comes over and stands, staring down at her as if he can't believe what he sees. Then he says, "Where've you been, beautiful?" In his breast pocket behind his four-pointed navy silk handkerchief is a little case. He takes it out and hands her a card from it. It says,* JEROME ALLAN MARCUS III Vice-President, Star Theatrical Agency. *And then Melinda Lucienne or Laverne Courtney thanks him and smiles her one-dimpled smile, mysteriously, like the sleeping beauty who'd known all the time about the prince coming to wake her. From then on her real life as a Star would begin.*

The day it happened Fanny had come home early, because she skipped school. When her mother left for the beauty parlor Fanny came out of the house with her and then walked around a while on the downtown streets waiting for the movie to open. That's what everyone called it, the movie: actually it was named the RKO Palace. At noon she bought the first ticket sold that day and went in.

She always remembered the movie they were playing that day, because it was the first time she had ever heard actors talk. To her infatuated sense Willis Lord and Catherine Dale were thrilling and beautiful persons, speaking poetry. She wanted to see *Their Marvelous Night* again, she had filtered out all the inexplicable noises that invaded the film and heard nothing but "I Love You" repeated again and again by the ardent hero to the pliant heroine in his arms. But she was afraid to stay later than two fifteen because her mother sometimes left work early.

She felt odd coming out of the theater in daylight. The dark stale air inside had seemed real. Now the outside daylight was a false, staged atmosphere. She walked the two blocks to the trolley stop, thinking how much the sun was like stage lighting. The movie's reality went on unrolling in her head, and she had the eerie feeling that she might meet Willis Lord or Catherine Dale at the stop, rather than the people who usually waited there.

On the trolley she fell into a dream. Enormous figures lived on the screen, breathing down at her in the dark. To her the actors and the characters were one; their screen love had united them in her mind. She imagined lovely rooms in which they must live, with windows to the floor and gauze curtains blowing in from a wind from the Sound or the sea. Or maybe they had an apartment on the top floor of a building in New York overlooking the Park, with a penthouse terrace full of potted trees and wicker chaise longues. From it they could see the river when they weren't in each other's arms gazing at the Park. The two actors loved each other gently, tenderly, exclusively, although there was another man who loved Catherine, hopelessly; they were all friends. All of them ate wonderful roasts but you never saw them chew their food. They made a great ceremony of mixing drinks in silver cocktail shakers, but they only sipped them and then put them down and forgot them. *They never did things like wash their hair or pick food out of their back teeth. They never had colds or went to the john or cut their toenails, or puked,* thought Fanny gratefully.

Riding past the drab, red-brick houses of Utica, Fanny conjured up again that *real* world and its people. She never gave much thought to the process of getting into this world because, in her daze, she was already there, even when she was at home eating at the card table with her mother and Jerryboy and listening to them argue about all the food he ate and the water he wasted in the bathroom. Fanny was a continent away from them and from the flat in Utica. She was Vilma Banky's houseguest in a duplex apartment. From a white boudoir she talked on a white telephone to Conrad Nagel.

That afternoon Fanny came home to an empty flat. She stretched out on the double bed in her mother's room and began to shape her eyebrows. She was trying to elevate the arch of the right one to look like Norma Shearer's. Supporting the magnifying mirror between her legs she bent her head toward it, holding the tweezers carefully so as not to pinch her skin.

Then she heard the key in the door and Jerryboy's heavy boots. He closed the door behind him, and she heard him turn the lock. She called out, "Mom'll be home pretty soon," but by then he was at the bedroom door, smiling at her. She began to feel queer.

He sat down on the stool in front of her mother's chest of drawers which was draped with an organdy skirt so it would look like a dressing table, and began to unlace his thick boots with his dirty hands, not looking down at all but smiling steadily at her as he did it.

"Bubbles," he said, "whatcha doin' home?"

"Nothing," she said, "nothing. Why are you?"

"Nothing special. Laid off for a coupla weeks. Goddamn plant shut down. Whatcha expect after the banks conked out last month? Everything's gone straight to hell."

Fanny had not heard about the banks or the layoffs. Her dream world did not allow for the realities of a crashing stock market or unemployment. But she could tell by the way Jerryboy's voice sounded that he wasn't paying much attention to the words he said. He was just talking to fill in until something else happened.

He stared at her, smiling that crazy smile she recognized. She'd seen him look at her mother that way. After dinner he'd fall asleep on the chesterfield for an hour. He'd wake up suddenly, sit up and grin at her mother, and finish the flat beer in his glass. Then they'd go into the bedroom. Fanny could hear the sounds, and then the name-calling, the terrible ones Jerryboy would call her mother and her mother's mumbled answers. There always seemed to be that time after the door closed when they hated each other and would shout the worst words they could think of. Then came the sounds of pain, and then something like Indian wrestling, Fanny thought.

When it was over she would hear Jerryboy slap her mother hard on the buttocks, she thought it sounded like. Her mother would cry out and then laugh. It was like a signal: THE END, like the fade when the movie was over. The next morning, when Fanny went into the bedroom for her clothes which hung in her mother's closet, she smelled sex, the thick, sour-blanket smell. That was all she really knew about it then, the sounds, the smell, the closed door, the names and slaps, and the ugly grin on Jerryboy's face beforehand.

He sat down on the bed, on the side away from her. Then he swung his filthy webbed feet up and crooked his arm under his head. He watched her as she started to pluck at her widow's peak. She had a small one to start with, but she was intent on making it deeper as she read you could do in a beauty-hints column.

He watched her without moving. Then he seemed to get annoyed at what she was doing. He reached over, grabbed her arm, and pulled her into the middle of the bed. Opening his fly he took out his thick red penis and then fastened her other, flaying arm firmly to the bed. He nudged her legs apart with his knee and fell on top of her, so hard that it knocked her breath away. He pushed. There was tearing, like a seam somewhere in her had ripped, and then she felt a hot splash on her thighs. Her eyes seemed to her to be filling with the same blood she was feeling between her legs. She blacked out.

When Fanny next knew anything she looked down and saw she was still bleeding a lot. She felt pain in a place she had not known the exact location of before. She had wondered about it, especially in connection with her mother. But always before she had an idea that the place had been made in her mother by a lot of different men pushing themselves into her until they had worn a way through, like a path beaten in the woods.

So. Violent things like this happened to her mother, and now to her. But it could not possibly be true in the movie world, the real world. She wondered: *After Willis Lord turned off the light and you no longer saw his profile and Delphine Lacy's and there was only the black screen—did the screen turn red with blood, not black? Was the silence pain? Did the cameraman look away in horror?*

Fanny lay there, bleeding. Jerryboy had gone into the bathroom. She could hear water running. She saw she was getting blood all over her mother's sheets, but made no move to get up. She pulled the blanket over her bloody thighs and went to sleep, as she always did when she was frightened. Just before she fell asleep she thought about how long it always took Jerryboy in the bathroom and how her mother hated that about him. She wondered how anyone could stay so long in the bathroom and come out dirty.

Fanny woke to the cracking feel of her mother slapping her face. She saw that judging look. Her mother had the blanket in her hand. Jerryboy was not there. There was no sign of him, no shoes near the door. Just Fanny, lying there in her bloody mess, her mother standing over her, slapping furiously at her face, first one side of it, then the other, like a funny man attacking the straight man in a vaudeville act.

She knew she had to get out of the flat. Her mother's appraising face had turned to stone. When she left for work the next morning without speaking to her daughter, Fanny got dressed, put on a pair of high-heeled shoes from her mother's closet, and took a trolley downtown.

The lobby of the Hotel Mohawk was crowded with salesmen and town girls who usually worked in the glove factory, but it was now closed indefinitely. The girls were all gussied up and looked at the men who were registering, or those reading the papers in square leather chairs around the lobby. Fanny stood near a paper palm tree taller than she was, hoping she looked as though she were waiting for someone she knew. She read the signs that said TODAY LUNCH ROTARY INTERNATIONAL and ELKS GREEN ROOM 12:45 PM. She thought if she stood there reading long enough some guy would say: "Hey, Blondie, can I buy you a drink?" because boys at school always called her that, and it was a common opener she had read about in *Screen Romances*. She would answer: "Why not?" It was illegal to serve drinks to fourteen-year-old girls, but everyone in school said she looked older. After that she would say: "My name's not Blondie. It's Laverne Lucienne."

All the men who came into the Hotel Mohawk, salesmen

for hardware or men's pajamas or farm equipment to the town stores, looked at her. Their shirts were stuck to their backs, their trousers hung low on their hips from sitting in their cars so long. Their luggage bulged with samples, dirty laundry, hair tonic, and bottles of Four Roses.

She waited, into the middle of that long afternoon. The stiff-mouthed, superior-looking cigarette counter woman watched her, and the bellboys looked at her sideways as they passed and repassed her, laughing. Her ankles ached from standing so long in her mother's shoes. But she was afraid to sit down in a leather chair where she felt she had no right to be. The woman at the cigarette counter had a high, teachery voice. She was talking to a salesman who asked for three of those. . . .

"You, Blondie," a man said, pulling his wet shirt away from his large stomach, "come on up and have a drink with me."

She looked at him and swallowed. She said, "Okay," and then she said, because by that time she knew what she was going to say after that, "Don't call me Blondie. My name is Melinda Courtney."

Once she had gone to live in the golden light of Hollywood, Franny remembered the East as dark and cold. The skies were always gray. The air felt as if it were about to snow. Everything back there was, to her, the color of fog and sidewalks. At night the skies were like school-boards, black and hard. There was no bright color back East that she could remember.

On such a gray morning she had left home for good. She could no longer stand her mother's stone silences or the pressure of the two of them alone in the flat. Jerryboy had been put out by her mother a few days after It happened. Fanny pocketed some bills from her mother's drawer, took a bus to Schenectady, and found a job waiting tables. She was given a room in the rear quarters of the hotel. For some time after she left Utica her life was serving blue-plate specials, and men.

She learned about eastern men. All the ones she met were going someplace. They were always planning for the future and making lists of places they had to get to at certain times. For a meal she had to listen to where they were planning to go this summer "with the kids," and the best way to get there: "You take Route Five until you hit Oriskany and then you . . ." Or they told her about where they planned to go when they graduated from someplace or to take courses at some other place. Plans. They were all full of them, and they loved to describe every detail.

Men looked at her and suddenly, it seemed, the plans they'd been telling her about opened up or held off for a minute, as though they were deciding whether or not to include her in them. But most of them were ambitious traveling men. They moved on fast, even faster now that the Depression had reduced their business. They went home to their wives, who were named Betty-Anne or Emmy-Jo, always two first names, one weekend in the month. They were up early in the morning to be first with their goods when the stores opened downtown. They liked to be there when the bank or the post office opened, sat close up for sporting events, and boasted they had the best seats in the the-ay-ter in Albany when it showed plays from New York. It seemed to Fanny that none of these men enjoyed anything very much, but they all had to be the first at it, and in the best location. Everybody was out of breath. Everybody planned, and then ran.

She spent three years working her way down through New York State from one hotel and restaurant and bar to another. Often she spent her nights with hotel customers in their rooms, listening to them talk about themselves before they laid her. They were always full of preliminary talk, mostly about their futures, like the futures in the grain market they told her they sometimes took chances on.

"Wait a sec, Blondie, while I leave a call. Operator, wouldya call me early, say six thirty. I've got to make Buffalo by three." Turning his confidences from the operator to Fanny, he would say: "Always try to get there early in the spring. Opened there and did pretty good. Expect I'll do even better this year. Before you come back, Blondie, could you fill this with a little water in the bathroom?"

She got to know what seemed to her hundreds of such men who ran around one upstate gray city after another, from one appointment to the next, stopping only long enough to invite her to share their dinner, or a drink so she would share their bed later. They were called at six thirty, and then she heard them splashing around the bathroom using all the water in the world like Jerryboy used to do when her mother would scream through the door to turn it off. They came out with a towel around their hips and stuffed their pajamas into their suitcases. "I'm off to Syracuse, Blondie. See you next time through. Be good now, ixnay on the heavy stuff, it'll ruin your looks, and don't take any wooden nickels, ha ha."

Fanny was almost seventeen when Judd Sampson drove her in his convertible down to New York City. It was his Christmas vacation from his last year in college. He, too, was originally from Utica, he told her, when they met in a hotel lobby in Kingston during a heavy snowstorm. They were both waiting, she for someone to ask her upstairs and he to be able to move his car back onto 9W for the trip to New York.

Judd said he was on his way to the City, she said she'd always wanted to see it, he asked if she'd like to drive with him if he ever made it out of Kingston in this snow. She went to her room at the back of the hotel dining room, packed her suitcase, told the man at the desk she was leaving, and, without bothering to collect the twelve dollars the hotel owed her for three days' work, got into Judd's Plymouth. It was the final lap from the city of her birth to the city of her dreams. She never saw Utica again.

After almost six hours on icy roads they arrived in the City. Judd had money. He drove to a hotel near Columbia University. They registered as husband and wife and were given a room so small there was nowhere to sit but on the bed. When the bellboy left their two suitcases on the bottom of the bed, Judd immediately began to unpack, putting his toothbrush in a drinking glass and settling his comb and brush squarely in the middle of the one dresser the room held. Then he lined up all his shirts in the top drawer, hung his ties on the rod of a hanger, and folded his trousers neatly over another. All of this took some time. Fanny lay on the bed, her feet propped on her suitcase, and watched him. She wondered if it was some new kind of fancy delaying action. He seemed frightened of her. Was he putting off turning around and looking at her by doing his housekeeping?

For some reason Fanny felt less exultant than she had expected at finally making it to the City. Then she realized it was because she had already been here so many times in her dreams. There was very little difference now except that it was not quite so fancy and it was very cold.

She felt sorry for Judd Sampson. He was still moving his things from place to place. She said: "Judd, are you cherry?" He turned to look at her, his face red, and said, "Yes, ma'am. Yes, I am."

Ma'am, she thought, *Jesus, I'm seventeen.* But she supposed he could not tell. They went out to supper in a delicatessen on Broadway and then, holding hands, they walked back slowly to the hotel through the snow. Upstairs they warmed up by leaning against the high radiator.

They undressed and got into bed. Judd lay on his side of the bed, very still. Then he started to talk. He told her how afraid he was of women and the black blood they had every month and of getting a dose from them. He said he believed fervently in God and was going to enter the Theological Seminary at Columbia the next fall to study to be a minister, if they would accept him.

They lay far apart. Fanny listened to him describe his sacred plans, his desire to serve God and His people, and to keep clean. He talked on and on: Fanny fell asleep listening to him. She was wakened at one in the morning by the sound of water running into the bathtub. She decided it must be because he had been lying close to her. When he came back to the bed she pretended to be asleep, and then she fell asleep and slept, without dreaming for once, through the night.

Next morning Judd said he had to go for his interview at the seminary. Fanny stayed in bed and watched him as he put on his black suit and white shirt and black tie, as though he were already a seminarian. After he was dressed he packed his suitcase.

"How old are you, Judd?" she asked.

He flushed. "Twenty-two."

Holding his black felt fedora and suitcase in one hand, he put the room key on top of the dresser.

"Stay as long as you like, Laverne. You're a beautiful girl, like . . . like the Venus de Milo or Gloria Swanson or someone colossal like that. I wouldn't do anything to you, even if I could. Even if I knew what to do."

Fanny stayed in bed all that day feeling good. She got up late in the afternoon because she was hungry. Under the key on the dresser she found two ten-dollar bills. The sight of them made her smile. It was the first time anyone had given her money for doing nothing, and she found that very funny, and very nice.

Fanny took the money and went upstairs to the roof restaurant to have dinner. She was given a table for two. Almost immediately a man came over and asked if she minded if he shared her table. She smiled and said no, although it was pretty silly: it was early in the evening, the restaurant was almost empty, and there were plenty of other tables. He said his name was Eddie Puritan and he was a talent scout for a movie company.

"Why do you laugh?" he asked.

"Mr. Eddie Puritan, you must be about the fifteenth or sixteenth talent scout I've ever met in my life. The hotels in Utica, Amsterdam, Albany, and Saugerties, New York, are full of them, wall to wall, all the rooms except those filled with hosiery salesmen."

"I *am* one, though. . . ."

"And they all have 'very tempting offers,' they always say, to make to me. Except nothing ever comes of them, only a few quick lays and a whole collection of fake cards I still keep, like a dope, in my suitcase."

Eddie Puritan went on insisting he was a talent scout. He told Fanny she was a beautiful girl and that he could arrange a screen test for her. He tried to take her check but she insisted on paying her own. She said, "So long, chum," and he said, unsmiling, "See you in the movies." She went back to her room.

When Fanny was leaving next morning, Eddie Puritan was in the lobby, with another man. Eddie introduced him to Fanny as Lou Price, and then he asked her name for the first time. "Melinda Lucienne," she said. The two men laughed. Lou Price said he was a literary agent, and Fanny laughed. He was about four-feet-eight-or-nine inches tall. She towered over him.

Lou Price looked up at Fanny. "You know, Melinda, Eddie is what he says he is. I can testify." Lou said he agreed with Eddie that she was beautiful. Fanny waited for the usual invitation to come back to his place and talk it over, the line that always followed the assurance about her looks. But Lou Price went on looking at her, and then he said:

"Trust Eddie. He's a good scout, ha ha."

Fanny asked Eddie, "How do you know I have any talent?"

Eddie Puritan had four gold teeth near the front of his mouth. When he laughed, as if she had made a very funny joke, she caught a gleam of yellow. He said: "Ha ha, I can *see* you have." His mouth was red and soft and ripe-looking inside, like a boy's. When his teeth flashed Fanny found herself staring into it. He said: "No, seriously, I didn't mean that. I really think you may have."

Fanny thought, *Well, so . . . I'll try it once more for kicks and see if it's true. Just maybe this guy is the real thing.* She told Eddie she had no place to stay in New York and almost no money.

He said: "Stay with us," and gestured toward Lou Price. They lived on East 33rd Street in a one-bedroom apartment. All that weekend Fanny slept on their couch that pulled out to make a bed. She signed some papers Eddie gave her, making him her agent. Lou Price witnessed the signing. In their apartment the telephone rang about every ten minutes. Fanny realized Eddie represented a lot of girls who weren't working at the moment, but even after she found this out she didn't lose faith in him.

He told her very little about himself. He had been born in Hollywood, a fact he seemed to find funny. "I've only met three other people who were," he said. "My sisters, and a man who works in set building on the First National lot." Since grade school he had known he wanted to work in pictures. Act, he had once thought, but no one he applied to would take him seriously. He was granted one screen test when he was eighteen, but his slender body looked matchsticklike on the screen.

"I almost wasn't there at all, honestly," he told Fanny.

So he settled for being a slate man. He held to the camera a slate on which was chalked the number of the scene. Then he moved it quickly off camera, erased it, and in the darkness behind the camera prepared it for the next take.

"That's all I ever did in movies," he said. "Until now. Now I'm on my way, kiddo. To do something big. With you."

Lou and Eddie were the kindest men she had ever met. People later said that Eddie rode caboose on Fanny's train to success and that Fanny would have become a Star even if Eddie had never set eyes on her. But Fanny didn't agree with that. She believed his was the magic first touch. Nobody else had ever followed through on their promises. Only men who wanted to lay her looked at her. Eddie acted like she *was* someone already, someone to be careful with, even take care of. Maybe it was true that he saw her as an investment, but she didn't think so at the time and that, Mary Maguire wrote in *The Fabulous Franny Fuller,* helped to salvage her battered sense of herself.

Eddie Puritan never touched Fanny except to help her into cabs, hold her coat, and take her suitcase from her. He made her feel whole and valuable for a while, not like the others whose eyes always seemed to be examining her parts, like people who buy only the pieces of chicken they like to eat. Eddie thought there was more to her than just her magnificent breasts and backside, her beautiful face and long legs. The others: their eyes would travel up and down her, stopping at the places they liked. They would whistle or pinch her, or make love-taps (they called them) here and there. She'd grown up to believe there was nothing else to know. She had given up on herself.

At first Fanny did not understand about Eddie and Lou Price. In her travels down from Utica she had never met any men who loved each other, and did not really believe in their existence. She thought they were inventions of the jokes men in the hotels had guffawed at.

In Hollywood she heard Eddie called a word she didn't know: "Where's that nance, your agent?" someone asked her.

Then she finally understood why Eddie treated her the way he did, doing everything for her and nothing to her. Even then she was grateful. She believed in his real feelings for her, his respect for her. *He must see something in me,* she thought.

After Premium Pictures said they liked the still shots Eddie had had taken of her and said they'd give her a screen test if she came out, Eddie and Fanny shared a compartment on the train to Chicago and then to Hollywood. All across the country they played gin rummy, which he had taught her, and talked about what it was going to be like when Fanny was famous. She could not get over his unquestioning faith in her, and the fact that he never once made a pass at her. She always remembered his fidelity and his gentleness when the hounds started coming down on her, and she could have had any agent in the business. He had been willing to work for Fanny Marker. On the train she confessed her real name to him, and by the time they had arrived in Butte, Montana, he had come up with a better one: Frances Fuller.

He was full of plans, a man who never looked back and so had wiped out of his memory every past disappointment and defeat. From the moment he named her, he never called her Fanny again. His nickname for her was Franny, and when he said it, the flat vowel and soft surrounding consonants rang with love. They talked about the parts Franny would be best in and, even, how she could move easily into character parts when she was older because it was obvious she would make a handsome older woman. They ate their meals together, slept one above the other on the hard, narrow Pullman bunks. All across the country they talked, exploring the strange ways of Stardom, and playing gin rummy for matchsticks.

In Hollywood Eddie Puritan worked hard for Franny. He gave up his other clients to do it. Although there had been some initial doubts about her weak, undeveloped voice (a sensitive point because studios were still paying off actors who had not survived the transition to sound) her screen test was fine: the wispy voice, carried in its entirety through the insensitive equipment, came out as a half-whispered, sex-laden invitation. After six months Premium Pictures began to give her good small parts. In the second year she was given a role in a picture called *The Daughters of Eve*. Six very blond girls—sisters from the Ozark hills—came to New York as a hillbilly act. Five went on to fame and all the tribulations of success singing as a group with a big-time jazz band. But Franny Fuller was the one who settled for love and married the charming, steady, adoring young farmer. In the scene which was to make cinema history—and her own career—she stood at the edge of a nightclub stage and breathed up to a handsome suitor in her half-whisper: "What's your name, fella?" She moved close to him, waiting for an answer, her breasts almost bursting the seams of her dress. In the audience of the dark theater, out of their uncontainable delight, men shouted their own names back at her on the screen. Franny Fuller was made, her flimsy voice at that moment translated into final proof of her extraordinary celluloid sexuality. She was nineteen years old.

At first, Hollywood fulfilled all of Franny Fuller's dreams. Her charm, her naïveté, her pleasure at all its curiosities delighted her escorts. Her salary rose with every picture, astronomically, it seemed, so she was able to move every year, advancing from furnished rooms to a furnished apartment, to a furnished house complete with gates and a resident caretaker for the three acres of grass, bushes, and trees that surrounded it.

"No flowers, please, Mr. Yee," she told the caretaker who was Japanese and wanted to make beds everywhere of canna lilies and geraniums, peonies and roses. He never questioned her instruction, so she was not forced to give her reason, that she hated to cut flowers or to see them cut, and she dreaded coming upon them dead on their stalks when they went uncut.

"Would you object to bushes that flower occasionally, like rhododendrons?" he asked politely. She hesitated and then said no, not knowing what they were.

The fate of her grounds did not long occupy her attention, for she rarely went out into them. Her first starring role, coincidently, was pastoral. *Tess* was a well-disguised version of the Thomas Hardy novel. Scriptwriters tailored the role to Franny's talents and anatomy, moved the scene to the American prairie, and produced a success story in the classic mode: girl of lowly origins wins a visiting Boston Cabot.

Franny worked long days. Her evenings were full. The

novelty of her innocent-looking beauty in Hollywood made her much in demand at dinners and parties. Every evening she had a date, sometimes two, one for dinner, another in the late evening for, on occasion, a screening or preview, and then supper. She passed easily from the eager arms of one escort to another, much as the chassis of a car moves from machinist to mechanic, her person, she thought, assembled, piece by piece, into Someone Important.

Parties: they were her best time, in the first years. She relied upon Premium's costume department for her evening clothes because she hated to go into shops. She would have rented everything she wore, if that had been possible. But it was not necessary: Lucretia Horn, the costumer, a dedicated and talented woman who wore mannish suits and pince-nez glasses, appreciated Franny's exuberant anatomy and provided clothes that contained yet glorified her full, young body.

To celebrate her ascent to genuine stardom, which meant that for the first time her name would appear above Brock Currier's in advertisements, on posters, and in screen credits, Eddie Puritan gave a costume party for Franny at his rented house in Malibu. Lou Price, by chance, was on the Coast at the time, and together they made lavish arrangements. A dance floor was laid outside under a rented striped canopy. Caterers set up tables around the periphery under small striped umbrellas, and trees were hung with Japanese lanterns.

For the occasion Lucretia designed for Franny a subdued floor-length gray cotton gown, with wide white collar and cuffs. Over her drawn-back hair she wore a Puritan bonnet, its small wings flaring out at her ears, the band at the back opening to show her discreet gold bun. The broad band, laid back across her forehead, made her look proud and aloof. On her breast, handsewn and emblazoned with gold thread, was a magnificently embroidered scarlet A.

It was Lou Price's idea, Eddie told Franny, seeing her puzzlement. He explained who she was intended to be, and what she had done. Franny liked the story. "Call me Hester," she told Eddie's guests at the party, and she moved among them, saying hello and she was very glad they had come, with all the grace and dignity she thought proper for the unregenerate adulteress.

Everyone was enchanted with her. Pierrots, clowns, Louis the Fourteenth, mandarins, Sherlock Holmes, cut in upon one another as the large jazz band played one nostalgic tune after another. Her partners allowed each other only a few moments with the Puritan sinner in their arms before they moved in to claim her.

An elaborate champagne supper was served by men in livery from long tables near the dance floor. Franny was escorted to them time and time again by partners who tried to prolong their time with her by offers of food and wine. Each time she accepted champagne from a fresh glass but ate nothing, because complex party delicacies that she could not readily identify confused her and she would not try them. "Hester is tipsy," she told a vampire with whom she was dancing. He grinned evilly at her and replied: "All the better to drink you in, my dear." Franny laughed loudly at that, and everyone dancing near her caught the infectious ring of her laughter and laughed with her. She felt exhilarated: no one knew, she thought gratefully, that she had no idea why she was laughing.

Franny came close to Eddie only twice that night, once to kiss him and thank him for the wonderful party. Later, at one thirty in the morning, when the gaiety was at its height, she looked around for him at the edges of the dance floor and did not see him. For no reason, she felt herself fill with darkness, as though her head had been forced down under a black photographer's dropcloth. Then, without in the least understanding why it should be so, the dark lifted and she had the sense that she had arrived, at that moment, on the summit of her life's enjoyment. *I will never feel this great again,* she thought. She could not fathom why she knew this.

Franny rested her head against the velvet shoulder of her partner who had told her when he cut in that he was Lord Essex, almost a contemporary of her Hester Prynne. The softness against her cheek, the guarded lights shining through the fluttering leaves of the trees, champagne moving through her veins and charging her skin, Eddie Puritan surely somewhere nearby loving her purely because she was, he made her feel sure, lovable and pure (he who had brought here all these famous people to honor her, as he had written in the invitation to the party): all this warmed the dark and empty core of her being, even as the black, imminent decline she felt on the edge of diffused through her senses.

She was desperate to find Eddie. At last she spotted him, standing in a corner of the garden talking to Lou Price and a woman dressed as a nun. Franny broke away from Lord Essex without saying anything to him. She had the feeling she had to move fast, as though whatever was inside her was in danger of leaking out, like those dolls whose split seams let out their stuffing.

Eddie took her hand and offered it to the nun. "This is Franny Fuller, Lillian. She's my client, my friend, my girl."

He turned to Franny. "And this—well, you must know. Remember *The White Sister?*"

Franny nodded. "Oh yes. I know you, Miss Gish. I saw all your pictures in—back home."

Lillian Gish smiled and patted her hand.

Franny nodded, feeling awkward in the presence of the famous face she had seen only on Utica screens. Then she turned to Eddie and asked: "Where are Delphine Lacy and Willis Lord? I thought you said they were coming. Are they here somewhere?

Eddie said: "I doubt they made it. Although the Studio assured me they'd come. Too bad. I would like to have had them meet you."

"Me? Oh no. I just wanted to see them in person. I used to dream about . . ."

She stopped, suddenly thrown back hard on the cobbled

coast of her Utica dream world. The blackness advanced with the pain of those memories. She had not thought of that gray world since her transmigration into Hollywood sunshine. She watched as two women dressed as gypsies claimed Lillian Gish, submerging her in loud, extravagant cries, taking her away toward the supper tables.

Eddie nudged Franny. "See that kid over there? She's the new child star at Fox."

Franny saw a little golden-ringleted girl in patent-leather pumps, a short pleated skirt, and a white frilled middy blouse. "Who's she dressed up to be?"

"Shirley Temple, I suppose. Which is pretty funny when you think that's who Fox hopes she will rival. Actually, she's almost fifteen. They've given her the idiotic name of Honey Moon."

Eddie took Franny's arm and propelled her along toward a group standing beside the punch bowls. At the center of the ring of men was a tall, elegantly dressed woman who seemed to be wrapped in black satin. Her head thrown back, a cigarette holder in the corner of her mouth, she was filling the air around her with smoke. In her hand was a half-full champagne glass. Her eyes were closed.

"Miss Gibson," said Eddie. "Have you met Franny Fuller?"

The woman opened her eyes, startlingly blue and blank. The men around her stepped back respectfully.

"No," she said, closing her eyes again. "I have not. On the other hand, has Franny Fuller met Gloria Gibson?"

Franny said quickly: "Delighted. *Really.*" She started to add that she had seen all her pictures but stopped. *That seems to be all I have to say to anyone here,* she thought.

Gloria Gibson smiled, pulled hard on her cigarette holder, and looked at no one. She pointed to one of the men dressed in the coarse jersey of a gaucho, his chest and shoulders broad and hard, his red hair cropped close to his head. "Meet my new husband," she said to the smoke-filled air.

The band started to play again, soft wailing music from

The Ziegfeld Follies of 1921. The gaucho put his arm around Franny's shoulders and said: "Let's dance."

On the floor couples watched as he led her through a series of intricate steps. She followed, weary and almost without will, drugged by the music and the champagne. The gaucho spun her around; in the whirl she heard the low lament of the music and her mother's voice over the tenor's: *He's my ma-a-an, he's my ma-a-an,* the saxophone wailed with the tenor, and her mother sang along.

Franny dropped her arms, looked toward the outer darkness at the edge of the dance floor, at the retreating lights in the trees. As the darkness seemed to break its bounds and move toward her, she turned away from the gaucho, walked through the other dancers, and vanished into the black garden.

Since Willis Lord's abrupt disappearance from the MGM lot, he had lost his taste for the public, and for the present. He lived alone with his immaterial past, his omnipresent fantasies, his liquor, a man of famous shadows reduced to anonymous existence. Alcohol had whittled away at his classic profile, giving it the rough outlines and uncertain curves of caricature. His nose was now dented and pinched, his sleek cheekbones turned concave, his once precisely trimmed mustache grown careless, ragged, and gray. The strict black hairline for which he had once been so celebrated had begun to retreat to reveal a flat plain of ridges and yellow skin. Hard liquor had taken root in his organs, twisting the twin plum-colored sausages of his liver into stones. Urinous yellow water had replaced his blood, he believed; bile ran riot in his veins, discoloring his skin.

Five years ago, *Their Marvelous Night* had been taken off the nation's screens by a distraught producer. Joe Pinsky heard his investment in the Great Silent Lover disappear under the choruses of customer laughter. A doctor had warned Lord, who tried to drown out the derisive sounds with gin: "Give up the sauce, my man."

There was no way. Gin was his mirror and his curtain, the flagon he offered to memory, the obliterator of his passion for fame. In two gulps, it carried him from the pain of his failure to the private pleasures of forgetfulness. He carefully hoarded what was left of his fortune in order to buy the magical mash and juniper berry, drank it slowly, reserving more solid swallows for his solitary evenings. Social, mannerly sips he kept for his cherished weekly dinners with his old friend, Delphine Lacy. During the day he assigned himself one taste, as he called it, an hour, enough to maintain the level of his self-regard. By means of such strategies, augmented by interminable games of solitaire, he had come through the years between his former eminence and his present obscurity.

He lived in a small, anonymous bungalow between the county line and Culver City. His house was ringed on all sides by others just like it in what was referred to as a bungalow court. From his kitchen window he could see the MGM skyline: battlements, towers, the spires of temples and the tops of skyscrapers close to the tips of minarets. It had been years since he had worked among those hollow structures, worked anywhere for that matter. And because friendships in Hollywood were spawned on contracts and levels of achievement (few Stars he had ever known fraternized with bit players or extras) he had abandoned his circle, those who had crossed the perilous Red Sea from silent films to talkies, even those, like him, who had failed the passage, and fallen into oblivion.

All except Delphine Lacy, a Frenchwoman whose father had some Irish roots. She was in her late thirties, tall, angular, with an almost androgynous body and a low, controlled, French-accented voice which Americans found intriguing. It was this voice as much as the mystery of her sexless body that allowed her to survive the coming of sound at the end of the twenties. Delphine Lacy's habitual look of profound sadness endeared her to the cheery Americans of the jazz age, as well as to the pessimists of the

Depression. Her much-publicized preference for private life, her aversion to the tricks and games of publicity, paradoxically, made her an object of intense curiosity to her fans, and to the avid editors of movie magazines.

Delphine Lacy and Willis Lord had made three silent films together at Premium. Indeed, as a result of carefully planted studio rumors, they were believed by the public to be lovers in what Hollywood liked to call real life. Willis Lord wanted very much to believe the rumors, even though he was aware they had been designed to promote *Passion Flowers* and *The Baron and His Lady*. He tried to advance his amorous cause with the beautiful but distant French star. Delphine, amused by his boyish ardor, listened to his plea but would have none of him as a lover. She claimed she had another, very secret, alliance. Willis was to learn this was her way of turning away pressing suitors. For the public, however, the hints of the Studio had proved persuasive. Their fans believed that the screen lovers gazed at each other with genuine love, carried over from the reality of their lives. Audiences settled back to watch, believing they were being made privy to the true romance of the private bedroom.

Willis looked forward all week to Friday, when Delphine would bring to his house a wicker hamper full of food and cook French dishes from her Gascony childhood. He sat at the kitchen table watching her, following her as she moved, in her loping, angular yet graceful way, from the cutting board to the stove. As she worked they talked, always of the past. Delphine brought to her friend a carefully censored version of Studio news of the past week: of their old acquaintances in the business who had died (for Willis rarely read newspapers and never the obituaries) and of the pictures that had flopped, an American word Delphine always smiled at as she pronounced it: it made her think of dank hair or the ears of a rabbit. She dwelled on box-office disappointments and studio trades, avoiding talk about success and progress of careers. She had learned that such subjects depressed him, made him even more silent, and destroyed his mood for the rest of the evening.

Willis's contributions to the conversation had been prepared during his long weekly silences. He liked to dredge up the buried fate of someone they had both once known.

"Rex Ingram," he said, as they sat in the living room waiting for dinner to cook, drinking the first glass of white wine from the bottle Delphine had brought. "Do you remember the picture he directed called *Trifling Women?"*

"No, I think not. I remember him only as Valentino's director in *The Four Horsemen,* and I once met Alice Terry who was his wife, I think. She was in that picture with Rudi that was reissued in the late twenties. I thought it was marvelous. *Marvelous."*

Willis nodded. "Yes. Both times. First in 1922 and later in 1926, the reissue. Both silent films. I saw each of them twice. They will never remake *The Four Horsemen* with sound, you can be sure," Willis said, grimly.

"Of course you are right," Delphine said, to comfort him.

"But I wasn't thinking of that picture. *Trifling Women* was strange. Ingram wrote it and then directed it. A man I knew named Ed Connelly was in it. One of its main characters was a huge chimpanzee who lived in a great dark cellar. The man who owned him was mad and lethal, as I remember. The chimpanzee was named Joe Martin. Connelly told me that Joe Martin fell in love with Barbara La Marr, the leading lady and, toward the end of shooting, would not let any of the men in the picture near her. They had to cage him when he wasn't involved in the scene."

"How strange," said Delphine.

"More than that. Ed said there was a scene in which he gave Barbara a necklace. The chimpanzee was so furious he leaped away from the trainer and almost choked Ed. Ed never forgot it."

"Were they shooting at the time? Did the camera get any of it?"

"No, the camerman was so frightened he kicked over the tripod. Too bad. It might have made a wonderful scene."

Delphine laughed. Bearing the wine bottle and her glass before her she moved toward the kitchen. "Lordy, my true love. I must do something in here. Bring your glass and join me."

Lord sat forward for a moment, staring at his dim, destroyed face in the mahogany surface of the coffee table. *Only a silent picture could have in it a monkey who loves a woman,* he thought. *Why did they give up all that . . . possibility?*

"Lord," Delphine called.

He picked up his glass. "I'm coming."

The wine that evening was especially good, a lovely Volnay Delphine had chosen to accompany her chicken dish. As they sat at the kitchen table, she toasted their long friendship. He countered with a toast to the jealous ape, and then they both laughed.

"On the set yesterday I talked to a woman, a dresser I think she is, who had known Marie Prevost," said Delphine, regretting at once that she had used the words "on the set." But she went on: "Do you recall her?"

"Of course. She was a victim of sound."

"Did you ever hear the details of her death?"

"I think not." Willis filled his glass. "Tell me."

"Well, of course, I cannot tell if it is all true, but this woman says that Prevost had this little dog. She locked her door in some cheap hotel in Hollywood, and began to drink from three bottles and to take some pills a doctor had given her to sleep. No one thought to look for her for four days, and when they did they found her little dog standing guard over her half-eaten body."

Willis took a long swallow of wine.

Then he said: "Mae Marsh, remember her? Whatever happened to her?"

Delphine shook her head. "I have no idea."

Willis said: "That story about the ape lover made me think of a picture I saw her in. She was a wild girl dressed in feathers and her best friend was a bear.

"She never did too well once Griffith began to fail. But

she made some fine pictures. Can't remember them all, but I do remember *The White Rose,* in which she played a lovely mistreated southern girl. Griffith liked that kind of delicate heroine whose strength was her goodness. I saw that picture many times."

"I did not see her that I remember. But I often think of Novarro in *A Lover's Oath . . .*"

"His real name," said Willis very carefully because his lower lip was growing stiff with drink, "is Ramon Samaniego, did you know that? He is Mexican, not Spanish as his fans think."

"So? I did not know. But I thought he was very good in *Ben Hur*. Wonderful. Like some Roman divinity."

"You know why, Delphine?" Willis asked, very quietly.

"Because he was a very fine actor?"

"No. Because that picture was *silent.* He was a foreigner, and had only a little English, but it did not matter. Because the stupid noises of animals and chariots and whips, and the inane chatter of gladiators and charioteers could not be heard. The idiot noises of lips sucking together during a kiss were not audible. Only the vision of a beautiful and brave man. Braver and bigger than the people in the theater knew themselves to be, showing them what he felt with his face, his body. That was what acting was. Now actors talk, and lose their divinity, their *elevation,* in a way. People who have to listen cannot dream, cannot be entranced, cannot *worship.*"

Delphine was silent.

"Silence brought us into a kind of communion. Noise—sound—talk—destroyed it. I am relieved to be away from all that—pandemonium, that acoustic hell."

Delphine said: "Is the chicken too heavy with sauce?"

Willis did not answer. He was thinking of the carnivorous fate of Marie Prevost, his mind moving in its customary backward and vertical shuttle.

He picked at his food. His left hand held his wine glass and he took long draughts from it, then filled it quickly.

"Try some of the good chicken, my love," Delphine said,

ignoring the shaking of his hand as he poured from the bottle, and the little spots of color that appeared on the linen mat at his place. "You must eat more, you know, to stay well."

He smiled at her, a look full of gratitude for her presence in his kitchen. She could not bear to insist further about the food. He said nothing, and stopped pretending to eat.

Delphine said: "Lord, dearest, do you remember that we said we might go to that late party for Premium's star, what's her name, I don't quite recall. It might be pleasant to get out a bit. Would you care to go?"

Willis said: "I don't think so. You go, love. I won't mind.'

But neither of them went. They sat together in companionable silence, she consoling him with her calm, beautiful eyes, he enveloped in his satisfying haze of gin and the distant past.

In three years Franny Fuller had become "a household name," Mary Maguire said. The Studio had long ago legitimized the affectionate diminutive bestowed on her by Eddie Puritan; the formal name was abandoned.

Franny's acceptance by the American public was immediate and enthusiastic. A man named Simon Sais ("Ha! ha! Hard to believe, huh?" he wrote to Franny) who had a fleet of trucks in Duluth, Minnesota, started a Franny Fuller Fan Club within six months of her first big role. Soon there were twelve such clubs around the country, the largest in Venice, Florida. Corresponding secretaries of the clubs wrote every month to their Star, informing her of their activities (picnics for members and their families, exhibitions of their scrapbook collections, matinee parties to her pictures, and evening gatherings to display and trade still photographs of Her). A fan club member in Martinsburg, West Virginia, wrote to her every day including Sunday: the press of letters from him, and all the others, and the requests for autographed photographs, became so great that the Studio hired a full-time respondent to handle Franny's fan mail.

Her appeal at the box office surprised even the Premium moguls who had planned a modest advertising campaign to familiarize the public with her person. It never proved necessary. After her first appearance, at the announcement of a new picture, lines would form, stretching like a great snake around the Loew's Premium Theater in New York, the Criterion in Chicago, the Paramount in Los Angeles. Theaters in smaller cities and towns would be crowded with customers long before the trailer, the Pathé News, and Popeye the Sailor had played themselves out.

Simon Sais wrote to inform Franny that *Tess* had been held over at the Zenith in Duluth for seven weeks. "We go every Monday night—twenty-two of us—and we are so glad they have not changed the show." *Silver Screen,* usually the springboard for rising stars, responded to Franny Fuller's exuberant, paying fans by a series of articles on her, each one outdoing the other in extravagant praise and almost wholly invented biographical detail.

She was famous. Premium Pictures was enriched. The secret lives of her fans were expanded by their dreams and fantasies, their social lives by club gatherings to talk about her and gaze at her glossy image.

As Franny flourished, Eddie Puritan declined. His face seemed very gray to her. He was always tired. He would fall asleep in a chair in her living room and sleep there all night. When he woke in the morning his eyes were brighter, his face a little less pale. He smiled at himself for having conked out that way, his wide, boyish, red-gummed smile full of gold flashes. He said, "See ya, Franny," and went home to sleep some more.

A doctor told Eddie he ought to go to the hospital for a checkup. When Franny went to visit him there (gathering together all her courage because she was afraid of hospitals and the sight of people suffering), he was lying in bed with a tube in his arm and a pipe running into his nose. Something was dripping into his vein from a bag hanging over his bed. Lou Price was there, dancing around the bed like a frenzied dwarf, making feeble vaudeville jokes, trying to distract

Eddie. Once outside Eddie's room Lou's manic look became strained. He told Franny that Eddie had cancer in his blood.

"His chances are not too swift," he said, and looked as if he were about to cry.

Once more Franny went to visit Eddie in the hospital. She saw very little of his smile or his flashy teeth. Then, in a few weeks, he seemed to get better. When he was able to leave the hospital, Lou took him back East. Franny was working on location in Nevada at the time and did not get to say goodbye to him. He died in New York, very fast. She never forgot him, even when her fortunes had moved far ahead of where Eddie Puritan could have taken them. Her mother had lowered her, judged her, found her no good, worth nothing. Eddie had seen beyond her outside and persuaded her of her own substantial reality. True, in his eyes she had caught an appraising look, but it was different: there she read his high estimate of her. She believed it, for a while.

All that came to an end with Eddie's death. After he was gone, she felt herself slipping, changing, falling. Pictures of her satisfied men's needs, the fumblings in the dark for the secret things men do, alone and in private places, to themselves and to women. The shadow of herself up there belonged to their fast, wet dreams. Men stuck her picture in their footlockers or tacked it to the inside of their college desks or pasted it up on locker doors in gyms. She imagined she could see her name FRANNY FULLER painted across their hot eyes as they looked at her. She was this thing men paid to look at in the dark, their hands twitching at the sight of her, their peckers stiff against their flies as they watched her shadow.

Eddie Puritan, the agent of her real self, the slate man for all her inner takes, was the only one (until she married Dempsey Butts) who thought Fanny Marker was a person. And then, of course, he died.

3

The Quarterback

Dempsey Butts was a small, lithe boy, twenty-two years old when the Mavericks of San Francisco signed him up a week after his graduation from college. He hated the idea of going to the West Coast to play football. But he had a passion for the game, and for the kind of solid, out-of-doors, sweaty, hard-pounding, second-effort life he'd been taught to respect by his family who were his other passion.

Dempsey's father, Wendell Butts, was the Sunday minister of the Open Bible Church. The rest of the time he farmed three hundred and fifty acres of feed corn and soy beans, and raised Poland China pigs. Dempsey's mother, Emma, was a pale, slight stick-figure of a woman with a wilted, unsubstantial body and a thin, kindly face. She had been the daughter of a farmer and was now a farmer's wife as well as the mother of four loving and athletic sons. The effort of all her roles seemed to have consumed her until there was little left but her small bones, her pale wrinkled skin, blue-veined legs, and gallant, fragile, bony head. She was less a woman than a sparrow. She fixed on her husband and her "boys" the bright beam of her birdlike eyes, loving everyone she looked upon. They in turn respected and loved her frailty and treated her like a convalescent.

The Buttses' two-story white-frame house with a green veranda that went around three sides, ringed by a few wind-breaking cedars, three silos, and huge white barns, was the hub of their lives. There they slept and ate, played and rested, joshed, and said their prayers, and asked their little concerned questions of each other: "Better today, Maw?" and "Still hungry, son?" and "Any of that plum jam left?"—loving queries that made up most of their conversation.

Their house was a good quarter mile from their nearest neighbor's; it was, somehow, self-sufficient. Everyone in it felt surrounded by warm, protective mutuality. Before the family settled down at any gathering, for a meal or on the veranda in the early evening where they told jokes or made farm plans or gossiped about the outside world, they went through a familial ritual of checking: "Did the bandage hold right on that ankle, Tun?" or "Pretty good day for drying, Maw?" and "Find the stuff from the store I picked up, Dad?"

The Buttses were selfless, generous people who took on a strong sense of themselves only when they were assured of the wholeness and safety of those around them. The climate of the family was masculine, all the children being boys. This accentuated the small flame of frail femininity that burned in Emma Butts. Gentle, almost humbly ashamed of their gross good health and utile bodies, the Butts men hovered over their wife and mother, carrying things for her, waiting on her, in a synecdoche she always used when describing them, gratefully, to the neighbors, "hand and foot."

None of the Buttses smoked or drank, or much liked to read or even listen to the radio except for the baseball games. Now and then on a Saturday night they all went to the movies in Prairie City. But their pleasures were primarily muscular. They loved large meals, working outdoors, throwing footballs to each other or kicking them against the barn. They walked because they loved the feel of dirt roads and grassy paths under their feet, they talked to each other about the farm, the seasons, sports, they drove farm machinery with the pure pleasure that came to them from visible accomplishments and physical activity.

They loved the rituals of Sunday, the early-morning baths, clean clothes, ties and shined shoes, then the wait on the veranda for Maw. The five men drank their coffee together there, standing up, looking out at their fields. There was the customary jostling for position when Emma came down looking like a bird shining after a rain, to go to church with them. On her narrow neck she usually wore oversized white plastic-ball beads. They made her look pathetic and proud.

"Spiffy. You look right spiffy," said the Reverend Butts to his wife.

Three sons squeezed into the back seat and one sat over the hump in front to give Maw enough room. The church was only a few miles away, in the heart of Prairie City, and had a congregation of sixty-eight. Wendell Butts read the service and then delivered his sermon. It was full of down-to-earth sense, his "grass-roots approach to living and to God," as he liked to call his sermons. His figures of speech were invariably athletic. He talked of his service to God as being "God's waterboy." Fighting against sin he described as "keeping the opposition, the Devil, off balance." A happy family was an "all-star team." To the farm families and the townspeople in the congregation these football references proved Butts's acquaintance with the wider world. He made them feel cosmopolitan and knowledgeable. To the Buttses listening with admiration from their pew, his allusions combined in a cheerful, Sabbath way, their abiding interests: God, football, the farm, and their love for each other.

The Buttses took great pride in good health, even Emma who had little of it herself but seemed to be sustained by the display of theirs. The oldest son, Dempsey, was small for a football player, with much of his mother's gentleness about him. He was "wonderfully put together," as she said. He could run very fast and for long distances without getting winded. His muscles lay smooth and flat on his bones; nothing bulged as he moved. Everything in his body operated with the greatest economy. Even his corn-silk hair lay flat against his narrow head. His brother, Tunney, younger by a year, was taller, darker, and much heavier, like their father, with unusually wide shoulders, long arms, and broad, capable hands. "A born pass receiver," his father said when Tun had attained his full growth and had already decided he wanted to be a farmer.

The young twins, Sully and Shark, loved football too, but their eyes were poor, the result of an overlong stay in incubation after their premature births. Good-naturedly, but without much hope, they ignored their handicap and practiced incessantly, throwing the football between them as they walked to high school or helped their mother in the truck garden, priding themselves at not hitting any tender shoots. "Old Four Eyes" they called each other: their names were Sharkey and Sullivan. In his youthful passion for the sport of boxing, Wendell Butts had bestowed the names of famous fighters on his sons, "as incentive," he told them later, "to work hard and be good, really good, at something."

As was only fitting for the eldest, Dempsey was the first to obey. During his last year in high school he led his team to the state championship; the University in Iowa City sent a scout to see him play. He was offered a scholarship to the University of Iowa which had a coach known throughout the middle west for building winning teams.

Demp was not much of a student and ignored attending a number of his more difficult college classes. Yet he squeaked through. In the spring he made the track team. His height and weight (by dint of forcing himself to eat starches he finally made one hundred and sixty-five pounds), the swiftness with which he moved, his accurate eye and arm, made him a natural quarterback. He played fast and hard, with perfect concentration on every play he called, every pass he threw.

On Sundays he went to an Open Bible Church near the University. Usually he was invited back "to the house" to have dinner with the minister and his family. The minister had a daughter, Edna-Mae, who was Dempsey's age. She was a healthy-looking, suntanned girl with hair exactly the color of Demp's. She tried to interest him in herself. But he was too involved in football and in watching his weight and getting enough sleep. So he would leave the minister's house almost as soon as dinner was over, and never seemed to notice Edna-Mae's attentions.

His classmates found him likable but very strange. He had none of their extracurricular interest in beer, women, jazz, and cars, an odd guy for a football player. Behind his back they called him "the Lady," but he was too sensitive, too tough-spirited, and too damned nice for them to allow him to hear the epithet. In his senior year he was able to throw accurate lateral passes and had compiled a record, for his league, as a ground gainer. The coach boasted to the professional scouts who began to attend the Iowa games on Saturday afternoons that Demp was calling the plays without help from the sidelines.

As president of his graduating class Demp gave a short speech after the valedictory had been delivered at commencement. He charmed the audience with his gentle, boyish smile, his deep-blue, sincere-looking eyes, and his genuine team-effort sentiments. A week later, so eager was he to play professional football, that he signed on with a new team on the West Coast, the Mavericks. Then he took a job on a road-building project near Des Moines to earn some of his expenses and to toughen up for the team.

In mid-July he was due at training camp. Demp went home to Prairie City for his last weekend before he had to leave for the Coast. On that occasion there was very little gaiety among the Buttses. It is often true that, for an unhappy family, an unaccustomed gay note is sounded when a member departs, as though a break in the pattern of the usual communal misery raises the hopes of everyone in something better to come. But when the Buttses knew that Demp was leaving for the West they gathered Saturday night at the dinner table in a funereal mood. When he was a college student, Demp had been only forty miles away; he had come home often. Now the threatened long distance made the break between them and their first son, their brother, very real.

At dinner, Emma Butts's pallor frightened them all. She appeared to have lost some of her life force or to have presented it to Demp, like a fond parent who gives up a favorite possession to a departing child. Tun, torn between the pleasurable feeling at his ascendancy as the oldest son at home and a deep sense of loss, covered his confusion by talking constantly and too loudly. Full of pride at Demp's success, the twins were silent.

Reverend Butts alone sensed what was happening to his wife. He knew that Emma existed, in a vital sense, for him and for her sons. He understood that Demp's departure would seriously diminish her and, to a lesser extent, all of them. But he was luckier. Sustained by his strong sense of God's will in all things, and by the hard, physical work he had to do, he would survive. He was not so sure about Emma. Tunney was moving fast into Demp's place in the family, if only in his own eyes which, after all, the Reverend Butts thought, was the important way. To the twins, Demp's leaving was not so vital. They had each other and many friends; people were always attracted to them by their composed and happy duality.

But for Emma: it was more serious. Her pretense at contentment, her determination to make these last hours at home happy for Demp, cost her so much that in the evening, after she had washed up the dishes, set out the fruit for later, and the family were settled into their usual places on the veranda, she had "a little sinking spell," as she called it. She had to be helped up the stairs to her bedroom, her husband's arm about her waist, the four young men trailing helplessly behind "to see Maw upstairs." They all felt they wanted to donate to their almost spectral mother some of their sturdy bodily tissue and energetic blood.

Demp was terrified. He blamed himself for his mother's

weakness, reproached himself for his selfishness in wanting to be a football player more than a son and a farmer. If she sickened he alone would be responsible, he told himself. For the first time in his life he felt the burdensome misery of being so cherished, and helpless in the presence of maternal love.

The next morning Emma was recovered, enough, she said, to go to church with her family. At once the air cleared. Demp's guilt melted, the Reverend Butts relaxed in his pulpit at the sight of Emma there among her four boys, his beloved wife and friend in the chipper straw hat and flowered silk dress she had bought in Younkers in Des Moines. On the ride back to the farm they all joked with each other. Dinner was eaten in an atmosphere of high spirits and teasing born of their intense relief. When it was time for Demp to leave for the train at three, there was no visible break in the determined familial cheerfulness.

"Kill 'em, boy. Don't worry. You'll survive."

"Show 'em how Iowa boys can play."

"Don't eat too much, Demp. If you get too fat you'll be a better target for the smear."

"Real desire, boy, real effort," said the Reverend heartily.

"Remember now, the playbook is the Bible," said Tun. The Reverend frowned at this irreverence.

Demp nodded, said yes to everything, and groaned as if in pain at the sentences intended to spur him on.

"Write when you get there, son," said his mother softly.

Demp told her he would. Clowning with his brothers and his father, he gave a handoff to Sully and then faked a run between the twins and through the dining room archway. It was hard for anyone to be serious in the presence of his resolute tomfoolery.

His mother kissed him and patted the sleek blond back of his head which she loved. Then she sat down on the veranda to watch Reverend Butts bring the car around. Demp waved from the car, his heart full of gratitude at the way they all clearly loved him. His mother seemed to have recovered from her look of loss. In his last sight of her she had turned away and was chatting with Sully, one hand on Sharkey's shoulder. Relieved and high-hearted, Demp talked to his father during the drive to Des Moines, about getting a hired man to help with the harvest, about his own future if he was lucky, and his intention, once his salary started, to help out by paying for his lost labor. They were back on safe grounds of ordinary masculine subject matter. The Reverend Butts found it easy to respond to his son.

The trip to San Francisco was very long and hot. Demp spent it sitting up in a coach in a happy state of anticipation, dozing occasionally, waking to think of his press notices in the *Daily Iowan,* of the stadium he would play in which he had seen only in photographs. He pictured himself in the blue and gold uniform of the Mavericks: *Goll-ee, the Mavericks. Think of it, me with the Mavericks.*

Demp arrived, hot, tired but exalted by his hours of daydreaming on the Union Pacific coach. At the dormitory of the college outside of San Francisco where the team was training, he found a telegram for him saying his mother had died in her sleep Sunday night, eight hours after he had left Prairie City.

Two years later, in early July, Dempsey Butts, now first-string quarterback of the Mavericks, went south with a carload of fellow players to see the sights in Hollywood. They had five days off to relax in. Two of them they spent walking aimlessly up and down the streets near Hollywood and Vine in the vain hope of seeing a Star. On the third night they gave up and went to a Mexican bar on the outskirts of Beverly Hills. They all ordered tequila, which none of them had drunk before. After the first drink, they decided they liked the place and stayed on, enjoying the darkness, the unabashed seediness, and what they took to be the authenticity of El Chico, following all the synthetic glitter and white plastic of the Hollywood tourist places. After two tequilas even the name of the place seemed very funny and therefore good to them.

"No Ciro's *this,* eh, Demp," shouted Amos Settle, pounding the table. Settle was a fullback, an enormous, rawboned, red-faced Kentuckian with a fondness for what he called "living."

"This is *it,* eh? This is living."

"Olé, said Demp. He felt fine, light-headed and happy, for the first time in three days. The sort of banging-around they had been doing, from bar to bar, poor restaurants to pretentious hotel lobbies (where they sat mornings to read the green sports pages and write postcards) was not for him. He liked plain home-cooking, a regular schedule of work-outs every day in the week, and a well-washed comforter on his bed at night. He was willing to put up with hand-to-mouth hotel existence for the sake of the game he loved, but he felt that in his free time he ought to return to the clean, settled, familiar world of a place like Prairie City.

No longer listening to the talk around him and fiddling with his tequila glass, he sat, watching a girl come into the bar. She went past their table toward a seat in the far corner of the dark, tunnellike room. Wearing heavy, unlaced boots, she clumped as she walked. But he could not miss her legs. Scratched and streaked with dirt, even in those boots he could see they were fine legs. Demp watched her drop heavily into a chair at a corner table. She ordered something, he could not hear what, and then the waiter brought her a beer. He watched her sip it. It was hard to see her face under the brim of her canvas cap and behind the wide green sunglasses she wore. He wondered: *Why does she need them in here? She must be bats or something.*

He was used to the farm women in Prairie City who dressed in men's work clothes, but for some reason she seemed different. Under the drab jacket and pants, he sensed a girl, not a woman. He wondered at the bulky clothes. Watching her steadily, he was the first on his feet when he saw her head go down on the tabletop.

Bill Eddy had risen too. "That guy back there is drunk already. Pretty early in the day." He looked, then laughed, and sat down.

Demp moved as fast as if he were avoiding a red-dogging. He was halfway to the back of the room before the others noticed he had gone. He slid into the chair beside the girl. Her head coming down had pushed over her glass. He could smell the spilled beer. Her hat had fallen from her head onto the table; he saw her hair, silk, yellow hair. *I knew it,* he thought. *She's just a kid.*

"Are you all right?" His voice was hoarse with concern. He pushed her hair out of the beer, but she did not move. Then he heard high, wet sounds. She was crying. His heart beat so fast he thought he would pass out, feeling the terror he always had when a woman cried in his presence.

"Hey. *Hey*. Stop that." He tried to lift her head from the table, but she shook it away from his hands. He sat still, waiting. Suddenly she twisted and lifted her face. Her sunglasses, askew, fell into the beer, and he saw her face. At once he knew who she was—the purity of those eyes, bright and childlike from fresh tears, the unmistakable glow of that face on which the dirt was streaked, the caked pieces of black on her eyelids, that cleft in her left cheek, the sharp, lovely peak of her hairline. He recognized, of course, and at the same time (he was to remember this as long as he lived) he knew, beyond any doubt, that he loved her.

"Franny Fuller," he said aloud to himself and then, too late, realized his mistake. She heard him, pushed back from the table, and stood up, pulled a bill from a jacket pocket and put it down in the beer. He stood up as she brushed past him. He could smell her—sour, unwashed, female. He gestured to the boys at the table, a low, hip-level wave with his right hand as though warning them off. Behind him he heard someone snicker. But so intent was he not to lose sight of her that he did not respond and, for that matter, never saw those men again on that trip.

A few doors beyond El Chico's he caught up to her.

"Whoa there a minute. Wait up."

She stopped and whispered, "Leave me alone, Please."

"I can't," he said, feeling his heart turn over with pity. "Let me help you. Please."

"You can't help me. Go away."

Demp walked beside her and said nothing. Her shoulders shook, she shuffled along in the thick boots, her blond hair pouring out of the cap she had jammed down over it.

"Where are you staying?" he asked.

"Where am I staying," she said.

"A hotel? What hotel? A house?"

She hesitated a long time. Then she said: "The Y."

"Oh, come on. Someone like you at the Y?"

"Someone like me," she said. There seemed to be some obscure comment in her flat repetition of what he said to her, but he could not understand what she meant by it.

"A movie star, like you."

They arrived in front of a building that looked to Demp like a Y. He waited for her to stop but she shuffled on, as though she had not noticed where she was. *Or maybe,* he thought, *she made that up about the Y.*

"Why do you wear all those clothes in this heat?" he asked. She was now walking faster, breathing in small gulps, and sweating profusely. He could smell her warmth mixed with the must of coarse khaki.

She made no reply, but she walked more slowly. Once she stopped so abruptly that he fell against her. He thought he would not be able to stand up under the furious beating of his heart. Then she turned and he followed her into a dark-brown, curtain-fronted bar. Without seeming to look at anything she headed for a table at the rear.

Demp sat beside her and ordered two beers. He could read the name of the place, scrolled backward, on the front window: it was Castellano's. The walls were decorated with faded, unframed pictures of the Bay of Naples and Lake Como, crepe-paper streamers, and religious banners left over, he imagined, from the celebration of some Italian festival.

The waiter brought the beers, nodded to Franny Fuller without recognition or interest, picked up the coins Demp had put down, and wiped the table around the bases of the two glasses. Then he went away.

"Does he know you, Miss Fuller?" Demp asked.

"No. But I come here now and then. I have a lot of places I go to now and then around here. It takes days to go to all of them."

"Why? Why do you do it? Go to these places like this, I mean."

"They're dark. And everyone in these places is alone and down. Like me. Here it's dark and I'm alone and down, so I feel at home here in bad times."

"But where do you sleep?"

"In one place or another. A little bit at a time. I go home when I'm dead, really dead tired, and sleep for three days, almost. Everything is better for a while, until I go down again. Then I come back."

"Are you ready to go home now?"

Franny Fuller looked at him, her face streaked with beer, weariness, and despair.

"I'll walk you home if you're ready to go," Demp said. He took her damp hand. She let him lead her out of the bar. She pointed down a street. The walk seemed interminable to him. Twice they sat down to rest on stone walls. The hills grew steeper, the houses farther apart, and then disappeared entirely, invisible behind high hedges.

"Where are we?"

"Beverly Hills. I live up here."

"Is it much farther?"

It was. When they arrived at a stopping place, it was four-thirty in the morning. The first faint signs of a break in the black of the night could be seen behind the roof of her house. The walk in through the gate and toward the house seemed very long to Demp who was now tired. Franny Fuller, her head sunk forward, had to be pushed along.

No one came to the door when Demp used the heavy knocker. He looked questioningly at Franny Fuller whose exhausted eyes were almost shut. She reached out and turned the knob. The door opened.

"Holy cow. Don't you lock this place?"

"Lost the key," she whispered.

They came into an entry hall as large and round as a ballroom, Demp thought. He followed her to its end, then into a huge living room in which every lamp was lit. Franny stared into it as though she had never seen it before, turned and walked on, down a hall lined on both sides with black-framed glossy stills from her pictures. She stopped before a half-opened door, pushed it open and went in. Demp followed her.

Suddenly he couldn't see her and, utterly confused, he stepped backward to the entrance of the room to find a light switch. He snapped it on. In the sudden flare of light he saw a bedroom almost as big as the living room. At one end was a broad, fur-covered white bed and white bearskin rugs everywhere. The room seemed to be without windows. Or, if they were there, they were covered by some kind of white silky drapery which hung from ceiling to floor on every inch of the walls.

"Wow," he said. "This is some swanky place." Franny Fuller had almost disappeared into the depths of a white chaise longue, her drab clothes and filthy boots the only color in the thirty-six-foot square of white the room contained. Demp knelt down beside her and pulled off her boots, holding her ankles gently as he tugged. Her legs were limp, she wore no socks, and her feet were very dirty.

She seemed to be asleep. He shook her and she stirred. "Do you have a maid, or something?"

"What for?" she asked without opening her eyes.

"You know. To help you undress. And you need a bath."

She opened her eyes. "No bath," she said. She pulled her feet under her, lay down, and seemed to fall asleep at once.

Demp gave up. He pulled the fur spread from the bed. It turned out to be twice as big as he thought, and he had some trouble folding it neatly, the way his mother always had done when she put blankets away for the summer. He put it over her, snapped out the light, and closed the door. After two wrong turns he found the living room again, took off his shoes, put out all the lights, and lay down on one of the room's three couches, the one nearest the door.

Afterward he couldn't remember why he hadn't left. He doubted she would remember him when she woke. She seemed to be in some sort of daze, from beer, from exhaustion, terror: he could not make out the cause. But something in her look when she did focus on him, the grime that covered her face, her hands, her feet, her need to be cared for, watched over, until she woke, and the absence of anyone around who might do these things for her, compelled him to stay.

Tired as he was, he found he could not sleep in that enormous room. His bladder was bursting, and he was worried about not having a toothbrush and a razor in the morning. He thought about missing a night's sleep and what it would do to his weight. He knew he would not be in shape for the long drive north tomorrow. He would miss the practice scheduled for the next day.

He must have dozed off. It was midmorning when he woke, oppressed by the silence and worried about getting back. The place gave him the hollow feeling of a funeral-parlor reception room. Shoes in hand, he walked through two halls until he found a bathroom. He urinated, stripped, showered, and, finding no razor in the cabinet, powdered his face and neck with a feminine-smelling talcum he found near the tub.

He went in search of the room in which he had left Franny Fuller, and found her, still on the chaise longue, in the same position as when she had fallen asleep. When he pulled the drapes open, she raised her arms over her face as if to exclude the light. Outside a great park of grass and trees stretched out in every direction.

Somewhere in the vast house he heard a telephone ring, muted and dull. He had no idea where it was so he made no move to answer it. On and on it rang, as though the caller expected Franny Fuller to put off answering it until the very last minute. Finally it stopped.

Dempsey moved a white stool and sat beside her. He pulled her arms gently away from her face and began to unbutton her stiff jacket.

"Miss Fuller," he said, the awe in his voice making it sound hoarse, unlike the way he was used to hearing himself.

But she was asleep and he could not wake her. She seemed without life, her body weighed down with an unconsciousness so profound that her muscles locked against his attempts to stir her. He felt helpless in the presence of such stillness. He was a man to whom being alive meant motion: even as he waited on the bench to be sent in to play he stood up often, shifting from one foot to the other, his hands moving, his arms wrapping themselves around himself, jogging in place, throwing an invisible football to a nonexistent receiver.

When he could not wake her, he substituted a chair for the stool and sat beside her, watching her sleep. For two hours the only sound in the room was the creaking of his small chair, inadequate to the restless switching of his weight on it.

At noon she was still sleeping. Demp knew if he was not back in Hollywood by three he would miss his ride. He tried once more to wake her. He knelt down beside the chaise and carefully, as though he was handling his mother's best company china, lifted her head. In the presence of her beauty under the dirt, the remains of beer and tears, her crusted eyelids blue with make-up, and the yellow-silk hair that fell everywhere beside her face, he found it hard to breathe. She was the culmination of all the women he had ever looked at with longing, the women whose pictures, in seductive poses, had formed his daydreams and, oddly, at the same time, she was the frail, fading mother he had seen for the last time, unable to be roused by his love, in her coffin in Prairie City.

His chest ached with longing, with love, as he looked at the sleeping actress. A fantasy took possession of him. The

Beautiful Girl was lost, inexplicably deserted and in some nameless trouble, and he had found her and carried her to an enchanted white castle. By virtue of all these things, she was, by the rules of fairy legend and sport, *his*. He could not explain this new certainty that possessed him but, working over her to remove her foul clothes, he knew that his new love, born last night in back of the Mexican bar, could not be thrown off. He would have to stay with it at all costs. It was no longer possible to escape.

Pouring her from one side of the chaise longue to the other, he managed to remove her jacket and pants. She wore nothing underneath. Aghast, he pulled the fur spread over her, at the same time wanting to look again, excited, and yet feeling there was something unsportsmanlike about taking advantage of her as she now was. He stayed in the bedroom all afternoon while she slept, moaning now and then in her sleep and then, as evening came on, beginning to talk incoherently. He heard the telephone ring again and again, more insistently, he felt, at every call. He knew he was already in trouble, not having started back with the others. He could imagine the coach's furious outbursts reproduced on the sports page. With his mind's eye, he read the story of his defection, and he estimated the size of his fine. But still he sat there, looking at her, loving her.

Finally he got up. By now it was five and beginning to be dark. He closed the drapes, left the room, and found the kitchen. There were yards of cupboards. He opened them all: they were almost empty. In one he found four boxes of zwieback. In the refrigerator, which was twice as large as any he had ever seen before and painted yellow to match the rest of the kitchen, he found five milk bottles filled with grape juice, and nothing else. A wave of cold air swept out of the box as he removed one bottle and quickly shut the door: he shivered. He took two glasses from a cupboard and a box of zwieback, piled everything on a tray, and took it back with him to the bedroom, not wanting to leave her alone long enough for him to eat in the kitchen. By nine o'clock he had been back to the kitchen twice, all the zwieback but a few at the bottom of the last box was gone, and he was light-headed and somewhat sick from the juice. After the first mouthful he had realized that it was heavily laced with gin.

At midnight she woke up. He had been asleep himself after all the grape-juice gin, the lights blazing, his chin on his chest. At her first stirring he sat up and waited. There was no doubt about it; she had taken possession of him. He felt her presence in his breast, in his loins, behind his eyes. She was no longer separate, independent flesh but part of him, living on his breathing and kept alive by the furious beating of his heart. Awake now, she looked at him for a long time, unblinking, as though she was not seeing him with her wide-open, bright-blue eyes and yet had no desire to look away at anything else.

"Have you been here for a long time?"

"I have," he said.

"How long? I mean, how long have *I* been here?"

"Since late last night. Do you remember walking home?"

"Some. I remember you in the bar, with that cropped hair and shining face. What are you, a soldier?"

"A quarterback."

"A *what?"*

"Quarterback. I play football. You know, for the Mavericks. In San Francisco."

"The Mavericks," she repeated, giving the words an odd, flat, prehistoric sound. Then she said, "What are you doing here?"

"Waiting for you to wake up, mostly."

She laughed. It was the first time he had seen her face that way, the famous, classic view, her dimple cutting deep into her cheek, her eyes lit by a pinpoint of blue fire that burned so bright it was beyond his understanding. *What was that queer light?* She pushed her hair back with both hands, holding them to her head and smiling at Demp, the pose he remembered from posters outside theaters in San Francisco showing her films and from the covers of movie magazines in hotel lobbies. It was unbelievable to him that she was here, the fur spread falling from her splendid breasts, unbathed, streaks of beer still on her face, with Dempsey Butts of Prairie City, Iowa, and the Mavericks.

"What's your name?" she asked, and stood up, leaving the spread on the chaise longue. She walked away from it toward a door at the side. Her body was a long, golden line of firm, beautiful flesh. Demp stared at her as she pulled the cord that moved draperies away from the windows. He could see a trickle of water running past the window into a black pool.

"Demp. Dempsey Butts." He spoke almost through clenched teeth, aghast at her unconcern about her beautiful nakedness, and then at the harsh, unpoetic sound of his name. Never before had he noticed how ugly it was.

"Hi, Dempsey."

"Demp."

"Oh. Yes. Demp. Hi, Demp." Then she asked:

"You know my name?"

He laughed.

"I guessed," he said. "Isn't it Franny Fuller?"

"Now it is," she said and laughed again, her throaty, choked-off laugh. "My name's really Fanny. Can you feature that?"

He laughed with her, sat down on the bear rug, and looked up at her.

"Oh, Fanny. Franny. You're a very sad girl, aren't you?"

She stared down at him. "Not a beautiful girl, Demp? Sad, not beautiful? That's a new one on me."

"I mean sad . . . and dirty. You need a bath something fierce, and some clean clothes. And you cry, and sleep all the time, and leave this palace for crummy joints down there and dress like a bum and don't seem to care—what you have, what you *are.*"

"Demp, you're a chump. I know what I have. But what use is it? I'm afraid all the time. Of everything. Of being found out for what I am, whatever that is. I don't know. Did you ever see that postcard of me?"

Demp admitted, blushing, that he had. Back at training camp one of the boys had three of them inside the door of his locker.

"Well, I'll tell you a funny thing. Everybody thinks I minded that picture of me in the nothing on those cards everybody bought. Mary Maguire in her column said I hated them. You know something, Demp? I didn't. It was printed at a time like this, when I thought I'd lost myself and maybe my mind. But when I saw it, all that curvy pink flesh of mine, it was reassuring. *That* was what I was, who I was, and it was good to know about it. To see it."

"Why don't you take a bath and get dressed, Franny, and then we'll go find something to eat?"

"What time is it?"

"About one, I think."

"In the morning?"

"Yes."

"I'll go pee, and get some clothes, and then we can find a place."

"Franny, don't you like being clean?"

She seemed to be considering the question gravely.

"No, not really."

"Okay, then. Get dressed."

But it never got to that. Franny came out of the bathroom and said she wanted to stretch out on her bed for just a minute, to rest, "and then we'll go." Demp lay down beside her because he could no longer keep a distance from her after all those hours of wanting her and waiting for her to wake up, and loving her.

She turned her bare, lovely body toward him, and he made love to her in a tender, almost boyish fashion. She lay still and let him do what he wished. He moved gently, even quietly, afraid of frightening her or hurting her, feeling instinctively that she could be hurt, or frightened, during this act. She watched him, listening to the rising sounds of his delight in her. When he was finished and had pulled away, she rolled over on her side so she could see him better. Now he lay still, his eyes half-shut, his legs sprawled and loose, used up and astonished at what he had just been permitted to do. *Demp Butts, with* her, *my God. . . .*

A few minutes later he had recovered. He sat up to look at her, his round eyes and narrow, sunburned face just above hers, breathing in the acrid smell of her body and the remains of his semen.

"Don't leave me, Demp," she said. Her bright eyes were opened wide. "I don't care what you do, but don't leave me alone."

"Only until I can square things with the team," he said. "Then I'll be back. Nothing could keep me away. But I've got a contract. I've got to let them know where I am. Then I'll be back."

"Tonight, Demp. Not tonight." Her voice was high and thin. He could not bring himself to say, the sooner the better for him.

He stayed the rest of the night and the next day and then the next and the next. They lived together in the bedroom as though it was the only room in the house. The room began to feel like a sheltering hut in the forest. They finished the grape juice which by now was half gin because Franny kept saying it needed to be watered down. Then Demp went out, using her white Cadillac, and bought food and cooked it for them. She ate very little of it, but he finished everything he had cooked. She drank the new bottles of grape juice and chewed childishly on the replenished zwieback for which she seemed to have a craving and ate some of a quart of ice cream, covered with chocolate sauce he had found in the cupboard. She would not touch the steak or canned vegetables or broiled tomatoes he had fixed.

"Don't you ever eat anything but those dog biscuits and ice cream?" he asked at the end of the fourth day. By now time had stopped dividing itself into days and nights, into mealtimes and times to sleep. The draperies permanently drawn, life had become continuous, slowed down only by the short naps she took. But she insisted he stay awake while she slept so he lost even his customary sense of mutuality with the rest of the human race. For long periods he thought he was the only person awake in the world and then, when he slept, the only one sleeping. The act of eating meals was uniquely his, too.

Her gratitude to him for his presence was profound. Like children, they set up a ritual in which he played the nurse and she the patient. They played house in the bedroom and bathrooms. They made love or rather, he made love to her. She seemed to permit him entry into her only to guarantee his continued presence, but she took no active part in the ceremony.

Finally he persuaded her to take a shower with him. Afterward he dried her with a huge towel as she sat immobile on a fur-covered stool, her eyes half-shut. He chose a robe from a walk-in closet crammed with clothes, and she put it on. He brushed her hair, fed her with small bits of food when she would not make the effort to eat herself, and then made her lie down when he wanted to make love to her. After each act of love she rewarded him with her charming, warming smile, and a touch, a brush of her fingers to his cheek. Except during the sexual act she never came closer to him of her own accord than to touch him, momentarily, with her fingers. When she permitted him to, he slept.

He noticed the ends of her fingers—blunt and red; she bit her nails until they disappeared into the angry flesh at the tip of her fingers. He wondered aloud at this. She told him it did not matter. The make-up people pasted false ones on if they needed to photograph her hands. Or they used someone else's unbitten fingers for close-ups.

The bedroom became a kind of nursery, a timeless, encapsulated place where they lived as loving children. Slowly she seemed to recover. On the last day and night of their marooned life she talked more to him than she had before. They spoke of their careers, he told her about football.

"If I'm still in it," he said, ruefully.

"Why wouldn't you be?"

"I'm AWOL from training camp for some time now."

"So am I, from the Studio. There'll be hell to pay, I suppose. What day is this?"

Demp had to go into the kitchen to study a wall calendar hanging behind the door. He came back. "Sunday," he said.

She was a week late, she said, reporting for the picture. But the first week didn't matter that much. It was mostly fittings and briefing on the part, so she might just get away with it. From under her bed she fished out a soft, bulky book, her script, and began to look into it. The long separation from the world was almost over. Franny, Demp saw, was making small overtures toward return. He knew he was now free to speak of his own plans.

"I can get a train out tonight, or a plane if I'm lucky," he said.

Her head bent over the typed pages, Franny seemed not to hear. It was always to be this way. As her need and her panic receded she became almost indifferent to her rescuer upon whom, hours before, her very survival seemed to depend. He told her he would be back as soon as his schedule permitted. He told her he loved her, and wanted to marry her. To all his sentences she smiled, as if from a long way off, and said nothing. She was at her white dressing table when he bent to kiss the top of her head, and he realized that she was revived and beautiful in the mirror image that he saw. It was the image he shared with the world. As he got to the door and looked back she was already absorbed in doing something to her face, staring intently at it in a hand mirror. She said nothing more to him. He called a taxicab from a phone in the entrance hall and then walked out to the hedge that surrounded the property to wait for it to come. Standing there in the same clothes he had put on a week ago, he felt curiously unlike himself.

Waiting, he had a vision: he saw a row of starched white shirts on the hooks behind his bedroom door in Prairie City. The sight went away as quickly as it had come, and he was left on the road in Beverly Hills, asking himself questions: What had he done with this week? What would he tell the coach and the team he had been doing? For that matter, how would he explain it to himself, tomorrow? Whom had he saved? He didn't know. And had he lost anything? He couldn't tell that either. He had the disoriented feeling of an amnesia victim slowly groping his way back to identity.

The taxicab came. To his long-cloistered eyes, the driver looked very strange, like a man from another planet. Telling him where he wanted to go was an exertion. The words sounded odd to his ears, as though he was using a language new to his tongue or moving painfully from long silence to unaccustomed speech.

All the way to the hotel, where his bag, he discovered, had been left for him with the bell captain, to the station, to San Francisco, and then out to the camp, he could not shake the eerie feeling that he had returned from visiting the Wizard of Oz or the Castle of the Sleeping Beauty or the Enchanted Forest. Something almost supernatural had happened to him. But he told no one where he had been or whom he had been with. He accepted the disciplinary measures issued against him for his absence, and agreed without protest to pay the large fine. He had a sense that none of it had anything to do with him, Dempsey Butts, the lover of Franny Fuller.

The feeling persisted. He found he was not listening to what his teammates were saying, he could not keep his mind on memorizing the plays the coach was trying to teach him, he was indifferent to the reprimands, the threats, the warnings. Three weeks later, certain he was sealing his fate with the Mavericks, at least for this season and probably forever, he asked for a few days off, went to the station, and took a train to Los Angeles. He was going, he felt, to rescue the enchanted princess in her castle, drawn back there by an invisible silken thread unwound from the magical ball she had given him.

Franny had insisted on a New York ceremony because a series of personal appearances in that city brought her there and then too, she told Dempsey, "My life began there, with Eddie Puritan."

By the time eight of Demp's friends from the team, players, two coaches, and one of the owners, had assembled downtown at City Hall, it was late in the day. Luxuriating in the numbers and the warmth of the whole gathering, Demp still was consumed with impatience. He sat with Franny, holding her hand, moving from one side of the bench to the other, afraid she would forget he was there. She seemed to have retreated into a daze, aware of what was happening yet not personally involved in it. Demp had the feeling he should be snapping his fingers before her eyes, if only he dared, to keep her awake. In the bleak, brown-painted waiting room which smelled of generations of anxiety and clothing, full now of other nervous couples dressed up for their own occasion, apprehensive and uneasy in these official, decayed surroundings, they all waited for Demp's family to arrive.

They waited for almost two hours.

The room grew heavy with heat and breathing. The other couples had, one by one, disappeared into the room marked Chambers and not come back. Outside, newspaper reporters and photographers clamored for pictures of Franny and Demp, but the clerk in charge of the waiting room had been instructed by the city magistrate not to let them in. At five thirty the Butts family still had not arrived. By then Franny was in a state beyond recall. She sat far back on the inhospitable brown bench, her feet pulled up under her, her profile seeming to be carved along the silky grain of her fair skin and tousled blond hair, immobile, looking utterly terror-stricken.

Demp's family had been very late getting to New York on

the train which had broken down for hours outside of Chicago. From Grand Central Station they went to the Astor Hotel to change their clothes and then had some trouble getting a taxicab to take them downtown in the rush hour. At quarter to six they arrived at City Hall, sweating in their unaccustomed dark suits and shirts and ties, silent with awe in the presence of the athletes and the Movie Star.

Demp pulled Franny to her feet and led her over to his father. He had carefully planned the introduction and he carried it off well. "Dad," he said softly, "this is Franny. Franny, this is my father, the Reverend Butts."

Franny whitened under her careful make-up. Demp had told her that his father was a minister, but until she heard him introduced the fact did not seem to pose any serious threat to her. She stared at him, her brilliant blue eyes wide.

"Hi ya," she whispered. Demp put his arm around her. "He's a great guy, Franny. Don't let him frighten you. He only looks serious because that's his job."

Franny managed a smile. The Reverend Butts reached out to pat her shoulder but only managed to reach Demp's arm.

"She's a real beauty, Demp," he said appreciatively, as though Franny were not there. "You're a real lucky fella. You've really called the right play this time." Demp could tell his father had rehearsed the speech many times.

Franny did not understand this reference. She had frozen again into an attitude of deep absorption, like a sentinel standing guard who dreams of being somewhere else. She held Demp's hand, desperately trying to find a sticking point for her attention.

"What time is it?" asked Demp of two of his teammates hovering just behind him, their eyes fixed on Franny. In his excitement Demp had forgotten to wear his watch.

"About six."

"I'll see if I can find the magistrate."

While Demp was gone his teammates and the Buttses stood around in small whispering groups, like people waiting for an overdue airplane. There was none of the usual premarital gaiety because, at the center of the room, wrapped in visible and impregnable solitude, the bride-to-be kept lonely watch, involved only in communicating with herself. Excluded from her notice, the men in the room did not feel free to approach her, could only look at her, amazed and confused by her beauty, not comprehending her isolation. Like Blake, they questioned fearfully, not so much the object she was as the daring hand that had framed it, the imagination that conceived it. About her perfect body and face there seemed to be something infinite, mythic; it kept men at a distance. Not moving closer to her was a discipline they enforced upon themselves, a religious exercise. They were, they felt, in the presence of a great Mystery.

Demp came back. "He's not here anywhere. No one can find him. They say he may have left the building."

The magistrate had, a half-hour before. Furious at having been kept waiting for more than an hour and a half (the assigned appointment had been for four), especially by celebrities to whose whims, by virtue of the bench, he felt superior, he had clapped his black fedora to his bald head and stomped out, muttering to the clerk about football players and movie stars. Even an apologetic telephone call, when Demp learned where he was, would not bring him back. There was nothing for everyone to do but leave.

After Demp's half-hearted attempt to set a time for the next day, half-hearted because everyone but the Buttses and Franny knew that his teammates had to leave very early the next day for the West Coast, the players went back to their hotel. Demp had invited them all to a celebratory dinner at the Astor after the ceremony but, once they saw it was not coming off, they left the waiting room discreetly, without mentioning dinner.

Demp was relieved. Outside, the reporters had gone to find telephones to report to their papers the story of the nonmarriage. Photographers stayed on to take pictures of the solemn-faced couple, and of the Butts family looking down in embarrassment at their shoes. The players formed a wedge and moved past them so they got shots only of their broad backs. Franny and the Buttses took a taxi uptown, after Demp had called the hotel to cancel the dinner. Franny had not known of this plan.

"Where shall we all have dinner?" Demp asked Franny in the cab, holding her two cold hands in his. The twins sat on jump seats facing them, the Reverend on the other side of Franny, and Tunney up with the driver behind the glass divider.

The Reverend looked glum. Even though it had been their lateness that had caused the cancellation of the ceremony, he felt there was something ominous, something very wrong about the whole event. His exclusion from performing the rites, by virtue of their decision not to have the ceremony in Prairie City, was a sign to him that all was not well with Demp and this odd, beautiful, silent girl, that this marriage was, somehow, an uncommon solution, a compromise, for an enigma the nature of which he could not plumb.

"Not awfully hungry, Demp," Franny said.

"Oh, Franny," he said, infinite pity in his voice. "Come on. Have some dinner with us."

"How about Jack Dempsey's? I've heard a lot about that place," said the Reverend.

"Great!" said Sharkey, bouncing in his seat.

"We can't eat there, Father," said Demp gently. "People would mob Franny in there. It has to be somewhere quieter."

The question was resolved by simple division. Franny and Demp went to the hotel suite he had reserved for them at the Astor with the promise that he would join his family later for dessert and coffee. The Reverend, by now hardened into disapproval of everything that was being done, and the other Buttses walked up Broadway to Jack Dempsey's. Demp called room service and ordered two dinners. But when they came, Franny was not hungry; he had to eat them both.

Demp entertained her by talking about his family. Of all of them, only the twins seemed to interest Franny. He had caught her watching them during the wait. That night she asked about them. "What are they like?"

"Like?"

"I mean, when they're together. Do they act like one person, the same person?"

Demp was nonplussed. "I don't know. Sometimes, I suppose. They're very much alike and sometimes you think you're talking to one of them and it turns out it's the other. Sometimes they tease and won't tell you who you're talking to."

"No, I don't mean that. I mean—well, I don't know, I don't know how to say what I mean. Do you think that, when they look at each other they see themselves?"

"I don't know. Why do you ask that?"

"I guess because I think it would be wonderful to find out about yourself, how you look, what you're like inside, from your twin."

"It would be strange, wouldn't it?"

"Oh no, Demp. Not if you really didn't know. It would be wonderful."

Dempsey never made it to Jack Dempsey's.

Next morning, deeply contrite, Demp breakfasted with his father downstairs in the hotel's coffee shop. He outlined in great detail the plans for the day. "The magistrate will marry us this afternoon, he says. The team guys can't be there, but you will be . . ."

The Reverend did not reply.

"Won't you?" Demp suddenly took fright at his father's silence.

"Demp, do you really think you can be happy with this girl?"

"I don't know, Father. But I love her. Right now I'm more worried about her being happy with me. I'm not so much, you know."

The Reverend was looking at the sports page of the *Daily News* as he drank his black coffee. A headline said NO HITCH

FOR SOLID CITIZEN BUTTS, FF. Beneath it was a picture of Franny and Demp leaving the waiting room. Demp was scowling into the camera, his dark tie pulled away from his opened shirt collar. Behind him the Reverend could see himself. Inexplicably, in the picture Franny was smiling, that charming, all-embracing smile that had succeeded on the screen because it seemed to include in its warmth every adult male in the world. It was the only time in that unfortunate afternoon and early evening, thought the Reverend, that he remembered her smiling. That smile, he thought, must belong to her profession, must be evoked only as a public thing.

"Why do they call you Solid Citizen in the papers, Demp?"

"Oh, you know. From a small town in Iowa, preacher's son, no drinking or smoking, all that. The guys on the team called me that, and some sportswriter picked it up."

"Sounds sort of scornful, doesn't it, to you?"

"Well, I suppose it is, when you consider that most of the other guys live it up more and get into the papers a lot because they have fights with guys in bars who remind them of their fumbles or something. I'm kind of a quiet one, I guess, so that's how I come by it."

"How about this marriage? Will you still be Solid Citizen Butts if you marry this movie star? And another thing I wanted to ask you. Doesn't she have any family, a father or a mother? Who are her people?"

"Hard to say, Father. I really don't know anything about them. She's never mentioned anything about them. But I love *her*. That's what matters. And she needs me."

"Yes, I'm sure she does. But I'm worried about you and what will happen to you, Demp. Do you need her?"

"I love her. That's about it." Demp stopped, and then he said, smiling ruefully at his father, "The only thing I regret about it all is, well, you know, I wish Maw could have been here."

"Yes," his father said, and folded his paper. "Well, what

are we going to do now? Want to get Miss Fuller and sightsee with me and the boys? We've never seen anything here, and we thought we might like to go to the Statue of Liberty."

"I'll ask Franny," said Demp, without hope.

Upstairs, Franny was still asleep. On the floor on her side of the bed was a round pile of discarded clothes from the night before that reminded Demp of cow plop on the farm. He picked up the clothes and neatly folded each piece on the chair. Then he sat down on the bed and shook her gently.

"It's almost eleven, Franny. Do you want to go to see the Statue of Liberty with Father and the boys and me?"

"For God's sake, Demp."

"Well, then, can you be dressed and ready by three? The appointment with the magistrate is for four. And someone from the Price Agency is camped in the lobby. He's mad as hops because you didn't let them know about yesterday. I mean, today."

"Demp, don't leave me. I'll get up if you stay."

"And bathe?"

"Okay, Demp. And bathe. If you stay."

So he did. His father said nothing when he told them he couldn't come with them to the Statue of Liberty and that he'd meet him and the boys at three forty-five. At City Hall.

"Business as usual," said Sharkey, the family joker. "We'll be there."

They were all assembled on time, the magistrate, now flattered into good humor by the attentions of the press, was in a jovial mood. He told reporters he remembered something Bernard Shaw had said, and that he thought this marriage might well produce a prodigy, a beautiful football player or an athletic movie star. The reporters chuckled dutifully at this, practiced as they were at responding automatically to remarks by public officials, no matter how foolish.

Demp and Franny were interviewed by reporters as they

left the magistrate's chambers. Demp talked nervously, in a tight voice, to hide Franny's silence. Yes, they were honeymooning right here in New York. No, he was not willing to say at what hotel. No, they were not returning to Hollywood after that, he had been given some time off, and so had Franny. Yes, Franny loved football and expected to come to as many of the games as she could before shooting started on *The Mermaid and the Shepherd,* her next picture. No, not before next month. They'd have a lot of time together first. Yes, the Reverend Butts (a gesture in the direction of his father who said nothing and stared at the cameras) approved of the marriage. Why else would he and his family have come east from Iowa to be at the ceremony? Yes, these are my brothers, Sharkey, Sully, and Tunney. Yes, named for the . . .

"And how does it feel to be Mrs. Butts, Miss Fuller?" Franny looked at the questioner. She appeared to be almost alseep, standing up, her eyes wide open.

"*Who?* Oh, yes." Bulbs flashed from all corners of the room. The photographers wanted shots of her with everyone. They caught her from every angle, expressions of delight, ordered by them, crossing her face and evaporating into her hair, her eyes remote but lovely, her upturned nose alive and tilted toward them like a sharp warning of some inner storm, her famous smile, with its unilateral dimple, flashing out instantly when called for and then retreating fast, like a timid pedestrian at the changing of the light.

The photographers were still taking pictures as the wedding party climbed into taxicabs. One of them caught Franny looking back, crouching to enter the cab, Demp's hand on her buttock. The picture was picked up and syndicated, with the story of the famous marriage, at the top of Mary Maguire's column in the *News.* Arnold Franklin, the poet whose first verse play had just been successfully produced on Broadway by the Atelier Company, sat in his study in New York reading the morning papers. He always went through two, the *Times* and the *Daily News,* for the great variety of language and rhetoric they afforded him, he said. He studied the picture of Franny Fuller and her new husband, Dempsey Butts, in the *News.* Outside his closed door, Arnold Franklin could hear his wife, Naomi, running the vacuum cleaner with her characteristically angry, jabbing movements. He stared at the celebrated face in the paper, and at Butts's incongruously placed hand, at the cab driver's leer and the mindless faces of bystanders on the periphery poking their faces into the camera's eye. *She looks like a small animal, caught, at bay. Going to ground but still trying to smile. What an incredibly beautiful woman,* he thought.

The first two years they lived together peacefully. Franny's career went well; she advanced to roles the Studio called "serious." She played a French *cocotte* whose mother had been a madam, and who yearned for legitimate family life. She was wildly successful in her first musical, in which she danced (after weeks of tutoring by a New York choreographer) and suggested convincingly a song-and-dance star of *The Ziegfeld Follies* because another singing voice was substituted for hers.

The Depression, which had dampened the real life of most Americans, had an inverse effect on the films Hollywood produced. Sensing correctly that escape films, garish and lavish musicals, and lush costume dramas would raise the spirits of the population, Hollywood filled its already elaborate Palaces with palatial films. It was the Golden Era of the golden film capital, and Franny Fuller, its golden girl, served it well. Her pictures were touted as "pure escape": In those depressed years that was felt to be the best that could be said for a movie.

The economic recovery did not make itself felt until war clouds had been gathering over the European continent for some years. Despite the deep isolationist feelings of most of his parishioners, Demp's father was urging upon the young men in his church, and his sons, the thought of service to the already involved neighbor to the north. Demp decided to offer himself early to the armed services of his own country, a move he knew would please his father. But for some reason he could never understand, he was turned down by all of them. Even the Air Corps, said to be accepting small, athletic men for the cockpits of pursuit planes, did not want him. Something about his kneecaps, they said, although he had never felt anything too much out of the way with them. He accepted their rejections cheerfully and went back to playing football.

For three years he tried to adjust two inflexible schedules so that Franny and he could meet at one coast or another. He lived with the fiction that if only these could be straightened out they would be able to return to the unvarying, tideless love they had enjoyed with each other at the start. Finally they were able to arrange a month, whole and uninterrupted, together.

In that month, he tried hard. They stayed at a friend's house in Greenwich Village. It was the Christmas season. Walking through Washington Square on cold evenings, having dinner at the Jumble Shop and the Colony (where the neon had failed on its sign and the blacked-out final letter gave them much hilarity) on 8th Street, going to movies and then to dingy Village night clubs: he was able to do all these things with her in relative privacy.

They were together for long periods of time without speaking to each other. At first Demp regarded this as an advantage, a sign of their closeness. Then he realized it was because they had nothing to say to each other. The silences began to make him uncomfortable. They spent less and less time out of doors, more days and nights in the back bedroom of their borrowed house, lying side by side on the bed in a strange communion that represented not marriage, not sex, not the concelebration of the rites of pleasure, but merely mutual peace. Outside the snow piled up in the streets and in the little backyards. A cold wind rattled the panes of glass in their windows. Demp felt like a refugee who had found a warm but temporary haven. "We are," he told Franny, "orphans in the storm."

Everyone else in the city seemed to be celebrating hectically. England was at war, and there was a feeling it was only a matter of time before it would be in these streets and bars.

Demp and Franny spent New Year's Eve in the bedroom. Franny sent Demp out to buy champagne and zwieback for a midnight snack. They took the binoculars to watch the parties in the neighborhood. One was in progress on the third floor of an apartment house on Charles Street. Sitting cross-legged on their bed, passing the champagne bottle back and forth between them, they watched four couples celebrating the New Year in a climax of hilarity. Three of the men, all of whom seemed to be wearing pajama tops in place of shirts (later Demp decided they were wearing Palm Beach shirts, *not* pajama tops), held a fourth man at the window's edge, his head hanging over the sill, a steady scream flowing from his O of a mouth, or so they thought watching through the closed window. They could hear nothing.

"Like a silent movie, isn't it?" said Franny. She seemed exhilarated by the spectacle. "What do you think they're doing?"

"Depends on how drunk they are."

"You know, Demp, what I like about binoculars? The feeling that just for this moment, this once, someone else is being looked at. Secretly, you know . . . ?"

Demp nodded. He had never felt burdened by the eyes of the fans upon him. But he was one of many on the field. He could understand how the one always watched would feel relieved at being at the other end of the glasses. The binoculars trained on the party, he saw one of the women, her face a massive grin, pour brown-colored liquid into the open mouth of the upside-down victim, who was now gasping and coughing. He passed the glasses to Franny.

"Look. I think they're trying to drown him."

"What's that they're pouring? Scotch?"

"Can't tell from here. Might be. Or tea. Or even urine."

"Oh, Demp, how terrible. Make them stop." Franny

began to tremble, still staring through the glasses at the window across the way.

"I'm just joking, Franny. Come on over here and lie down with me. Forget about them."

He should have known better, he thought, than to have made that joke. He had learned that threats of catastrophes like this poor drunk being half pushed out of a window would not move her, but she would be badly shaken by an indignity like urine in the mouth. Oceans fascinated her, but she was terrified by small ponds in which the water came to her knees. In anonymous crowds she felt safe; a single man staring at her threw her into a panic. They spent the rest of the night lying chastely together, his arms around her while she shook or sobbed in terror. Finally she fell asleep, and he watched the pale, flat New York City dawn break over the patch of river.

At the start of the new year, after a month borrowed from each of their lives, their peeping-tom existence ended. The games played themselves out in the borrowed house while Demp learned there was no way to rescue and re-create the good moments he remembered from their past. Franny went back to California to work on a new picture and Demp went with her, for a while. There were still two months before training camp opened.

But he could not stand waiting for her in the house with no provision for physical activity except a strangely shaped swimming pool that had a crack in it somewhere and would begin to empty itself soon after it was filled. After a week in Beverly Hills Demp took a train across the continent to Florida where he had arranged to meet some teammates for a month of fishing and conditioning. Their marriage was over. He was relieved to be returned to the world of men and movement, away from the static, isolated, sleepless world of Franny Fuller Butts.

Of course (Demp always reminded himself later) no one, after the first hour of their marriage, ever called her that. That was the least of his concerns. He knew he would never be able to equal her luster. But he never worried about her name. No one in his right mind would tie a name like Butts to this fragile, luminous child. Sure, it served a quarterback pretty well. It was even kind of descriptive. It was fine for a blunt, down-to-earth preacher of the Open Bible Church and his sons. But neither the name nor the concept of marriage which it represented could be fastened for very long on the golden child-woman he had married.

Demp had been in Florida for three weeks when the telephone rang in his hotel room at three o'clock in the morning. He struggled to the surface of a sleep so profound he was almost drowned in it to hear Franny whisper: "Come right away, Demp."

"What. . . ? Oh, Franny. What's the matter? What happened?"

"I can't tell you now, but you've got to come over here."

It must have been the time, or the idea of the distance between them that she had diminished by her command "come over here," or perhaps the week at the Keys he was looking forward to, that made him, for the first time since he had taken her home three years ago and stayed almost a week, say, "No, Franny, I can't come now."

"Demp. No fooling this time. Please come." He heard the sound of urgency in her whisper, but to his ears it was an old sound. He thought it probably signified that she had run out of grape juice, or couldn't find her eyebrow tweezers, or was getting panicky because her supply of Benzedrine or Seconal or Nembutal was almost gone. Or Olivia her housekeeper was on her day off. So many similar emergencies of the same magnitude, at five in the morning or at one in the afternoon as he was leaving the locker room for the field, had made him jump and run, at once, as if he had been called upon to rescue a child from a burning bedroom. This time, he thought, he would not go, he could get away with it, just this once. . . .

"Are you coming now, Demp." The question came

across the wires in the form of a flat command. This made him angry.

"No, Franny, I just can't. Won't you tell me what's the matter?"

"I can't tell you. Just come here."

This time the sorceress's whisper, the siren's song, did not move him to act on her behalf. He said goodnight to her and, thinking he would call later in the morning to see if he could get her to tell him her "troubles," he went back to sleep. In the morning when he called, Olivia answered. She said Franny was not there. Demp was angry, asked no questions. Before Olivia had a chance to say anything else he hung up. He decided she must have gone to work, having recovered from her night's panic, and he put it all out of his mind.

A week later he read in Mary Maguire's column in the *Miami Herald: ". . . FF is resting quietly in Cedars of Lebanon. Exhaustion, the Studio says, although rumor hath it that it may be more serious. . . . Ol' Johnnie Barleycorn, maybe?"*

Demp made rapid airline arrangements and got back to the Coast that night. At first he had trouble getting in to see her. A hospital guard had been stationed on her floor, another guarded her door against the persistence of the press. For once he decided to pull his weight.

"For Christ's sake, get out of my way. I'm her husband."

Franny lay in bed in a room banked with flowers, like a funeral parlor. The odor of slowly dying roses was overpowering. She was curled up in the center of the bed, wormlike, a small inert curve, almost a remnant of humanity, her wild, bright hair the sole evidence of life. He knew she was awake, he could tell, as he stood beside the bed, by the slight motion of her eyeballs under her blue eyelids, but she would not respond when he spoke to her.

"Come on, Franny. It's Demp. Talk to me. What happened?"

She would not talk to him, or even look at him. She had

cut the thread of her confidence in him and he could not get her attention. He left the room and waited near the guard until her doctor came and then went back into the room with him, standing in the corner so that Franny would not see him. He watched the doctor take her pulse and blood pressure and listen to her heart, while she lay inert and unresponding. Then the doctor reached under the covers, pulled her legs apart and bent down to look. From where he stood Demp could see nothing of Franny but her yellow hair and the raised white sheet.

The doctor asked Demp to step outside for a minute. In a few moments he came out, shut the door behind him, and walked over to Demp. He was a hearty, sleek-looking young man with thick-lensed glasses.

"I'm Doctor Harry Bernstein," he said, thrusting his hand toward Demp. "Of course, I know who *you* are. I saw you play last year when I came to Frisco for a convention. You're . . ."

"Yes," said Demp, too preoccupied to notice the doctor's outthrust hand. "What's wrong with Franny—uh, Miss Fuller. I mean, Mrs. Butts." There was something slickly professional about the doctor that confused Demp. He wanted only to hear what he had to say and then to be rid of him. "Tell me."

"She's had a miscarriage."

"You're kidding. How could that be? You must be wrong."

Doctor Bernstein's professional manner did not desert him. His medical training had elevated his view of himself to a place where he disliked at sight anyone who challenged anything he said. But he valued Franny Fuller as a patient and he was determined not to antagonize her husband.

"A miscarriage," he said firmly, and then added, "Of which she was not entirely innocent."

"You're a liar, a damned liar," said Demp. He clenched his fist in Doctor Bernstein's face. "Why would she do something like that?"

The doctor held on to his temper with difficulty. "You're

her husband, Mr. Butts. You ought to know the answer to that better than I do. Let's call it what I think it was then, fella, shall we? A self-induced abortion. Like that better?"

Demp abandoned any attempt to make sense of what Doctor Bernstein was saying. "I don't understand," he said lamely. "I didn't know."

"So." Suddenly the doctor knew he had the lead. With Demp in this bewildered state, attack in any direction would succeed. "I had a bad time, believe me, patching up what she did, or had done to her, I don't know for sure which. I couldn't question her properly without letting every damn scrub nurse and intern in this hospital know about it. Not to mention those reporters hanging about, gasping for news every time I go past them, like fish out of water. So, fella, just say thank you, Doctor Bernstein, for doing what you did. Don't give me any trouble. And don't ask a doctor questions if you're not prepared to hear the truth."

Demp started toward the door to Franny's room. Over his shoulder, but not stopping, he said in a flat tone, "Thank you, Doctor Bernstein, for doing what you did. And Doctor, don't call me 'fella.'" He opened the door to Franny's room and went in. She was still stretched out in the same position but now her eyes were open. He knelt beside the bed.

"It's okay now, Franny. You'll be okay."

"Go away, Demp."

"Okay, I will. But I'll be back. Tomorrow."

"No."

"What do you mean, no?"

What she meant was that she didn't want him anymore, even tomorrow. So much she said. Under the simple words he heard the rest, that he had failed the last of her impossible tests and was to be permanently expelled from her presence, like the peasant boy who loses the princess because he ignores the witch's instructions. He kissed her gently on the forehead, told her he'd see her soon, and went back to the house to gather up his belongings.

"Goin' on another trip, Mr. Butts?" asked Olivia.

"You might call it that, Olivia."

"We've been havin' a time out here, you know that?"

Demp wanted to know the details, but he couldn't bring himself to ask. Large, brown, motherly Olivia, her fat arms folded over her heavy bosom in the classic posture of maternal judgment, didn't wait to be asked. She launched into a lengthy narrative which muddled together Franny's discovery of her pregnancy, her frantic calls all over the country in an effort to locate him because she had lost the itinerary he had left with her, and Olivia's discovery of her in bed in the morning.

"Blood everywhere, see, and Miss Franny lyin' there, starin' at me, not sayin' nothin'. I do wish you'd been here, Mr. Butts, it was awful, jess bloody awful."

"Yes," said Demp, turning back to his packing.

"When we expect you back, Mr. Butts?" she asked, carefully. Olivia understood that the details, which she could not resist supplying, had wounded Demp.

"When Mrs. Butts calls me," said Demp, "I'll come. I'll leave a copy of my schedule."

But she never called.

4

The Poet

Liberal, sensitive, intellectual, critical, cynical: Arnold Franklin had always managed to subdue the forces around him to his master plan for himself. At CCNY he had edited the newspaper on his own radical terms while still able to compel the admiration of the college's administration for his competent student journalism. At the very moment he was being praised by the president he attacked him as reactionary and niggardly. Franklin published his own poetry in the college literary magazine; his work was much admired and emulated by other poets among the students.

Franklin combined his poetic talent and his fondness for the theater by writing plays in verse. His first, *The Lemming,* written two years after college, was performed by the Atelier Company. It was violent, radical, shocking, and vaguely poetic. But he possessed what Lawrence Langer, in writing about the play, called a genuine sense of theater. *The Lemming* did so well on 14th Street that it was moved to Broadway. On the Sunday of the week before the Broadway opening, in *The New York Times,* Franklin lashed out at Broadway audiences who were, he wrote, the natural enemies of what his play had to say. The article was a brave piece of defiance, effectively bolstering both his ego and the ticket sales at the box office.

Soon after his graduation from college, Franklin married Naomi Kaplan, a woman of his own age. Naomi was a well-fleshed, passionless woman whose single concern since her girlhood had been to be married like her mother and her friends, and then to play in some game or other every afternoon of her life. She had no desire for children. But these things she disguised successfully from her "intended," Arnold Franklin, who was dazzled by her pose that she was devoted to poetry, to the higher life of the mind, and to the underlying passions of the body that sustained it.

After their marriage she cooked elaborate meals for herself and Arnold, not so much for his gastronomical pleasure as for her wish to report to her women friends the routines she employed and the menus she devised.

Naomi possessed a certain measure of loving kindness which she reserved for her friends. Her husband bored her, indeed, almost immediately after the excitement of the wedding was over. Their wedding night ended the promises her body seemed to hold out for Arnold. She suffered his ministrations to her in bed as if she were enduring with heroic fortitude some kind of painful and undeserved trial. When a friend came by one evening to talk about the formation of the Abraham Lincoln Brigade to go to Spain she found herself hoping that Arnold's radical zeal would take him there, thus providing her with some relief from what she considered unusually heavy sexual demands. But it did not happen. Arnold's poor eyesight would never have allowed him to take his place among American antifascists.

Except for her progress reports to the "girls" at the bridge table, she had little sympathy for Arnold's agony over his writing. She was impatient with his presence in the apartment all day long. She longed for private, feminine hours such as her friends had, time to do things to her body and her face without fear of his walking in upon her. Except for the luster of his name which was beginning to be well known in New York, giving her a certain amount of standing with the girls, and his income, sporadic but adequate when it did come, Naomi had no need whatever for him.

She was astonished when he finally told her he knew this. It had never occurred to her that theirs was not a complete and ideal marriage. What was missing? she asked. What else *was* there?

Arnold moved out of their apartment and took two rooms in the Ansonia, a Broadway hotel full of retired, elderly Jews living on their interest and coupons, and theatrical young girls involved in obscure productions in the Village from which they hoped for a break. In this hotel Arnold was a personage, treated with respect by the staff, stared at in the restaurant and in the aged elevators by the inhabitants who rented their rooms by the year.

After a time Naomi reluctantly agreed to a divorce. Arnold submitted to the unsavory pantomime that the State of New York required as evidence of infidelity although he insisted that "it" be done in a midtown hotel where he wasn't known.

In two years he was free. Naomi returned to blessed singleness. She kept her married name, the apartment, generous support, and gave herself over wholly and with pleasure to her wide circle of women friends. She was an Amazon warrior who had won a costly victory over a male army, not one whit diminished by her losses. Now that she was free of him, Naomi displayed a compassionate affection for her former husband, like a proud owner recalling a prize horse from his stable that had gone lame after some major victories.

She ate a great deal, grew fat, and began to play bridge for a penny a point.

Arnold Franklin's concept of life, formed from his parents and prolonged into his marriage to Naomi, was bourgeois. After his divorce he became more conventionally settled than ever. He insisted on being left alone amid all the orderly impedimenta of his literary life. He required a well-arranged, dusted set of rooms to live in, a neat periphery to the methodical and productive-looking confusion of his desk.

He had abandoned the Ansonia and taken a house, which he sublet from a friend, on Washington Square.

He told himself that his appetite was delicate and capricious and at the mercy of his creative urge. This was a fiction. The truth was, he got hungry three times a day at the same hour every day. He went without eating only when he had some strong, self-punishing point to make by staying away from the table.

All his habits were equally compulsive and meticulous. He liked drawers full of rolled socks, starched shirts, and pressed undershorts. He told the woman who came in to wash and iron that he liked his handkerchiefs pressed into a folded triangular shape that slipped effortlessly into his breast pocket. He drank two cocktails before dinner, never more, and nothing, ever, afterward. He wrote during the same hours every day, and for this activity he required good light. His eyes were weakening and he wore bifocal glasses.

He wrote always in the same manner, on legal-size, lined yellow paper with a carefully chosen English Parker fountain pen and blue-black ink. He did his best work seated in a particular chair, his pipe and tobacco at his right side and a hassock near his feet for those moments when he felt the need to stretch his legs.

At four in the afternoon, after a short nap, in good or bad weather, he took a walk. He liked to leave the house and walk through the streets and mews of the Village at the exact time he knew the maid was in the process of preparing dinner. His excursions were timed to bring him back at six, when the evening meal would be waiting for him. Sunk in upon his poetic problems, he preferred dinner to be solitary and silent. Occasionally he broke this rule and invited a female friend to dinner. He was patient with what he considered her pointless chatter because he had trained himself, under his parents and Naomi, not to hear too much of it, and because it seemed a small price to pay for the subsequent evening's pleasure in his bed.

These occasions were always without pressure or strain.

After a pipe, while she smoked cigarettes, they would talk a little, and then retire for an hour or so upstairs, after which he would offer to accompany the lady back to her quarters. Somewhat perplexed by the courtliness of his demeanor, she would nevertheless know it was time to leave.

By eleven Franklin was always back in his study. The last hour of the evening was reserved for a reading of the day's work. His invariable bedtime was midnight, a time determined by the amount of sleep he knew he needed and the length of the comprehensive news report on Hitler's advances he listened to every night on the radio. Because his chest was deemed weak (as his mother always reminded him) and his eyes even weaker (this of course was a fact, not a maternal opinion), his connection to the war was only peripheral. True, his verse plays took on a slight patriotic coloration.

But the order and precision of his working life remained the same. At five of twelve he arranged the yellow paper in a neat stack and filled his pen for the next morning, emptied the waste basket and the ashtray, and locked the doors. He removed the telephone receiver from its cradle, lowered every shade in the house, closed all the doors to every room, and settled down to sleep in a rear bedroom chosen because it was small and situated away from the noises of the Square. He disliked being disturbed during his undeviating eight hours sleep, in preparation for a routinely creative morning.

Before he was forty, and as a result of the careful strategies of his life plan, Arnold Franklin was a success. He was one of the few American poets able to live on the proceeds of his published poetry and his successful verse plays. His poems were read and explicated in literature classes in universities; he lectured at Harvard, at Carnegie Tech, and at other smaller places. His critical writing, incisive, often witty, and always pitiless, appeared in the literary quarterlies and in the small magazines. He was always in demand to read his own work. Hollywood made inquiries about his availability to do the scenario of *The Lemming*. He said he was not in the least interested.

Arnold's poetry turned to the right with the years and took on a new, ethnic significance. The fierce, adolescent, proletarian sympathies of his college years that gave his early manuscripts such stunning force gave way, with the predictable nostalgia of maturity, to strong sympathy with the despairs and urban failures of his lower-class Jewish family. With this new, stern honesty came the sympathies of his readers. Even secure, white Protestant admirers could identify with his compassion for the outcasts, the self-aware fathers and self-sacrificing mothers, guilt-ridden sons and overwrought daughters that populated his poems and plays. *At the End of My Rope,* his third and most successful play, achieved a perfect amalgam of social indignation and ethnic *angst,* all of it couched in highly charged free verse.

His work absorbed all his days, and much of his nights. He was now concentrating on a new manuscript, a rendering of *The Tempest* into modern terms. He might have gone on this way, working almost all the time on *Tempest Two,* as he intended to title his long poem, had Lou Price not bothered him late one afternoon.

All that day the writing had gone well. He was halfway through the revision of a very difficult section when Price rang the doorbell.

"Are you home, Arnie?" he asked foolishly when Arnold opened the door.

"What do you think? Decide for yourself."

"Okey doke. I'll start again. Can I come in? It's four thirty. Time to cover the keys and bring out a bottle and a coupla glasses."

"So it is. Sorry, Lou. I've been working and forgot the time."

Price inspected the living room, at the end of which was Arnold's worktable and typewriter. "Looks pretty orderly for a day's work."

"You can't really tell. I hide the waste basket behind the couch."

Price was Arnold's literary agent. He was one of those Lilliputian men who makes up for his lack of stature by an abnormal show of toughness. In truth, he was a man with an unusually gentle nature, devoted to the service of others. Arnold and he had been friends in college, where Price was business manager of the newspaper Arnold edited.

"I work better when everything's in order," Arnold said. Price knew this. Even in the editorial office of the campus newspaper, before Arnold could put a word on paper, he had to square away everything on his desk, clean the typewriter keys, open and answer the mail, and empty the ashtrays. Sometimes he so tired himself out with essential housekeeping tasks that he had no energy left to write, a consummation Lou knew Arnold deplored but still could not prevent.

Arnold mixed Lou a drink and sat down opposite him across the coffee table.

Lou asked: "Doing anything tonight?"

"Not that I know of. Thought I'd stay home, have Josie get dinner for me, and then work some more. You're welcome to stay. She always cooks enough for the cast of *Hamlet.*"

"Thanks, but I haven't had dinner at home since I was fifteen. If the plate doesn't come covered with a silver protector I can't eat what's on it."

"Tough. Maybe Josie can send out for one."

"But I wanted to tell you. I have a swanky dinner date and I thought you could join us if you want to."

Arnold said nothing. Usually when Lou Price let him in on a date it was because he had a middle-aged client, divorced, widowed, or maiden, he thought might be good for him. Lou considered human relations part of his job. A bachelor himself, with unconventional sexual preferences, he believed everyone else should be married, settled, and working at top speed and effectiveness to provide him with salable manuscripts at regular intervals.

Arnold asked: "Another client?"

"Not like that at all. This one is something. Franny Fuller."

"Surely you joke. Why would she want to have dinner with you?"

Lou stretched his miniature legs before him. Most of the time he sat down, at tables, at his desk, or on couches, because he had an idea he looked taller that way. Actually, seated beside a larger man, he took on the appearance of a ventriloquist's dummy.

"I knew her a long time ago, through an old friend, Eddie Puritan, who was her first agent. My agency handles her now. She's here for a few days. I've been assigned to dinner detail tonight."

"How nice for you. I thought she had a husband. That football player."

"Not anymore. She's between husbands, as they say out West. Mary Maguire says the rumor is she's going to marry her new leading man, some boy actor, the one with the jug ears, what's his name, the one who made a comeback when he was eighteen, yeah, Jimmie Lombard. But we haven't heard anything about it back here, at least not from her. But whatever. Tonight, Arnie my pal, she's mine, all mine. And yours."

Arnold was bored by Lou's narrative, uninterested in the prospect. He wanted to get back to his desk before dinner. He drank off the last of his gin and stood up.

"Thanks, but no thanks, Lou. I'll sit this one out."

Lou handed him his glass. "That's very rude. Aren't you going to freshen up this dry ice?"

In the end, loosened by two gins, his concentration broken, and realizing he was tired of his own company in that room all day, Arnold agreed to go. They took a cab uptown to pick up Franny Fuller at the Plaza. Lou went to the desk to call to say they were there. She said all right, she'd be right down.

They waited in the lobby for almost an hour. Twice Arnold decided to leave, and started to, and twice Lou stopped him. Finally she came down. There was a great stir in the lobby. The patrons of the hotel, rarely interested in celebrities, stood in their places that evening to look at Franny Fuller as she came through the lobby from the elevator. Lou Price rushed to meet her. She smiled down at the small, immaculate man in patent-leather evening slippers, his thin, oiled black hair glistening, his voice high and delighted. Arnold stood back, watching.

Lou said: "Franny, this is Arnold Franklin, the poet. Arnie, this is—"

"I know," said Arnold. "How do you do."

Franny Fuller continued to look down on Lou's shining head as though to quell his excitement. Then she turned her astonishing eyes, blue, depthless, and childlike, unseeing yet all-embracing, shallow and still full of a curious nameless glow, on Arnold. They all stood there, the interested spectators keeping their distance, forming a vague rim around them. Lou Price tried to set Arnold and Franny in motion.

"Let's get going," he said. Arnold did not move. He stood looking at Franny Fuller.

"I hope you don't mind my barging in on your dinner," he said. He realized he was staring at her but he could not look away.

Franny Fuller said nothing.

"Let's go," said Price. "I have a cab waiting."

In the cab Franny Fuller sat between the two men. She looked ahead as though she were memorizing the driver's number, name, and picture on the card hanging on the dashboard. Then she said flatly, "The poet." Clearly she had never heard of him before.

"Oh yes," said Lou eagerly, launching into a long account

of Franklin's career beginning with what he seemed to consider its high point—their college friendship.

They went to the Roof Garden. An enormous orchestra played Cole Porter and Irving Berlin songs under a roof painted with stars and light-blue, floating clouds. Men and women in evening clothes drifted over the waxed floor, appearing bemused by the music and their memories, reclining against each other in nostalgic languor.

Arnold asked Franny Fuller to dance. She shook her head. He found himself wondering if all contact between them had dried up irrevocably when she heard what his profession was. He fell into a silence of his own, leaving Lou Price to carry on.

Lou's head turned to and fro, he babbled on, becoming the comic fulcrum of a conversation now reduced to monologue. He talked to Arnold about Franny's new picture, about the prospects of shooting on location in Arizona. To Franny he jabbered on about what a great honor it was to represent a poet who might win the Pulitzer Prize some day.

Arnold tried to catch Franny Fuller's eye. But she was staring ahead, apparently unaware of him. Her blue eyes seemed to have clouded over and turned dense, fixed upon the water tumbler as if she expected it to overflow at any moment. He asked again, "Will you dance with me?" There was a long pause. Then, sounding far away, she said, "All right."

They had plenty of room in which to move. People on the floor recognized her at once, her whispered name spread through the Roof Garden, and everyone on the dance floor stood back to watch her. They asked each other: "Who's the man she's with?" No one seemed to know. Astonished at how much more beautiful she seemed "in person," as they said to each other, than on the screen, they remarked upon every one of her features, her piquant lost-child look, her deep single dimple, her flood of gold hair beginning at the sharp point of her forehead, and most of all, her splendid, swelling breasts that strained against the seams of her dress.

No one looked very long at Arnold. People seemed disturbed by his anonymity, by his clear unworthiness to be dancing with Franny Fuller: He felt himself to be conspicuously balding, middle-aged, nearsighted, thin, weak-muscled. But with this beautiful girl in his arms he grew, suddenly expanding into bulky life, elevated to a new height, merely by his closeness to her. Having always thought himself to be Someone, he could not fathom why he should now suddenly have become fluent, graceful, handsome, commanding, *filled out*.

They danced four numbers together. Once started Franny was unwilling to stop. She seemed unaware that people were leaving the dance floor and others had come to take their places. Arnold knew their dinner was waiting but was afraid to suggest they go back to their table. Later, he was to learn that Franny Fuller was oblivious to food. After the first bite of anything she would grow bored, and after a few mouthfuls, like a child, she would have to be reminded to go on eating.

As they danced he became aware of an urgency in his body. She clung to him, hid her eyes in his shoulder so that only the cascade of blond hair could be seen by the onlookers. She moved willingly, even eagerly, to his direction, as though she had abdicated all will to him. He was *leading*. After his years with Naomi, who disliked dancing but took control of their movements when he had persuaded her onto the floor, and after his few attempts to dance with the arid, determined young New York actresses in his plays, this was a new, fine feeling.

They danced on. Back at the table, Lou Price ate his salad alone. Franny Fuller said nothing to Arnold, and he was prevented from speaking by her silence. His own muteness began to bother him. He started to say something. Franny raised her head to look at him solemnly without seeming to see him in particular. He fell silent, stopped by the imploring blankness of her look.

The band put its instruments on their chairs and left the stand. Arnold led Franny Fuller back to the table. She ignored the roast beef on her plate and ordered a Roof Garden Delight, an elaborate concoction of ice cream, whipped cream, nuts, chocolate syrup, and maraschino cherries. For the first time in the evening her interest appeared to be aroused as she described to the waiter exactly what she wanted on the Delight. When it came, she ate voraciously.

She finished it all, tipping the tulip-shaped glass up to drink the last brown drops. Then she smiled at Arnold for the first time, and asked him to order another.

"Same thing?"

"Uh huh."

They sat for a while in silence. Franny played with the glass and her spoon. Then she said: "Does everyone call you Arnold?"

"Yes. Or Arnie."

"Arnie," she whispered in her famous half-voice. "The way I'm called Franny."

My god in heaven, he thought, *I'm hooked.*

The waiter brought Franny the second Delight. Her face lit up and she ate it without once putting the spoon down. *Only while she's eating that sickening mixture,* thought Arnie, *does she seem to be here.* The last spoonful consumed, Franny lapsed into unmoving, blank silence.

Arnie said: "Will you be in New York long?"

Franny looked at Lou who said: "Until the end of the week."

Franny nodded.

Then, for no reason he was able to remember afterward, he breathed in deeply and said: "I'd like to show you the place I have just bought in New Hampshire, if you have the time."

"I'd like to see it," she said.

Arnie and Lou took her back to the Plaza, going through a rear door of the hotel to avoid the crowd of autograph hunters that had gathered on the front steps. They stopped at the door of her suite. Arnie said he would pick her up at eleven on Wednesday for the excursion to New Hampshire.

That was to be the first of Franny's escapes that Arnie was to witness. He arrived at the Plaza promptly at eleven o'clock and called upstairs on the lobby phone. The hotel operator reported there was no answer. "You must be mistaken," he insisted.

"No, sir," she said. She checked her lists. It was right there, she said. Franny Fuller had left the hotel at ten thirty this morning.

"Did she say where she was going?"

"No sir, she did not."

"Do you know when she plans to return?"

"No sir, I do not. She didn't say."

Three weeks later Franny called Arnie to apologize.

"I had to go out," she said by way of explanation.

He was glad to hear from her. His dreams had been full of her face, he had trouble settling down to his writing routine, the platen of his typewriter seemed to have become pitted by the unexplainable presence of her blue eyes every time he tried to insert a new sheet of paper. He thought nothing of the inadequacy of her explanation.

"That's all right, Franny," he said. "When can I see you again?"

"Right now," she said. "I'm at the Plaza."

It was nine o'clock at night. He had just settled down with his pipe and his pages for rewriting. He took a cab and was at the Plaza in twenty minutes. When he called up she told him to come upstairs. She was in a feathered white negligee, a script in hand.

"I called you because I remembered you said you were a poet. Lou Price just gave me this. I don't understand what it's all about. What kind of part is this? What do they want of me? I don't know how to do anything so complicated."

In her anxiety she said more to Arnie in that minute than he had ever heard her say before. He took the script and followed her into the bedroom. She got into bed, and he sat on a small satin dressing-table chair to read.

It took him more than two hours to get through it.

Franny said nothing, and then she listened closely as he began to explain the text to her. Tired of the uncomfortable chair, he moved over to the bed and then, still talking, he stretched out beside her. After a few minutes, he put the script on the floor, took off his clothes, got into the bed, and made love to her.

Arnold stayed the night. He ordered breakfast sent up to the room. He went on talking to Franny about the mindless little script she had been given to study. In the afternoon she lay still while he made love to her. By early evening Arnold began to feel imprisoned.

"I'm going to make a phone call to some friends, Franny. We need to get out of here. I think you'll like them."

The Cairnses were out. He left word that he'd called, from Franny Fuller's suite at the Plaza. A few minutes later they called back. He talked eagerly to Patrick, feeling he had at last made contact with the outside world. Franny was asleep. When she woke he told her he had spoken to the Cairnses and they were coming to have dinner with them.

"Downstairs. All right, Franny?"

"All right," she said. He felt elated that she had agreed to do something more than the limited acts they had been repeating in the overstuffed hotel room.

Two hours later Pat Cairns called from downstairs. Arnold went downstairs to meet him. Mollie was with him. They all greeted each other ostentatiously, with the excessive embraces and exclamations of persons somewhat uncertain about their real feelings for each other.

Both genuine affection and professional suspicion characterized the long friendship between Arnold Franklin and the Cairnses. They had been the first people to do his verse play, at their Atelier. The three had never been able to decide among themselves who deserved the greatest portion of credit for it, and this made them uneasy. When they reminisced about *The Lemming*'s progress from the Atelier Company to the Broadhurst on Broadway, it was always with the caution of diplomats approaching a solution to a delicate international boundary question. They hedged about their own share in its success, unusual for a serious play in free verse. In their conversations they tended to assign credit too liberally to each other, while secretly convinced that it belonged solely to themselves. Arnold's private view that the play and its poetic language were the thing, seemed untenable to the Cairnses. They had cast, directed, and produced other successful plays whose scripts had to be almost entirely rewritten during the six weeks' rehearsals and knew how much depended on execution. Of course, this had not happened with Arnold's meticulously composed play. But because they had all been deeply involved in an historic hit, regardless of their precise degree of responsibility for it, they had grounds for their warm professional relationship.

"Where shall we dine?" asked Pat. He was tall, broad, and fatherly, tending to fat in his middle age, with a shock of grizzled hair, and untamed, tangled eyebrows that gave him a surprised look. In his acting days he had held his wiry hair back with heavy grease. Now his role as mentor of a highly regarded professional acting school allowed him to have it rise naturally from his head, affecting a kind of comfortable and lovable eccentricity. He was an easy man, a favorite subject for Hirschfeld's Sunday-morning cartoons in *The New York Times* theater section whenever a play he directed was to open that week on Broadway. The tangle of his hair and eyebrows could always be relied upon to harbor at least three of Hirschfeld's hidden Ninas.

"The Persian Room. Then we don't have to fool with taxis and all that," said Arnie. "I'm starved. I'll call up to Franny and tell her where we are."

They made their way to the dining room, Arnie walking between the Cairnses, holding Mollie's hand in comradely fashion. He had always gotten on with Mollie, who was self-effacing and therefore, in his eyes, charming. Well into her fifties, she was still pretty, in the way that Irish women are who keep the precise, fine outlines of their faces despite an increase in the bulk of their bodies. Mollie was heavy—

she and Pat had taken on weight at almost the same pace. They illustrated the cliché often used for married couples that they grew to resemble each other.

Mollie's voice was unexpectedly high and strident. She had worked hard on it with all sorts of speech teachers but had never been able to lower it much. In its tones her students could hear echoes of the shrill, happy, Irish girls she had once played in Dublin's Abbey Theatre. But her point of individuality was her clothing. She liked ethnic dresses and collected Hawaiian mumus, Indian saris, and the heavy, woven blouses and skirts of the Mayan Indians. Draped over her heavy body, below her small, pretty face, her colorful, exotic clothes distinguished her from the conservatively dressed theatergoers as Mollie Cairns, herself.

At the door to the Persian Room they were immediately recognized by a theater-wise *maître d'hôtel* who gave them a table not far from the piano. They ordered drinks and waited for Franny. When she had not appeared in an hour, and they had drunk four rounds, Arnie made a lame excuse. Without bothering to call her again (Arnie sensed that if she had not come down by now she was not going to respond to his coaxing), they ordered dinner. Arnie said nothing to the Cairnses, about Franny's other nonappearance, knowing there was nothing he could do about her.

They ate at a leisurely pace, talking theater and literary gossip. Patrick outlined his plans for the reorganization of their school's faculty—fewer full-time people and more visiting professionals. Economics, he said, as well as quality. He inquired if Arnie might not like to teach there for a semester or two now and then. To each of Pat's sentences, Mollie added footnotes in her high, quick voice, like a scholar explicating a text. Arnie said he would give it some thought.

Over coffee, having avoided the question delicately thus far, Pat asked Arnie about his "relationship" with Franny Fuller. While Arnie hesitated, Mollie overcame her natural reticence about other people's conduct, especially creative people whose outrageous behavior she always accepted as normal, and brought herself to ask: "How did you ever get involved with . . . a movie star?"

Arnie was full of scotch, wine, and after-dinner brandy. In the unaccustomed disorder of his senses, he did not say what he planned to say, that he had known her, really, only a few days. Instead, to his amazement, he heard himself telling the Cairnses that he intended to marry Franny Fuller.

They both listened attentively, Mollie trying hard not to show her dismay at the news. They were anxious for details which would, to their doubting minds, make some sense of a union between their friend, the shy, sensitive, talented poet, and the famous motion-picture star whose turbulent life they had read about in the newspapers' gossip columns. Arnie then provided them with a chronology of the admittedly short time he had known Franny, the depth of his love for her, omitting any account of *her* feelings which would have required much fictionalizing. These, he had to say to himself as he talked optimistically to the Cairnses, he knew nothing about, not even if she would consider marrying him.

Like all couples who have stayed together despite violent temperamental differences, the Cairnses liked to hear about the marital intentions of their friends. Their intermittent clucks and *my*s were signs of their understanding, their superiority to the usual cautions of more conventional auditors, and their pleasure at being the recipients of such a startling piece of news.

Arnold had almost finished his short saga of Franny and himself when the lights in the Persian Room were dimmed. A spotlight moved slowly across the heads of the patrons to the piano, where it hovered for a moment, and then stopped. Diners reached for their coffee cups and dessert plates and pulled them closer, seeming to fear that in the darkness which accompanied the entertainment they might be separated from their sustenance.

In the bright circular light there appeared a woman of uncertain age, her harsh dyed hair glittering, the rough texture of her face unavailable to disguise. She appeared to have been pressed into youthful lines without being young. When she had taken her place in the exact center of the light her name was called, like an incantation, from all the corners of the room. The applause was loud and rhythmic: "Helena! Helena!"

Annoyed by the interruption, Arnold stopped talking to listen to the singer. Helena went through her repertory of blues songs, all alike in their wailing lyrics. Her voice had long since disappeared under the weight of her affected delivery, her arms followed a pattern well known to her audience. Like a snake charmer evoking a cobra, she raised their enthusiasm to a pitch far beyond their first delight at her appearance. They seemed to sway toward her as she embraced herself with her familiar floury arms.

Arnold's attention wandered during Helena's performance. Unlike the other listeners, he felt no nostalgia for the aging Helena. His youth had been spent in less elegant places, his ears were tutored by more natural sounds: *Josh White and Leadbelly are more my style.* He played with his empty water glass, making overlapping circles with its wet bottom on the table cloth. Like Arnold, the Cairnses, too, had already used up their quotient of interest and had begun to think of other things. They never noticed the singer throw her arms above her head in a vast, self-congratulatory gesture. It was her signal to her admirers of the end of her act.

The chanteuse gone, the lights back on, Arnold and the Cairnses were freed from forced attention, able now to talk to each other. The cheers and applause gradually died down.

"Depressing, wasn't it?" said Mollie. "She's getting on."

"That's the nice thing about show business, though," said Patrick. "People look at a used-up performer and see her as she once was and love her and behave as though she hadn't changed in the least."

Arnold said: "I suppose."

Patrick could tell he was worrying about Franny upstairs. He said, "Go on up. We'll take care of the damage."

"Not at all. Let me." Arnold took the check, signed it, and wrote Franny Fuller's suite number on it.

"Thank you. Very nice of you," said Mollie. "Why don't you and Miss Fuller come down to the Atelier tomorrow?" It was her effort to equalize Arnold's assumption of the check.

"I'll ask her. You never can tell with her. She might like that. I'll suggest it to her. And thank you for your patient listening. I'm afraid I did run on."

"Not at all," said Mollie. "I enjoyed it."

"Thanks for the feed," said Patrick."

Arnold told her to wear something plain. In the taxi he looked closely at her for the first time and saw she was wearing a sheer black, sleeveless dress cut to her cleavage and clinging close to her hips and upper thighs. Over her arm was a thin, gauzy scarf.

"Did you think the color would make you less visible?" he asked, amused at her innocence but vaguely irked at the target for all eyes she would present.

"It's all I have, Arnie, that's plain like you said."

"Well, yes, plain, I suppose. But there just isn't much of it."

She made a gesture of helplessness and threw the black shawl around her shoulders, obscuring her bosom. At the door of the Atelier, Arnie could tell by the slowness with which she climbed out of the cab that she was searching desperately for reasons not to go in. He decided to give her no chance for escape. Taking her arm, he moved her gently in front of him and opened the door to the old townhouse.

The Cairnses were waiting for them. They came at once from a back room, full of polite, welcoming gestures and vapid talk. Arnold introduced Franny to them. "This is Franny," he said proudly, forgetting to give her their names. Mollie said, "I'm Mollie Cairns," and then smiled at the futility of having to be told who *she* was. Patrick mumbled his name, staring at Franny, trying not to look at the expanse of breasts that was visible under the scarf.

As they walked toward the rehearsal hall Mollie caught glimpses of the famous profile. Opposed to the movies as an art form, she had never seen her in a film but she knew her face well from newspapers and the framed still shots in front of movie theaters. Mollie felt disturbed by Franny's beauty. She belonged to the school of the theater trained to distrust flagrant good looks, believing that a handsome actor was likely to be a poor actor. She could not accept Franny Fuller for anything more than she appeared to be, a magnificently endowed young woman whose fortune was her face and her breasts, her hips and fiddle-shaped backside, all blown up to eight times human size and moved by a machine across a giant screen, a lavish vision—but hardly an actress. Looking at Franny made her remember the skinny, odd-looking little actresses in Dublin, physically hampered by too little chin or too much nose, who had overcome those defects or hidden them completely in superb performances.

None of that, she thought. She led Arnold and Franny Fuller into the hall where a group of students was seated around a large, bare table. Patrick brought a chair for her. Arnold found his own. The Cairnses sat with them, a little behind the students. Patrick introduced them all around. After the first curious, surreptitious glances at Franny, the students turned their attention away from her and Arnold and back to the discussion of their scripts.

"They're working on their version of a play of Arnie's, *Survival of the Unfit,*" Patrick whispered to Franny. "During these first few days of rehearsal they talk the roles out until they begin to understand them, to get the feeling they're moving inside the characters. Then later they will begin to incorporate action, expecting they'll know better how to move and walk and sit after these preliminary talks. They try to work from the inside, from some kind of interior understanding of everything concerning the character, how he clenches his muscles when he's mad, the way her body tenses when she's afraid, his attitude, no, well, rather, his stance when he hears something he likes or doesn't like. That sort of thing."

Franny nodded. *They work from the inside,* she thought. *What in hell does that mean?* What *inside?*

Mollie had been listening to Patrick's *sotto voce* to Franny. When he stopped she said in a low voice: "But there's more to it than that. Once their understanding of the character is as complete as possible, then they need to *be,* not just portray, but to be, to feel at that moment on the stage as if they *were,* that person. In other words, you are not showing emotion as you think it might be, but you are, you see, feeling it, being yourself moved by it, before the eyes of a live audience."

Franny said, almost timidly, "But then it's not acting really, is it?"

"The best acting, actually," said Patrick. "Because it isn't acting except in the broadest sense."

Franny stared at the students in front of her. Engrossed in their study, they paid no attention to their teachers or the visitors, did not even seem to be aware of themselves. One boyish-looking actor, pointing to the script before him on the table, burst out in a constricted voice: "But I hate this guy. Really despise him. What do I do with that? How do I handle that?"

The instructor, who looked the same age as the students, said, "Keep remembering how much you dislike him. It will help you in the part. Especially if you believe, as somebody else just said, that he hates himself. Right, Mr. Franklin?"

Arnold scraped his chair forward. "You're quite right," he said, the pedantic tone of his youth creeping into his voice. His hands moved with swift gestures, his eyes flashed behind his glasses, lighting on student after student and stopping at the instructor. He sketched out in fluent sentences his concept of the character. Then he began to talk knowingly about the character's father. The students switched around in their chairs to look at him. The boyish-looking actor, still on his feet, stared down at the playwright. At one point he broke in upon him to ask a question. Arnold was all understanding, all patience. He stood up to make an abrupt, cutting motion with the side of his left hand against his thigh, to show what the self-hating character might do at a moment of tension in the play.

"I'd like to hear what *you* think now," Arnold said, gesturing toward the students. He moved his chair so far forward that he was now in their circle. Tumbling over each other in their eagerness to speak to him, to test their insights on the creator of the character, they interrupted each other to offer one opinion after another, the women in stage-accented, controlled voices from which all trace of regional origin had been studiously erased, the men in smooth, low-register tones. In their efforts to establish the precedence of their views they grew heated, even angry, with those who disagreed with them, as if they had been discussing a person related to them by blood.

By the time Patrick Cairns entered the circle to make a suggestion, they all appeared to have forgotten that the father of the character did not appear, was not even referred to, in the play. Patrick was pleased at this obedience to his dictum that it was important to create a whole childhood for a character one was to play, complete with friends, homes, fears, grandparents, toys, games, etc., and then, "from this unnecessary welter," he said to them now, "raise up the character." They all listened with respect to what he said, couched as it was in his authoritative, carefully maintained, Anglo-Irish accent.

Mollie had been impelled by her interest in what everyone was saying into moving her chair into the area of discussion, leaving Franny alone on the periphery, beyond the waving arms, animated faces, sparkling eyes, and colliding opinions, beyond all the evidence, astonishing to her, of heated minds at work on a purely imaginary project. She did not move closer. She said nothing.

The boyish-looking actor insisted with great force that when *his* character walked he was sure he pounded his heels. "It is essential to my concept," he said, pounding his fists rhythmically on the table to simulate the action of feet. "Does he crack his knuckles, do you think?" asked a girl with long, dark hair and an impish twist to her lips. "And if he does," said a boy with hair cut in close, caplike fashion, "does he usually do it sitting down or standing up?" The class laughed at the little joke. The young actor sat down, looking somewhat miffed.

During the rest of the afternoon, until the Cairnses invited Franny and Arnold to tea in their office, the two of them attended three rehearsals, a dramatic reading, a class in movement and dance, and one in eurhythmics. They watched a young director block out a scene from *Richard III*. At four thirty, after tea, Patrick asked Franny if she would like to talk to a group of students interested in the techniques of screen acting.

"Oh no. *No.*"

"Informally, of course. They're all admirers of motion pictures. Would you do it?"

Franny appeared frozen at the thought. She shook her head again. She refused to go back to watching a group work once the idea of talking to them had been suggested to her, countering Patrick's suggestion with one of her own.

"But I might like to come back some time and . . . go to some classes in acting or something as, well, a student, you know. Could I do that?"

Mollie answered before Patrick could. *"Delighted,* Miss Fuller. We can arrange it any time. You could attend for any space of time that would fit into your schedule. A few days, a week, a month, anytime at all. We'd be *so* pleased."

Mollie wasn't being polite. Her enthusiasm for the project was genuine. As she spoke she was silently stage-managing Franny Fuller's attendance at the Atelier, choosing a photographer to take many informal shots of the famous movie star having lessons, listening to Pat's lectures on the Way Theory of Acting, participating in improvisations with the young students, perhaps even taking a part (small: after all, she *was* a novice in the theater!) in a play. Mollie could visualize a new edition of the Atelier catalogue. Among the action photographs of students at work, a clear one of Franny Fuller herself, being instructed. . . .

Patrick, whose visions, without consultation, often paralleled Mollie's, said: "What would you like to do most? What sort of class, Miss Fuller? We could easily arrange it so that it would be scheduled for you."

Franny said she thought "the talking through of character." She repeated the clause that seemed to have impressed her: "how you work from the inside." Her whisper filled the little office. Arnold laughed, embarrassed at the idea of this voluptuous beauty, overflowing her insufficient, vulgar dress, the woman he loved in spite of himself and all the difficulties raised by her fame and her ignorance, working seriously to learn acting. He covered his lapse by a display of enthusiasm for the project:

"It would be fine for you, Franny. It *is* a different approach from . . . films," (he hesitated over the words, trying to stay on this side of politeness) "you can see that."

Nothing came of it. The whole idea of the stage and the school terrified Franny. She was like a bather at the edge of a cold ocean who is persuaded, against her will, to test the water and then, chilled at the first touch, retreats to the warm beach. A few days later she told Arnold she had to fly back to Hollywood for retakes on the picture she had just finished. Mollie was always to remember her secret plans for Franny Fuller with regret and some guilt. It was a conspiracy she had entered into with herself, to use Franny for her own ends. She felt like a philanthropist who plans to leak to the press the extent of his charitable contributions.

Franny was in Hollywood when Arnold Franklin, miserable in New York without her enlivening beauty, flew to the Coast, rented a car, and drove to Beverly Hills. He found her lying out beside her half-empty swimming pool, asked her to marry him almost at once, and then flew home, full of delight with her agreement that she would come to New York for the ceremony when the retakes were completed.

From *The Fabulous Franny Fuller* (As Told to Mary Maguire):

My marriage to Arnold Franklin, the famous poet, was a great day in my life. I went back East as soon as *Pot of Gold* was finished. Arnie and his whole family, except his father who had to work that day, met me at Idlewild Airport. I loved his mother at first sight—she was so warm and kind to me. From the very first, his sisters, Lucille and Ruth, treated me like one of the family.

There was a crowd of reporters at the airport. They took pictures of us all, Mrs. Franklin kissing Arnie, and Arnie and me kissing, and Arnie's sisters kissing him. My hair is blown every which way in those pictures and the sun strikes Arnie's glasses and makes him look blind. But we both look happy. And we were!

We drove into New York in the airport limousine because the Franklins had no car and Mrs. Franklin said that taxis were too expensive on the Island. I remember that Arnie got mad at a man sitting behind us who kept poking his head forward. Arnie shoved him back and told him to mind his own d—— business. I thought Arnie was going to hit him! I could see how much he loved me! That day I really felt good about everything!

We stayed at the Plaza, where I always used to stay, because the Franklins only had a small apartment in Brooklyn, and Arnie's house was lent to a friend. But we went there for most of our meals. How Mother Franklin could cook! The first night we were there, I met Arnie's father. This was harder than meeting his mother. His father is a very quiet man and I couldn't tell what he was thinking about me. He worked downtown, he said, where he was a salesman for a knit-goods company. He shook hands with me when we met and seemed very reserved toward me, I thought. I didn't know whether it was because I wasn't Jewish or because I was in the movies or because he disapproved of the way I looked. I did try to dress right that evening, high-necked, loose dress and all that. But of course I didn't come out looking like Lucille or Ruth. I felt that in Mr. Franklin's eyes something was wrong with me somewhere. I made up my mind that I was going to win him over!

The wedding was held in a reception room at the Pierre. Arnie had made all the arrangements. I wore a light-blue dress—after all, I'd been married before and so had Arnie, who wore a new light-gray suit he'd bought at Brooks Brothers. Lou Price said he thought I should wear white, but I didn't want anybody to think I was trying to be something I wasn't. Arnie looked wonderful in his light suit, more like a Californian than a New Yorker.

His father wore a dark suit and didn't seem happy, but the rest of the family were swell to me, really swell. I met all Arnie's aunts and uncles and his cousins and their children before the ceremony. Arnie's grandfather didn't come. Mr. Franklin said he wasn't well. Arnie seemed upset that he wasn't there. I have never met him. I've heard he's very old and almost blind and was once a famous religious scholar, or something like that.

We were married by an old friend of Arnie's mother, a cantor. I couldn't understand any of the Hebrew in the ceremony, but I enjoyed it all. There seemed to be a mystery about that language. Very few people there knew what the cantor was saying, I thought. But everyone listened very respectfully. Lou Price was Arnie's best man. Since he was the one who introduced us, it was wonderful to have him there although he looked funny, being about half as tall as Arnie. The Cairnses were there too, old friends of Arnie's from the theater whom I knew too—I once visited some classes at their school and enjoyed them very much.

During the ceremony I thought about Eddie Puritan and wished he had been alive to come. I loved that guy. I suppose Lou Price must have been thinking about him too because he looked sad a couple of times. I wished I'd thought to ask Dolores Jenkins, my stand-in and friend, to come East for the wedding. Except for Arnie and Lou there was no one there I really knew.

The Franklins were wonderful to me. Mrs. Franklin said she thought of me as a daughter. Mr. Franklin didn't say much, but I think that was because he didn't like all the fuss the press was making outside the door where Arnie and Lou had insisted they had to wait until after the ceremony was over. There was a wonderful supper after the wedding. After it was all over we had only a week before I had to get back to Hollywood to start work on a new picture. So Arnie and I drove to his place in New Hampshire.

He had a lovely old farmhouse there, very old, but he'd fixed it up and it was very comfortable. We stayed there for six marvelous days. We were divinely happy. A couple of reporters followed us there from New York. Arnie made an agreement with them: If they could take some pictures of us, me in jeans and a work shirt and Arnie cutting wood, the kind of pictures they seemed to want, they would go away and not bother us again. They took some great pictures and then they left.

We walked a lot in the woods, Arnie taught me

to cook some of the things he liked to eat, and we talked and talked. It was a divine time and, as I've said, I've never been happier.

But like all good things it had to end. Arnie was beginning to work on a long poem. He told me something of what he wanted to do in it. It was fascinating for me to be in on the beginning of a great thing like that. At the end of the week we drove to Boston and I flew back to Hollywood. Arnie had to go to New York to see a publisher who wanted to bring out a book of his poems. He promised to join me in Beverly Hills in a few days. . . .

Arnold Franklin went to Hollywood to be with Franny. The reasons given by his agent, Lou Price, to Mary Maguire, suited the American dream of marital bliss and success into which the press had cast Arnold and Franny. By good fortune, reported Mary Maguire, Franny's contract to do a new picture had coincided with the offer made to Arnold Franklin to write a scenario from one of his plays.

FF, ARNIE, OK PIX, *Variety* reported. Mary Maguire made an ecstatic lead paragraph out of it:

> DELIRIOUSLY HAPPY, ARNIE FRANKLIN FOLLOWS FF TO COAST FOR START OF HER *THE LONELY ONES*. HE WILL DO THE SCRIPT FOR HIS OWN NEVER-PRODUCED PLAY. . . . FF WILL WORK AGAIN WITH HER FAVORITE (SHE SAYS, BUT WE KNOW BETTER) COSTAR BROCK CURRIER. . . . THE PRESS IS DELIGHTED WITH FABULOUS FRAN'S NEW NAME. NOW THEY CAN WRITE FFF . . . OR EVEN FFFF, FOR FABULOUS ETC. FRANKLIN.

Activity in Hollywood's studios was hectic when Arnold arrived to begin his sentence, as he referred to it, as a screenwriter. Heads of the little city-states which each studio constituted felt, unanimously, that the fierce realities of the war demanded more "upbeat" entertainment for "our boys" overseas. While these pictures were in the works some leading men left for the services, and some female stars donned elegant uniforms in which to travel to entertain soldiers and sailors "live," or in which to sell war bonds to well-to-do war-industry workers.

Hollywood responded to overseas death and destruction with musical accounts of gay shore leaves, filled with dancing sailors and obliging, tap-dancing beauties. Bored homefront audiences loved them, the more absurd and unlikely the better, and attendance records, even at afternoon performances, were at an all-time high, reported Mary Maguire, in those words.

Hollywood and Beverly Hills shocked Arnold. Lou Price had warned him about the untidiness of life on the Coast. But he was unprepared for the lack of visible day-to-day progress in the lives of the people he met. Scenarios were written, scenes shot, sets and costumes designed, and background music composed: these things he knew happened, but he had no idea when all of it was accomplished.

Everyone was constantly out of their own houses or away from their offices "for the day," visiting other people's swimming pools, lying in redwood loungers in wet bars at the back of someone else's beach house. Or, it seemed to him, everyone was in automobiles, snakelike lines of them on the way to another house, to "The Club," to a preview, to Ciro's or Romanoff's. "You go on ahead, we'll follow," was the substitute Hollywood sentence for "goodbye." Arnold found himself perpetually following someone he knew only slightly to a place he'd never been before in a car to whose other occupants he was a total stranger.

In the early months of their marriage, when friends and acquaintances were often at her house, Franny seemed content. She didn't say much, but she liked the house to have other people in it, especially at night when she had trouble sleeping. This came as a surprise to Arnold. In New York he had known her to sleep interminably, and he had worried that she was ill. At first Hollywood seemed to awaken and exhilarate her. She wanted to "show" him her friends. It turned out that her friends were far less interested in him than she had thought they would be. After the first polite exchange, they would turn back to talk movie gossip with Franny.

Arnold felt pigeonholed, filed away under "Franny's husband," of the same order of things as Franny's electric organ which, in fact, had arrived at Fullerton (the synthetic name bestowed on her house by Premium's publicity department) at the same time as he had, a wedding gift from the Price Agency. No one who visited them could play the instrument, nor could Franny. Arnold tried, fitfully, but hated its fraudulent tones. For him it became another of those vestiges of movieland's civilization that filled the houses he visited: the Pla-Pal Prohibition hidden bar-radios to which no one seemed to listen, elaborate electrical devices for mixing drinks that no one wished to waste time with, and gardening tools of such ingenuity and complexity that the Japanese gardeners found them intimidating.

These unused machines offended Arnold's sense of strict economy. He spent the little time Franny permitted him alone trying to follow the optimistic directions that came with the electric organ. The brochure read: "With just a few minutes' practice and the ability to follow the numbers of the chords, anyone can learn to play this magnificent organ at the first try." He never progressed much further than the first set of chords.

Confusing as this way of life was, after a little while Arnold was able to bring some personal order out of it all. When everyone started off, in a great burst of energy and hilarity, for Another Place, he would manage, in the confusion, to be left behind, go to his typewriter, and turn out some dialogue for the script he was trying to complete. With the legend of Scott Fitzgerald in his memory, he worried about drinking and "not producing." He welcomed any sudden turn in the social tide that moved people out of Franny's house and off to some Other Place. He had no trouble with the technique of preparing a movie script after spending some days with writers from the studio and reading a number of their finished scripts. His trouble was in finding enough consecutive time in which to produce something that seemed to him to have value.

But, in the long run, his adaptation to the Hollywood environment proved insufficient. Fanny changed as soon as shooting started on *The Lonely Ones*. Fanny: Arnold found himself calling her that once he learned it was her real name. Introspective as he was, he never tried to explain this usage to himself. The beautiful woman Franny receded into Fanny, the child he had begun to know best. She stopped seeing her friends, she came home from the studio exhausted and often, strangely frightened. She lost the delightful exhibitionism that had made her such a joy to be with in public, the sly wiggle of her bottom, the flash of her innocent and radiant smile, the sway of her walk. She turned back in upon herself—and him.

For the first weeks of shooting she worked hard and, it seemed to Arnold who sometimes came over from his office to watch her, did very well with the part of Robin, a tough, dockside girl in love with a murderous labor-union leader. One night he woke to hear her crying in her sleep. Next morning she said she was sick and could not go to work. From then on, and until the destructive cycle had run itself out, a major part of Arnold's days and nights were spent in an effort to get her to "do" something, get up, go to the Studio, go to sleep, eat, or refrain from eating (ravenously) sweets or the same food repetitively day after day. For days she ate nothing but minestrone soup which she insisted Olivia buy for her in an Italian place near Hollywood. She would not eat Olivia's homemade variety.

Getting her to the Studio now was an achievement in subtle persuasion and logistics. Keeping her there often meant he had to stay with her, doing almost nothing himself because he could not learn to write or rewrite amid all the clutter and noise of a Hollywood stage.

Arnold noticed that Franny seemed affected by the presence of strangers watching her on the set. He talked to Reuben Rubin, the director, about excluding them while she was working. Reuben looked at him oddly, as if Arnold were making the request out of a perverse need, perhaps a jealousy, of his own. But Reuben ordered that no visitors be admitted to the set. For a while this exclusion seemed to help, until Franny's period of almost marathon nonsleeping began again. Then her nerves seemed to rise to the surface of her skin. The least sound disturbed her, making her forget her lines or her instructions about movement. Sleeping pills put her to sleep, temporarily, until early in the morning. Four weeks after shooting had started Arnold had trouble waking her because she'd taken four pills the night before.

His role now expanded from that of social companion to solitary, day-and-night nurse. He told no one, not even Keith Andrews who came to the house often because he was handling Arnold's business affairs "from this end," as he said, Lou Price having declared he would operate only from New York. "I despise Hollywood, I can't breathe there," he claimed.

Arnold knew his reticence about Fanny's life was due to an odd kind of pride. He could not help feeling that if she did not sleep or eat properly it was, in some way, his failure. Looking at himself as he dressed in the morning (from the day he arrived he had been upset by the number of mirrors in his bedroom, in all the bedrooms in Beverly Hills, he surmised, and not only in bedrooms but also on every available wall in spaces where, back East, paintings would ordinarily hang), inspecting his thin legs and arms, his inconsequential body diminished by his large head, seeing at close range myopic eyes and high forehead that marked him as "intellectual," he would probe for the source of this feeling. Was it possible that he had been propelled this far into a fantastic existence by his pride in possessing this extraordinarily lovely child? Did she raise him up out of his ordinariness, metamorphosizing him into the American ideal of manhood? Was it (the thought chilled him) that walking, figuratively, two steps behind her, sitting close to her in her living room and listening to the foolish, self-absorbed chatter of her friends, he took on, in their eyes, a reflected glow, a halo of masculine conquest? Did he consent to live this Alice-in-Wonderland existence because, in spite of all the craziness, he felt more a man than he had ever been before?

He had married every man's dream, had acquired Eve for himself alone, the Cleopatra, the Helen of epic poetry, even though he alone knew he could rarely keep her awake long enough to make love to her or, when she was not drugged into a marathon sleep, get her into bed at all. He had climbed a mountain occupied by gods, heroes, and leading men. On this level what *he* was or had done meant very little. Who, in the mythical kingdom of *Photoplay,* Grauman's previews, adulatory audiences, semiliterate studio heads, and gossip columnists, had heard of him or had read his poetry? Fanny was the plum he had picked off, the prize he had won in a unique public contest. The world granted him a heavyweight crown, golden gloves, whatever else the champion was given.

Arnold suffered intensely, more without Fanny than when he was with her, because her presence evoked both his pride and, more and more often, his pity. Left alone, he pitied himself, and that was hard to bear. His work suffered from the synthetic nature of the assignment the Studio had given him. As unproductive weeks went by and he began to balk at the number of new scenes and rewritten lines required of him, the film's producer, impatient with the delays, ordered two veteran studio screenwriters to "assist" him. They were professionals who could produce scenes on demand, correct the poet's technical errors with dispatch, smooth over his blunders and ignorance by their experience and facility.

At first this relationship with the Two Competent Young Men (the producer had described them in this way and so Arnold referred to them for the duration of the picture) was agreeable. Of course, they knew Who He Was, and had read, or at least said they had read, his work. But after the first respectful pleasantries had been exhausted, their relationship veered in another direction. Firmly, they expropriated his play, then his script, and finally his confidence in himself. He felt like a by-the-week renter on a beach inhabited by all-summer residents. In a short time the Two Competent Young Men had made him feel like an incompetent illiterate. He couldn't wait for the picture to be finished so he could return to his old, productive ways, hidden away out of the hideous California sun in the dark house on the north side of Washington Square, sans pool, sans suntan, cocoa-butter smells, sans breakfast with the newspaper wit and wisdom of Mary Maguire.

He was never able afterward to remember the exact moment when the pleasure of being married to Fanny started to diminish, when delight in having captured the American Dream Girl gave way to apprehension about what he would do with her, and how he would survive her shriveling aura. His sense of triumph had been acute but short-lived. As early as the blissful days at the farm, when he had thought that, if they stayed long enough, Fanny would tell him more about herself than she had so far, he had sensed that something was wrong.

"Why do you want to know all those things, Arnie?"

"About your mother and your schools and such? Aren't they the kind of things you wonder about—you know, your wife's vital statistics and all that?"

"Most of it's in the fan magazines."

"Well, yes, the authorized version, but not what things mattered to you when you were growing up. Or hurt, or hindered you. What you thought about your parents. I don't know anything about you except that you talk very little and are very beautiful and that I love you and you say you love me."

She whispered, "I do, Arnie," in her famous voice. It was her screen sound, half-swallowed, sexy, and provocative, effectively turning away his interrogation. But underneath her professional delivery of the line Arnold sensed her need for protection from the facts about herself, her cry for help.

Once before, when he took her walking through the New Hampshire woods, he had heard the same cry. They went into a stream, he swimming to the deep center, she wading on the shallow edge. Suddenly he heard her cry out, "Arnie!" He swam over to her and stood up. She clung to him in terror, standing there frozen in the shallow water. He picked her up and carried her to the bank. She would say nothing about what had frightened her. From that time on, he tried to catalogue her habits and her fears, her curious life customs, her ways of advancing toward him, her methods of retreat, so that he could anticipate the crises that resulted from the unexpected, and from his unpreparedness. When she laughed he waited for the tears to come; in her deepest sleep he saw the signs of approaching, inevitable insomnia. As time went on, he attributed these transitions to the price she had to pay for being forced to embody in public all the yearnings for perfection of a daydreaming society. She became the natural and inevitable host to the private flaws in that perfection.

Of all her difficulties Arnold found it hardest to understand her distaste for sex. Her attitude toward activity in bed was the antithesis of her public self. Brimming with visible sexual energies, her breasts uncontainable in the slinky clothes she habitually wore, she was an undulating invitation, a pied piper's come-on, to every American male. In bed, she became a hostile Puritan, rigid with distaste for prolonged fondling, disliking the precoital rituals so essential to Arnie's own success in the act. She wanted it to be over fast, when she permitted it at all, not because she could not wait for her own pleasure but because her dislike of the whole procedure was so intense that she could bear just so much of the activity, and no more.

Early in the evening, dressed in a black chiffon nightgown, robe, and black fur mules, her hair a great blast of light in the sober disguise of her voluptuous body that her night clothes represented, she would begin to run through her catalogue of reasons for not having intercourse with him. The list was varied, covering every excusatory situation from sickness to weariness, in all degrees, from the natural cycle of feminine anatomy to headaches caused by nerves, nerves caused by conditions on the set during the day, the smell of his pipe, the humidity. In certain kinds of weather—overcast or too sunny, rainy or intensely hot—she felt particularly unwell. She took aspirin in grape juice and gin for many of her "conditions" (she had latched on to the word when she once heard someone talk about a heart condition), and other pills to sleep. Her favorite for staying awake was Benzedrine, which she used mornings when she had to be on the set early. Sometimes she took too many of these, and in unusual exuberation she would call her stand-in, Dolores Jenkins, and tell her to hold the fort, she was working on her part at home and would be in later.

To her public she presented a portrait of perfect health, an earthy, joyous spirit spilling over into girlish stunts, impromptu dancing, and liberal outbursts of kittenish good humor. Only Arnold knew the truth. He felt he was becoming a historian of them. Worse, he was beginning to feel that this was his sole function in their marriage, that he had been forced into this activity by his love of this sick, famous child and by his unseemly pride at having won her.

Alone in her own rooms at the other end of her rambling house, Franny suffered intense insomnia. But in Arnold's bed, in his arms and without sex, she would fall instantly into a sleep so deep that it was impossible to waken her. Wide awake, exposed to extreme and painful need by her presence, he would often play out the entire sex act upon her inert body, feeling like an expert bridge player driven to solitaire. After a few such experiences the sham pleasures of solitary orgasm began to diminish. He felt only the violations to his sense of himself that they caused. Ultimately, it would be impossible to distinguish between what he was "doing" to her at these moments, and his boyhood practices upon himself or even, he grimly acknowledged to himself, necrophiliac acts upon which Krafft-Ebing had been so explicit, in Latin.

Once her acquaintances stopped arriving and departing, Franny's house began to resemble a sanatorium, a clinic constituted for the sole end of preserving the Star and, only incidentally, Arnold Franklin's wife. When he married her, he had suspected what the order of their roles would be. But so confident did the *fact* of the marriage make him that he was able to delude himself into thinking he might be capable of reversing the order or, at least, of equalizing it. It had not worked. In six months, the Star, poor Franny and her private troubles, inadequacies, and rare public appearances, had obliterated the new Mrs. Arnold Franklin and all but extinguished, he had come to think, Arnold Franklin himself.

5

The Stand-in

Dolores Jenkins lived in the heart of downtown Hollywood in a four-room apartment above a Viennese bakery. The rooms were hers, and her mother's, in a way that few Southern Californians knew: They had lived in the same place for twelve years, renting it when they first arrived in the city and settling their small collection of family furniture and belongings there. Dolores never thought about moving. She had arrived in Hollywood with hopes for a career as an actress in films. She was too intelligent and too realistic to believe for very long that she was intended for miraculous stardom, but she clung to the hope that perhaps good minor parts might be offered to her.

Unlike many of the Golden Girls she was to encounter who were never able to abandon their dreams for stardom in order to earn even a modest living, Dolores settled for a job as a waitress in a studio commissary. She made enough to support herself modestly. After the first period of disillusion, that was all she asked of the outlandish Production that was Hollywood.

Dolores's mother, Billie-Jo Jenkins, was a widow, a tall, spare, sternly religious, barren-looking southern woman. Her husband had died so soon after their wedding that he had left barely a mark on her memory. To her mind Dolores might have been not so much conceived during a sexual encounter as carried into life from a competent but undisturbed egg, given birth to, and then reared as her exclusive product.

Billie-Jo was a nominal Catholic. Her faith tended to bolster her conviction of her undisturbed purity. She developed a comfortable, virtuous forgetfulness that "the act" had ever happened to her. Her brief contact with her husband, whom she had married for now forgotten reasons, had not interested her in the slightest; she had no desire ever to repeat the experience, even in memory. She settled into grateful widowhood, her baby daughter proof to the outside world of her respectability. At least once, she had tried It.

Now she considered men to be auxiliaries to her comfort. They existed to hold her bundles on buses when they did not give up their seat to her, they were asked to repair light fixtures and plugs in her apartment, and to fix the toilet when it overflowed. They were services rendered to her, naturally, since she was a woman. She managed on occasion to appear fragilely feminine and southern, weak and somewhat helpless—her Alabama accent contributed to the effect—but under it there lived a single-minded, unsexed woman who bent the world and her daughter to her purposes.

The Jenkinses had arrived from Anniston with very little money and high hopes for Dolores's success. Billie-Jo found a job almost at once in the basement corset department of the May Company. She "worked" heavy women into girdles. Seduced by her soft, lady's manner and subservient air, women let themselves go under her sympathetic efforts on their behalf, easing their difficult passage into new "garments," unaware that she despised them.

Billie-Jo used her store discount to furnish their apartment. Everything in it was in some way nicked, scarred, or stained, because she could not bring herself to pay even the employees' discount price for new furniture. She waited until floor samples, bearing the scuff marks of passing customers, were offered at half price or less. Living in a city known for its excesses, her mentality was framed by the contrary triumphs of getting along respectably on very little.

She knew that ordinary persons in Hollywood existed in this manner, below the glittering surface of the place, and she was proud to be one of them. She never regarded objects as "soiled" as the sale announcements did, but accepted them willingly because they were what she called dirt cheap, the bargain marked down.

As Billie-Jo grew older, what had once been a necessity became for her a positive joy. She loved the contest with the cost of living she had entered into, feeling an almost suffocating delight every time she managed to outwit the price tag. Her pleasure was intense, one month, when she received a bill from the May Company that failed to show a purchase she knew she had made. When the grocery clerk left out of his tally an item she had purchased, or when she was given a few cents too much in change, she was overjoyed. She gloried in rescuing an unmarked three-cent stamp from a letter to use it again. Like an invading army that lives off the land and relishes its ingenuity, Billie-Jo spent less and less money in Hollywood and gradually came to feel that, despite the disappointment of her hopes for her daughter, her occupation of the city was being supported entirely on the almost-free opulence of its careless superfluity.

Dolores observed with relief her mother's preoccupation with getting something for almost nothing. She realized that all Billie-Jo's frugal scurrying about, bargaining for the second-hand, the discarded, and the less-than whole, had put a healthy damper on her mother's cinematic ambitions for her. For her own part, Dolores saw how hopeless it was to expect a break into movies. Such fairy tales were not for her or for anyone she had ever known well in Hollywood.

Someone told her of a job in Premium Pictures' commissary. She was interviewed and got it. For two years she waited tables, serving the famous, near-famous, and about-to-be famous actors and lesser movie personnel until she heard (it was easy to overhear in the commissary because everyone connected with pictures talked at the top of their voices in order to reach the widest possible audience) that

Gloria Gibson's stand-in had fainted on the set that morning. Gloria was blond, handsome, big-boned, and well over thirty. Dolores, whose looks were of the same order although she was younger and not beautiful, left her station, still in her white uniform with blue collar and sash, and found Gloria's set. She talked to an assistant director about filling in for the afternoon.

"Temporarily, okay," he said. "But you might have waited until the body was removed."

Dolores laughed. "Where's the body? I heard she just fainted."

"Well, yes," he said. "The dope's pregnant, I hear. But she may be back tomorrow."

For once, Dolores's luck held. The pregnant stand-in stayed out three weeks with morning sickness. By that time Dolores's good nature, her ability to hold still for long periods, and her patience with every detail of the job, gave her permanent possession of it.

Gloria Gibson was a spoiled, erotic, self-loving woman with a vile temper and the kind of ripe figure that disturbed the netherworld of men's fantasies. She liked her new stand-in because Dolores had no apparent sex appeal, or "s.a." as Gloria referred to it. She approved of the fact that, if Dolores had once been good looking, there was now only vestigial evidence of the fact.

In the two years that she worked as Gloria Gibson's stand-in, Dolores changed the style and color of her hair whenever Gloria did, ran her errands, fed and walked her dog on the set, and listened patiently to her endless harangues against her husband ("that bloke, the bastard," she called him) who, she said, was "living on her," while playing around with a starlet at Paramount named Honey Moon, "that bitch."

Dolores never grew fond of Gloria—she was too imperious and too indifferent to all existence except her own and her dog's, who was named Lovey. But she understood the vast river of ignorance and insensitivity that flowed within her. Gloria was an empty woman, a beautiful and salable outer skin. From watching her, Dolores realized she had learned a truth about the movies when she discovered this. For a strange technical reason she could never quite fathom, the camera was able to suggest meaning and content in the slow lowering of Gloria's heavy, shadowed eyelid, like the sudden entry of the ocean onto a beach on a calm day. The less thought there was behind the movement, the more audiences seemed to understand. In the same way, they responded to the meaningless throb of a vein in a hero's fine forehead, his brows lowered with congested anger or passion, as they preferred to think of it. They assembled the details the camera flashed to them and made whole, complex men and women out of them, deluded by the larger-than-life twists of a colored mouth, the rise and fall of a beloved eyebrow, the flicker of light in a luminous eye.

Near the end of *Nefertiti's Passion,* Gloria's last picture, she was taken ill. Mary Maguire got the story first and ran it in exuberant capital letters at the top of her column:

> TIRED OUT, AT POINT OF COLLAPSE AND COMPLETE EXHAUSTION FROM STARRING IN THREE MAJOR PRODUCTIONS WITH ALMOST NO TIME OFF, GLORIA THE GORGEOUS GEE WILL BE RESTING IN PALM SPRINGS FOR SOME TIME. DR. ALBERT LEVY INSISTS. HUSBAND THEO, AWAITING ASSIGNMENT AT PARAMOUNT, WILL VISIT WEEKENDS. BOTH DENY RUMOR OF RIFT. BUT WE KNOW, *YOU* KNOW, GLORIA. . . .

Gloria's sanatorium was indeed in Palm Springs; her doctor had indeed insisted. She had locked herself in the men's room of a downtown theater and slit her left wrist with the razor blade she had brought in a handkerchief from her bathroom at home. Her husband could not be located. Doctor Levy had sewn and bandaged the cut wrist, and then committed her to a place called Rest Haven, with instructions that she be kept in a private room and watched day and night.

Surprisingly, no word of this reached Mary Maguire until a few days after she had printed the version of the story supplied to her by the press agents of Premium Pictures. The manager of the theater, aware of possible consequences, had notified the Studio before he did anything else. The Studio said thank you, they would call their own doctor, believing this move would provide security for themselves. But the revised version reached the Hollywood columns by means of the director of Rest Haven who realized at once his guest's publicity value to his Haven.

Mary Maguire printed it all, both the official story and the later, more accurate one, and she added her own ironic detail: The picture at the theater Gloria Gibson had chosen for her act of desperation was an old one, *Out of Sight, Out of Mind,* in which she had starred with her former lover, Brock Currier.

Gloria gone, the picture halted, Dolores was out of a job. It was as well. She had been putting off a physical examination she knew she ought to have and which, when it was over, sent her to the hospital for an operation. After a month of recuperation the doctor discharged her, saying cheerily, "We got it all."

Dolores reported back to Premium, and was in luck again. The stand-in for Franny Fuller had been severely sunburned on Sunday at Catalina Beach and summarily fired because of the condition of her skin under the lights. Dolores got her job.

At first Dolores found Franny hard to know, even harder to understand. She had none of Gloria's vanity; she never looked at herself in mirrors. But the odd thing was, Franny did not seem to be interested in other people either. She lived in some gray no-man's-land, a kind of gentle fog, existing without being aware of it, or of anyone. Her voice was wispy, high, frightened, like a child just discovered locked in a closet. When Franny spoke to her, Dolores noticed, her voice seemed produced by an inner mechanism that projected it between those opulent lips without her willing it.

And her breasts: Dolores regarded them with awe. They were high, erect and lush where other women's were often shapeless or flat or flabby. Composed of rowdy, uncontained flesh, they boiled up between her broad, soft shoulders. *Curious thing about those breasts,* Dolores thought. *She holds them before her, indifferently, almost cold to their presence. They seem to be separated from her, like falsies worn over flat chests.*

And her hips: they present the odd spectacle of being disconnected from her trunk, mobile, on their own. They move in circles as if to defy the forward movement of her legs. Like some great toy, she seems made of fascinating moving parts, a magnificent but curiously mechanical woman.

Franny was polite to Dolores, more than polite. She made an effort to say pleasant things to her although, Dolores noticed, rarely did she look at her as she spoke. When Dolores was first hired to stand in for Franny, she tried helping her, as she had Gloria Gibson, but she found this offended her. Franny wanted to do things for Dolores, to give her anything she might mention she needed or wanted. It was fatal for Dolores to say she was out of anything. Franny immediately sent for a carton or a gallon of it. Dolores thought perhaps Franny's gifts made her feel safe from involvement, as though the act created a protective distance from them.

At first Dolores let Franny have her way to see how long it would last and how far she would go. Her obsessive giving stopped abruptly, halfway through *The Princess and the Pomegranate.* On a very hot afternoon, Franny invited Dolores to share her dressing room during a break in the shooting. Dolores's was beastly hot and had no fan. "Try in here," said Franny, not looking at her but smiling vaguely and pushing her gently through the door.

Franny's dressing room was huge, decorated entirely in white and equipped with a white chaise longue and a giant fan that made it a haven from the heat of the set. They talked of how hot it was as Franny stretched out on the chaise. Dolores sat in an easy chair, her dress open at the neck.

"Back where I come from this would be called a heat wave," Dolores said.

"Where is that?" Franny's question sounded flat, like an incurious statement.

"Alabama. We lived there until I was eighteen. But out here it is bad form to talk about heat waves. It's not supposed to get this hot. So everybody says it's unseasonal."

"If you're hot, take off your dress. I've got all sorts of robes behind that door. Try the white one."

Dolores stood up, stepped out of her dress and reached for the white one.

"Very handsome," she said, generally, to the long peignoir of some extraordinarily thin material and a long neckline of feathers.

"Take it. I've got another at home just like it."

Dolores shut her eyes against this new donation. *Poor Franny. She doesn't know how to keep anything. To her the value of things lies in being able to dispose of them fast.*

Dolores turned around to face her. Franny's mouth was an O of horror.

"What's the matter?"

"What's that . . . thing you've got?"

Dolores pulled the white robe wide open. It was to be the only thoughtless act she ever committed against Franny Fuller. Later, it seemed inexplicable that she should not have realized what she was doing. She was to wonder: *Was I being vindictive? Do I envy her that extraordinarily perfect body?*

A great flat scar ran under Dolores's arm and up to the dividing point of her chest. With a final, pitiless motion she unhooked her brassiere and let it hang in her hand. Another violent seam dissected the left side of her chest on which there was no breast. The brassiere she held in her hand contained one full breast made of pads of layered cotton, sewn on to it, which her mother had put together.

Franny stared. Her bright-blue eyes widened in shock. The sight seemed to torture her, but she was unable to look away.

"What happened to you?"

For the first time in the unintentionally cruel pantomime Dolores hesitated. *How can I talk about all this to this frightened child?* Then she said: "I had cancer. A lump in my breast, small, like a pea. I thought when I went in that they were going to cut it out and I'd have just a thin little white scar there. But they said the lump was malignant and they took the whole breast and part of my arm here, too. Preventive, they said. But don't worry, I'm fine now."

Franny's eyes moved away from the ruin of Dolores's breast. She closed them. From under her lids, thin and blue as paper, tears poured down her cheeks. Dolores was suddenly frightened.

"For goodness sake, Franny, you'll ruin your make-up. I'm fine now. Lots of women have this."

"Oh no. Oh *no,*" Franny moaned. She brought her knees up, clasped them, and buried her beautiful head in her arms. She cried aloud, making sucking, gasping noises, her head moving convulsively, her hair falling around her knees.

"No. No, *No,*" she screamed.

"Stop that, Franny. Stop now." Dolores knelt down and shook her. But Franny was possessed by her vision of destruction. Her crying turned to shouting; she screamed defiance at what she had seen. Dolores pulled her dress on hastily and went to the door. She called for Reuben who came running, took one look at Franny, and went to find the set nurse.

At once all the activity of the set converged on Franny's dressing room. A doctor drove up to the edge of the set, leaped out of his car, and raced for the dressing room. In the confusion of persons working over Franny, and because she was not up to explaining to anyone what had happened, Dolores slipped out and walked back to her little box of a dressing room, *like an arsonist,* she thought, *leaving the scene of the fire while the firemen fight the blaze.*

No one worked any more that day or for two days after. Franny was taken home and stayed there to rest. When she came back to the Studio, she sought out Dolores in a new, pathetic way. It was as though she now recognized her as a partner to some inner wound of her own, as though her missing self was a parallel to Dolores's lost breast. Dolores understood the relationship. *At least,* she thought, *she has stopped giving me everything.* She guessed correctly about Franny's new feelings of hopelessness, as if nothing she had to give could make up to Dolores for her lost breast. So she stopped trying.

The picture proceeded for three uneventful weeks, until the day everything went wrong. Franny blew her lines four times, Brock Currier shouted angrily at her, she stared at him, turned on her heel, and went to her dressing room. Reuben Rubin watched his stars in silence. Then he followed Franny and knocked gently on her door.

"Go away."

"Oh, come on, Franny. It's me, Rube. Let me in."

"No."

"What are you doing?"

There was no answer.

"Are you coming back soon?"

Her silence frightened him. He rattled the doorknob.

"Franny?"

Brock Currier had followed Reuben at a distance. He came up behind him. "Ignore her. She's sulking, the filthy bitch."

"Go to hell, Brock. Every moment of this costs money. Franny?"

The door opened, and Franny, dressed in gray workman's pants, a black silk shirt, and wood-soled clogs, came out. "I'm sick, Rube. I'm going home."

The truth was, she *did* look sick. Great dark circles had worked themselves up through her faded make-up. The blue craters that were her eyes made her cheeks look sunken, and her blond hair, pulled back and piled on her head, gave her the suffering, withdrawn look of a movie spinster-type. After the dumb, lovable blonde married to an English lord that she had been playing a half-hour ago, the change was startling.

"Franny, you'll be all right. Stay here. I'll send Jay for Doctor Levy. He's right near here. Brock, for God's sake, *apologize.*"

Brock hated his part—the English lord with all his looks and manners who turns out to be a fool, manipulated by the curvy, ignorant farm girl from Oklahoma. He wanted it to be over so he could move on to better things. He said to Franny, not looking at her: "Sorry, darling. Lost my head. Let's have at it again."

Franny seemed not to have heard him. She took Reuben's arm and pulled him along with her.

"Please. *Please,* Rube. Don't be mad. I'll be back in the morning. I promise. You can use Dolores on the run-through of the next scene. Just today. I feel awful, Rube. No kidding."

He believed her. The pressure of her hand on his, even though he knew it was just a signal of her need, made him happy. His awkward, undersized Jewish businessman's body was suffused with joy, and he could not hold out against her. Her illness, he suspected, was one he had known something about when he was younger. It was dislocation sickness, a loss of a sense of place and self, a disease he knew to be ineluctable, one for which there is no amelioration. On the set he had watched Franny react to other players or, more often, fail to react. He knew she was searching for moorings, for a place to put her head, to house her nameless griefs, to shelter her sick heart. He longed to offer her consolation, his sympathy, something immense like an ocean or a forest of redwoods or the Hope Diamond. Instead, he said: "Okay, Franny. Take it easy. I'll have Jay drive you home."

Dolores Jenkins was sitting on the edge of the set holding wool for Charlene Emory, the script girl, when she saw Franny and Reuben walk toward the parking lot. Following at a respectful distance one of the assistant directors, Jay

Boardman, was struggling into his sports jacket as he walked. She put down her two handfuls of wool. "Be right back, Charlene. Hang on."

Running, holding her arm across her chest to keep her one breast in place, Dolores caught up with Franny and Reuben. They were talking, his head bent earnestly toward hers, but they stopped when she came up to them.

"I'll see you tomorrow, yes, Franny?" he said.

"Tomorrow. Yes," she repeated in her flat, toneless way, as though the exact use of someone else's words was superior to any response she could make.

"Take care of yourself," he said and kissed her lightly on the forehead. *The kiss of peace,* he thought, *between two priests*. He walked back to the set, feeling defeated and angry at the same time, like an athlete leaving the field in a fit of bad sportsmanship.

"Is there anyone at home, Franny?" asked Dolores. "Is your husband there?"

"No," she whispered in her half-voice. "He's in New York. Just Olivia, I think."

"Tell you what. Why don't you go to my place? You can rest there. My mother's there. I'll call her and tell her you're coming. She'll make lunch for you. She'll love to. Then I'll drive you home tonight. Okay, Franny?"

Franny looked at her, seeming not to see her. After a moment she said: "Your place. Okay."

She got in beside Jay in the black sedan the Studio kept on the lot for emergencies.

Dolores said to him: "Take her to Lilac and Vine. Number seventy-three. Right above the bakery. You'll be able to smell it a block away."

"Want me to wait for her, Miss Jenkins?"

"No, my mother will be there. And I'll be home soon."

Jay backed up carefully, went into forward gear, and started ahead slowly, as if he were driving the lead car in a funeral procession.

"Feel better now, Miss Fuller?" he asked in a hushed voice.

She did not answer. Slumped down in the seat, her head thrown back, she appeared to be asleep.

After Dolores's call, Billie-Jo Jenkins scurried around tidying up the apartment. She greeted Franny profusely, ignored Jay's presence, and ushered the Star into the living room. Jay hung about for a few moments, realized that his assignment, in Mrs. Jenkins's eyes, ended at her doorsill, and left, shutting the door quietly behind him. He was used to his function as errand boy for the Great, biding his time until, as a director some day, he would do some ordering around himself. With the recent spectacle of powerless Reuben Rubin in his mind, however, he was not so sure.

"Would you like to lie down, dearie?" asked Billie-Jo. "The chesterfield's very comfortable."

"The what?" An old, hated, buried world flooded into Franny's mind at the sound of the word.

"The couch, I guess you call it. Where I come from—well, never mind, here, try it." She puttered about, arranging a plump pink pillow neatly into a hollow in one cushion caused by defective springs. She had compensated for this imperfection the day the sofa arrived from the May Company and by now had forgotten that it had not always been this way. To her, no structural defect was objectionable if it reduced the cost of an object and then could be repaired with "something I had around the house."

Franny lay down. Billie-Jo removed her clogs and covered her with an afghan Dolores had crocheted during waits on the set.

"Now, dearie. Tell me what you want for lunch and I'll fix it while you rest."

Franny said, with her eyes closed: "Some grape juice, please, Mrs. Jenkins."

"Nothing to *eat?*"

"No, grape juice is fine. Nothing else." She was almost asleep as she said the last words, her energy having seemingly been exhausted by them.

After an hour she woke, sat bolt upright, and looked

around blankly. She seemed not to remember Mrs. Jenkins. The dream she had just had was still there, whole and terrifying.

Two little boys and Fanny Marker walked barefooted to the dried-up reservoir bed and then crawled into the pipe almost big enough to stand up in and it got darker and then black inside and there was some water full of orange rust like dried blood at the bottom of the black pipe and every sound of her foot on the pipe and the swishing of the water made a roar like a bull and all at once nobody was in the pipe but Fanny and she started to run to one end and banged her head and went down on her hands and knees and crawled in the bloody water and looked back and there at the opening was a great grinning face, the eyes crossed and a great red tongue hanging out and hair all over its head like tar and Fanny screamed and her scream came back to her like the high notes of a saxophone never stopping and Fanny crawled on, her knees scraped and rusty crying so hard she could hardly see, her hair in her face her heart echoing like a drum in that black pipe and at the other end oh jesus, another face, fingers pulling down the corners of the mouth and no teeth in it and the blood roaring in her ears as she tried to stand again and banged hard at the side of her head and slipped back in the muck crying and screaming, even after she remembered about the boys and recognized their faces and saw it was a game and then she put her head down and crashed into one face and fell out of the pipe hitting against the face that pulled away from her before her exploding head the roar the bull's roars the blood bursting in her hair and fright screaming flowing from her ears the roar and the blackness and the blood

Then she saw Mrs. Jenkins. She shook her head to wipe away the dream, the dream she had again and again since it had happened to her in Utica when she was a child. She smiled her instant, brilliant, distant smile.

"I was dreaming," she said.

"Tell you what, dearie. I just thought of a place near here you'd like to see. Put on your shoes and I'll show you."

"Outside?"

"Oh yes, but not far. Just about five blocks away."

As they came out of the building, Franny stopped, shocked by the glare of midafternoon California sunlight. She found her sunglasses in her handbag and then turned to look into the window of the bakery. It was almost empty except for white doilies on empty white plates. In the center on a pedestal a three-tiered dusty wedding cake bore aloft two celluloid dolls. Franny stared at them. The groom doll had stiff arms painted black all the way to his finger tips, the bride-doll was buried to her knees in the sooty white cake.

"Come on, dearie, it's not a bad walk from here."

Franny pulled a kerchief over her hair. In her workman's pants and silk shirt she looked waiflike, fragile. Billie-Jo took her hand, as she would a child's, and pulled her along. It was difficult to make much progress because Franny's clogs did not give as she walked. With each step her feet made a slapping noise, like the sound a circus clown makes with great false feet. Even so, no one on the street looked at her. The citizen of Hollywood, accustomed to nobodys accoutered like Stars, distrusts everyone he sees: Franny in clogs, work pants, and cat-eyed sunglasses looked like an imitation of Franny Fuller. No one paid any attention to her.

They arrived at a brick building painted black.

"This is the place."

A sign entirely composed of electric bulbs read WAX MUSEUM. Underneath, in gothic letters, a painted sign said MADAME TWOSO's and then, in black block letters, SEE THE STARS!

"What's in there? What is it?" asked Franny, backing away.

Billie-Jo put down two quarters at a window in the kiosk in front of the museum and took Franny's hand again. They went in through a black velvet curtain and stood uncertainly just inside, blinded in the darkness after the sunny street. In a few moments Billie-Jo saw a green arrow glowing.

"This way, Miss Fuller. The arrow says over here."

"What arrow?"

"Take off your glasses and you'll see it."

Together, like mountain climbers tied together and groping past a dangerous place, they moved in the direction the arrow indicated. Past another black velvet curtain musty with the odors of many hot, confused hands pushing at it, they were in a large, lighted room with recessed glass panels set into walls. Franny put her dark glasses back on.

Billie-Jo said: "Yes, I remember now. We start over here, dearie." Each window revealed a group of Hollywood stars, called *Greats* in the legends printed beneath them, in a scene from their GREATEST SUCCESS. Billie-Jo ushered Franny rapidly past the first displays—frizzy-haired Mae Murray embracing smooth, seductive, frowning John Gilbert; languorous, sulky Constance Bennett in the fierce arms of Richard Barthelmess; famous comics in sailor suits, horn-rimmed glasses, and police uniforms chasing women into revolving doors or falling out of skyscraper windows.

"Now, *here*. Take a look at this one, dearie. Take off your glasses."

Through her smoked glasses Franny saw herself. She was dressed in a black satin evening gown cut to a deep V in front. Two bulbous wax breasts pressed out of the cleavage of the dress. Waxy and painted so that it looked like the embalmed remains of someone she remembered having known well, her head was thrown back, her eyelids were lowered over glassy bright-blue eyeballs like giant marbles, and her lips, oversized, swollen, and bursting with jellylike red wax, opened as though to allow some last, vital ceraceous breath to escape. Vaguely, because she could not take her eyes away from herself, she was aware of two male figures flanking her, both in evening dress, both handsome, stiff, their marble eyes looking avidly at her.

She recognized the dress but could not remember the movie the scene was from; even the men were unfamiliar.

But the angle of that head, the deep dimple struck into the wax cheek *(with a hot needle?* she wondered), the silky hair pointed down that forehead—oh, she knew *that* one, that was the face she had worked on as a girl on her mother's bed, the day Jerryboy came home early to find her there. . . . Behind the glass, sculptured for all the world to see, was Fanny Marker who lived forever behind her, under her, like vegetables under a stone, and that was why it was so hard for her to breathe, to live.

"Don't you think that's a swell likeness? It takes you off just perfect, I think. Take off the glasses. You'll get a better look."

Franny made no move. Through the glasses the unlined face, the body, the glowing canary hair, were mercifully darkened, diminished. Bright lights shone down on her manufactured skin, grayed out and dulled into a twilight color.

"I look dead," Franny said aloud to herself. But Billie-Jo heard her speak.

"What's that?"

"That really is me," said Franny. "And I'm *her* stand-in, like Dolores is mine."

"Oh no, dearie," said Billie-Jo.

"Yes," said Franny in her flat whispering monotone. "See, just *look* at me. I tell you, look: I'm dead. Really. Dead."

A week later, lights were being arranged on the set of *The Princess and the Pomegranate,* and then shifted. Dolores Jenkins waited, changing her position at command, her face tilted upward and then lowered, then raised again. She held still until the lighting director said she could move. Dolores had developed a technique, an occupation to follow, while remaining absolutely still. She would freeze into the desired position and then hold it by thinking hard about non-thought. Sometimes her concentration on blankness was so intense that, when she was told to relax, it was an effort to obey. She was the ideal stand-in, unambitious for herself, unglamorous yet attractive in a quiet way, perfectly yet mindlessly still when she worked.

This day she had been working since seven thirty. The cameramen had been ready to shoot at nine and puttered around ever since trying to appear busy, because Franny Fuller had not arrived. Everyone on the set was trying hard to keep his temper, but every now and then a small ugliness broke out in some corner of the set: there was too little to do.

At the edge of the set Charlene was knitting another in an interminable series of sweaters for her nieces and nephews. On Franny Fuller's pictures the assistants cultivated hobbies, played tournaments of gin rummy or cribbage, began ambitious pieces of petitpoint with every expectation of finishing them during the inevitable delays in production.

Dolores had finished her posing. She came to sit beside Charlene, stretching her arms above her head, free to do this for the first time in hours. Often she was grateful for delays, but today discontent with the long wait had infected even her.

"I wish she'd get here. It's damn hot under those lights. I think they do all that fiddling around just to kill time."

"You can't prove it by me," said Charlene, her favorite expression for every contingency. Once Charlene, too, had dreamed of stardom. Now she despised every star on whose picture she'd ever worked. Close to forty, she looked faded and bitter. Her lost hopes colored her conversations.

"She sick—as usual?" she asked Dolores.

Dolores liked Franny, with a fondness born of intense, female, creature sympathy. She viewed her from her own secure, if lower, position, understanding the precariousness of Franny's elevation, and the price in terrible self-doubt she paid for her eminence. Dolores thought about Gloria Gibson, at the end of her career. Married six times, and then left alone by her last husband, she was ending her life in Palm Springs with a nurse in a cottage on the grounds of Rest Haven Sanatorium. Blank-eyed, her skin pink and dry under layers of badly applied pancake make-up, her eyes blackened by crusted mascara, the Star had not recognized Dolores when last she visited her.

Gloria asked: "Seen Norman lately?" Dolores remembered that Norman was the Star's second husband who had died fifteen years ago in an airplane crash. Dolores said no, she had not seen him recently. The aging Star then lost interest and turned away to talk to her nurse. Dolores said goodbye. For a moment, intelligence returned to the still-bright, famous blue eyes under the familiar, triangular, penciled brows. "My new picture starts next week," Gloria told Dolores. "I must be ready. I'm resting up here." Then her eyes clouded over as though Dolores, by making no response, had failed her in some obscure but crucial way.

The lives of those afflicted by fame were part of Dolores's Hollywood education. Other stand-ins were similarly learned. They belonged to an unofficial underground of mutual sympathy. Whenever they happened to meet they exchanged information about their "people," inside tidbits and gossip about their current loves and enduring terrors, their escapes into marriage, love affairs, alcohol, drugs, and delusion. For those forced to live out their sicknesses and ruined affairs in the public eye, Dolores felt genuine sympathy, almost sisterly love. She took no pleasure in their falls from glory, their plunges into the abyss of public neglect.

"This part has been hard on her," she said. She watched Charlene's hands whip yarn over the needle with one extended finger. "You really knit very fast."

"Hard on her? At fifty thousand for sixteen weeks' work? I should suffer so."

"You know what I mean. Working with someone like Brock Currier."

"Because he was a New York stage actor? What's that mean?"

Dolores was accustomed to defending Franny against all criticism. "Not only that. He's such a bastard, so hard on women."

Charlene smirked and brought forth her usual sentence for actors whose looks she admired. "Well, he can put his shoes under my bed any time."

Dolores laughed half-heartedly, and returned to the defense. "Franny can't take criticism too well. Every time he raises that eyebrow and smiles his crooked smile down at her she gets sick, I think."

"Tough."

"It is. You don't know her."

"For crissake, Dolores, how can a woman with those breasts and that fanny and that widow's peak have an inferiority complex?"

Dolores said nothing.

"Where is she this morning? Her call was for eight, wasn't it?"

"It could be that she overslept."

"Oh, come on. Arnold Franklin wouldn't let her. I hear he starts writing at five thirty in the morning."

"Maybe she really is sick. She's not very strong."

Charlene snorted.

The set emptied for lunch. Reuben Rubin stopped at Charlene's chair. Since the start of this picture he had grown thinner and looked more boyish. Dressed as he was in a gray striped suit, a vest, and a wide, gray-silk tie (as if to belie the stereotype of the Director) he looked like a worried haberdasher. He pointed to the script in her lap.

"See that for a moment, could I?" he said in his public-school, Brooklynese accent, superimposed on a thin base of Hollywood.

Charlene looked annoyed. She had a proprietary feeling about the heavy, bound volume, and disliked letting it out of her hands. Gathering her wool, needles, and knitting bag to her chest, she indicated by a shrug of her shoulders that Reuben could have the script.

"Bastard," she said after he had walked away, searching for something in the script as he went.

"No," said Dolores who liked Reuben's gentleness. "He's not. He worries about all the delays. They can never tell up above whose fault they are. I think he often takes the blame for Franny."

At two, everyone was back, slumped in chairs or leaning against the back of the set, the actors standing in attitudes that displayed their good features, their better profile. An air of universal impatience hung over the set.

Reuben Rubin had retreated into himself. Although the lighting on the set was now dimmed, he still wore his sunglasses, staring through them at the elaborate southern mansion which stood ready for use, like a vacant battlefield waiting for the moment soldiers would arrive to enliven it. He thought about the meaninglessness of everything here, the complex of lights strung up and wheeled into place, the make-up tables laden with restorative potions for faces and hair, the costume racks, the soundmen and cameramen mounted and ready, when nothing was being done, no pretenses being acted out. *The set,* he thought, *is like a track without runners, like an office building before and after hours, like a college dormitory during summer recess. It seems sullen, resentful of its desertion, reproaching its human defectors.*

Brock Currier shouted from where he leaned against a cardboard magnolia tree. "Did you ring her again, Rube?" Currier was dressed in a southern colonel's frilled shirt, immaculate white pants, and white shoes. His full, handsome mouth was tight with annoyance. He had been in this stiff outfit since eight in the morning. Now he felt deeply, personally offended, like a bridegroom who has been stood up.

"The boys did. Arnold Franklin said she'd be right here after lunch."

"It's right after lunch now. What lunch does the Great Poet refer to? I had mine an hour ago."

"Oh, come on, Brock. She'll be here. . . ."

"Look, Roo-bin boy, I'm damned sick of this, and you, and her. My contract doesn't call for . . ."

Reuben turned and walked to the other side of the colonnade, wanting to hear no more of Brock's self-righteousness. He disliked the actor, so ordinarily he was careful to treat him with consideration. But today his patience was worn thin. Between him and Brock Currier the weight of unspoken truths hung heavy. Brock's usual manner of drawing out Reuben's name was a subtle nudge at his Jewishness. It always succeeded in activating Reuben's memory: When first he had met Brock Currier as a boy in Chicago Brock's name had been Aaron Feldstein.

Another hour went by. Reuben came out of the tall box that served as his office and told his assistant to let everyone go home. He skirted the façade of the mansion and knocked on the door of an upright, coffin-shaped dressing room in which Dolores was redoing her make-up for the third time that day.

"Charlene there?"

"No. I think she went to lie down in the little girl's room." Charlene suffered from her "period," especially in the afternoon after a large lunch, and was often to be found resting in the ladies' lounge.

"Oh. Well. Tell her I've left her script on your step."

"Do you need me?"

"No. You might as well cut out. We can't do anything more today."

Dolores opened her door, holding her wraparound make-up coat to her chest. In half make-up she looked pale. The normal lines in her face had been erased by pancake covering and nothing had as yet been restored. She smiled at Reuben.

"No word from FF?"

"No word. No appearance. Nothing. You look like Ben Blue in that stuff."

"Pretty ghastly, eh?" Dolores said, agreeably. "Not much better underneath, either."

"Your call is for seven thirty tomorrow morning."

"Okay. Will she be here, do you think?"

"Better be. Brock's about to call his agent. Maybe even his congressman. A few more of these delays and Fleischer will drop her even if she is the Name in this epic."

The set was almost dark. Brock slammed the door of his dressing room and came down the two little steps, his crisp hair still wet from the dousing he had just given his head. Without make-up he was swarthy, masculine, and angry-looking. His fans mistook this look for passion and adored him for it. He himself mistook it for acting talent and overrated his abilities. On his way to beatification as one of Hollywood's "Greats" almost entirely on the strength of this expression, his hair curled endearingly about his ears, his vulgar, piratical teeth shone out of his dark face, and his one, perpetually elevated eyebrow suggested a subtle sexual invitation.

To him Franny Fuller was nothing special, just another dumb, blond female with a famous name, big boobs, a fat ass, and something loose in her belfry. Once, working close to her, he caught a warning look, a quick facial sign, of retreat into herself. Her lids had fallen as if loosened like a venetian blind, and her mouth opened, ripe and desperate for air. He thought he recognized that look as a cry for rescue, a signal of impending disaster.

Brock had long ago armed himself against the needs of others. Any suggestion that someone required something of him, anything more than a handout or an autograph, put him on his guard. He did not talk to his costar when the scene was over, and never after that was able to respond to her unspoken appeal. Today, in her absence, he felt afraid of her. He feared being halted on his way up by sympathy for anyone but Brock Currier of Beverly Hills, born Aaron Feldstein of Chicago, a boy-self buried so deep now that he rarely remembered it had ever existed.

He walked across the lot and toward his assigned parking space, saying nothing to anyone, trusting to the look he knew was on his face to convey his irritation.

Reuben saw him go and smiled at his back. *That horse's ass. Living in his dream of himself. The gentile loverboy.* Brock, *yet. All he is to me is a thin shadow on the screen, a name on a marquee, designed to rivet girls' eyes on my picture. That's all.*

The set was almost deserted. Except for one guide lamp, the lights were out. Seated low in his canvas-backed chair, Reuben looked at the fake door into "the downstairs hall of

Colonel Ashby's majestic plantation home, Ashend," as the script described it. He thought of Franny, who had failed to come out of that door this morning costumed in white southern-girlish splendor. Dolores passed him leaving the set, he waved to her, and went on thinking of Franny. Loving her in the cerebral, hopeless, boyish way that he did, he wondered what new hell she was inhabiting today, what there was within his poor power to do for her, how he would explain this expensive lost day to Fleischer.

Dolores, her face clean of make-up, with that curiously blank, mannequin look women have after they've scrubbed their faces, finally gave in to the fact that the empty day had tired her. She put on a long-sleeved cotton blouse, believing as did her mother that complete covering kept away the heat, and a white pleated skirt. Her car had been parked in a pool of afternoon sunshine, so she sat in it for a few minutes with the door open, the windows down. Then she drove her yellow Chevy slowly toward the studio gates. The guard waved, a gesture that always warmed her because it made her remember the days when, using every facial expression she thought to be effective (she had practiced them before a mirror), she could not get past this same gate. Once it had seemed like the Pearly Gates into Heaven for the Elect, the stellar Greats. She waved back and smiled wearily at the guard. *In and out without any trouble,* she thought. *Think of that.*

Her apartment was cool. Billie-Jo was in Alabama, visiting an old friend who was dying. Dolores had left the windows closed and the shades down when she went to work in the morning, unlike her mother's habit of opening everything to the California sun under the illusion that "the air is always cool." Dolores stood for a minute at the door, basking in the boxed-up cool air. Then she crossed to the window and opened it a crack.

Fragrant bakery smells came in, an odor she loved although she never ate the rolls and bread it emanated from. She ran too easily to fat.

After her shower she put on a kimono, a word her mother always used for "robe," and stretched out on the chesterfield with the telephone beside her. She dialed Franny's unlisted number.

Arnold Franklin answered.

"Yes?"

"This is Dolores Jenkins. I'm worried about Franny."

"Welcome to the battalion of the worried," Arnold said. "Don't ask me where she is because I haven't the faintest idea. She left here for the Studio at one thirty. Said you were picking her up at the gate. I've looked everywhere I could think of and called some other places, likely and unlikely. Nobody's seen her."

Dolores sensed that Arnold Franklin had no desire to speculate further upon where his wife might be. She thanked him and hung up. Poor Arnie, lately become a kind of keeper, with lists of places to check, a telephone exchange for everyone who wanted to contact the Star Franny Fuller.

Dolores picked at the remains of last night's tossed salad and ate a saucerful of cottage cheese. She thought about her loneliness, which usually afflicted her at mealtimes, and destroyed her appetite. *Without Mother here, for whom I care very little, actually, I find I'm lonely . . . odd.* She thought about Franny. *Is she lonely with Arnie whom I thought she loved? She must be, or she wouldn't retreat the way she does, like a coward in a war who goes backward as an officer urges him forward. So you can be loved and love and still be lonely.* There was some comfort in the realization. Dolores gave it all up: her own isolation, Arnold Franklin's bitter despair, Charlene's disappointments, and Reuben Rubin's curious sweetness, the day's whole accumulation of responses to the savage world of moviemaking. She stretched out on the couch with a glass of iced tea on the floor at her side, wondering with everyone else: *Where has our bonnie girl gone?*

At six in the evening Franny sat on a bench in a small downtown park off Hollywood Boulevard. She wore her usual camouflage, a workman's jacket, cap, and pants. Her hair was pushed under the cap. Part of her face was hidden behind large, dark-green sunglasses. Through them she watched a young girl walk toward her down the narrow park path. Franny thought she looked highly colored, blue around the edges, like a poor Technicolor movie. She was small and had an arched, broken-boned nose and no chin at all. Through Franny's glasses, her crinkled yellow hair looked orange. Her straight thin legs had little-girl's knobby knees, she wore a flared white taffeta skirt and a high hat with white plumes in front. Franny wondered what she was: *that outfit? that strapped-on funny hat?* She looked again at the way her face declined sharply from her lower lip into her neck. Franny shivered, terrified at the sight of the missing chin.

The girl carried a silver rod with a small ball at the end. When she was almost abreast of Franny on the bench she slowed down and smirked at her, a generalized, professional smile without recognition. Then she walked on.

During the long afternoon she had spent here Franny had rarely lifted her head to look at anyone or anything. But the young girl caught her diffuse attention: she focused on her, watching her as she passed, seeing her bobbing, jaunty little backside.

Realizing that she was being watched, the girl stopped abruptly, turned, and tossed the silver rod high above her head. She raised her chinless face into the air, half-buckled her legs, and leaned under the rod to catch it with her twisted wrist and thin fingers. To Franny she seemed to be plucking it out of the air, almost magically, as if it had not been she who had thrown it there. It seemed miraculous: Franny watched her as she turned out of the park, her triumphant little backside and blowing orange hair disappearing from her vision.

In a rare moment of understanding, Franny thought she recognized who the girl was: one of those people who knows exactly what she can do and who practices all the time to be able to do it like that. She believed that it didn't matter to the girl that her face fell off to almost nothing or that her hair sprang around her head like Christmas twine. *She catches that silver stick,* Franny thought, *and then she knows who she is and feels fine about it.*

Staring after the girl, Franny's eyes rested on a building, a red-brick school at the edge of the park. She turned on the bench to get a better view of the place. It looked like the schools she had known in Utica, except for the gold cross over the front door. The cross was made of two rows of electric light bulbs, now lit. It glittered garishly in the dusk. The building was squat and square, and seemed to sit heavily against its ribbon of sidewalk.

At the window in the upper-right tier of the building Franny saw the figure of a nun adjusting a shade. First the shade moved up a little over the middle band of the window and then down a little too far. Patiently the blank-faced nun jockeyed the shade until it was exactly even with the middle of the window. The cord with its little circle at the end swayed and then, as though in obedience to a higher will, settled permanently into the exact, geometric center of the middle panel of the middle strip of glass in the window.

Franny saw the nun disappear behind the red-brick wall and reappear at the next window. She went through the same motions there, and at the next window, and then at the next and the next. Like a figure in a Swiss clock she appeared on a methodical stroke to make her small adjustments, and then she retreated.

To Franny, watching her perform her maneuver on the windows at the first floor of the school—at the door she lowered a full-length shade to the floor—there was something inexplicably wonderful about this vision. The regularity, the completeness, the order; she thought she knew what the nun was feeling each time she disappeared from view: a satisfaction that this piece of action was finished and she could move on to another place and finish that. *Another one,* Franny thought, *of those people who knows what she is doing, and does it exactly and, even more, knows what she is going to do next. Will it all be the same tomorrow,* she wondered, *will she always be this exact and orderly? Does what she looks like have nothing to do with anything she does?*

It had grown dark. The lights in the school were now out, the building's windows had the look of some heavy-lidded bird's eyes, dim, partly asleep. Only the electric-bulb cross lit the air in front of the school. Franny took off her sunglasses; evening light returned to the sealed look of the building.

Cold now, Franny was angry at herself for having nothing to do, nowhere she wanted to go. She realized she did not know what there was to think about. She bit at her thumbnail and tore it off in one vicious cut with her shining teeth. For a reason she could not fathom, she felt deserted by the baton-twirler and the nun. The park was empty: only an occasional walker passed her, *on his way,* Franny thought, *to someone at home, maybe to his dinner.* No one gave her more than a glance. No one seemed suspicious of the drab, huddled little figure. The dusk had reduced her to a vagrant.

It was very dark now. Franny thought about the scenes she had watched while, for once, no one watched her. She envied the nun and the baton twirler, thinking how fine it must be to be part of an audience, watching but not watched.

A low red car pulled up and stopped. "There you are, Fanny," said Arnold, climbing out of the driver's seat of the convertible. "I've been on almost every street in this damned town looking for you."

"Who's that in the back seat?" she asked him, not moving.

"Keith. He's been helping me look for you."

Who is Keith, Franny wondered. *A poet? an agent?* Some friend of Arnie's from New York she didn't know anything about?

Arnold took her arm and helped her up. "Come on. Get in. We'll go home and have some supper." His tone was soft, as if he were persuading a child.

"What time is it?"

"Almost nine."

Franny fell heavily into the front seat. Keith said, "Hello, Mrs. Franklin." Franny did not answer or look at him.

The silence in the car was weighty. Arnold drove, gripping the wheel, sitting forward grimly. Franny put her head back against the blood-red upholstery and closed her eyes.

"Let me off at the next corner," said Keith. "My car's in Janet Faith's driveway up the street. Only a step."

"Okay," said Arnie, turning the wheel with that odd, badly coordinated jerk he used for all his bodily motions, as if he were bolted together at the joints. "Call me tomorrow. My heartfelt thanks for your company."

"Nothing. Nothing at all." Keith climbed out of the back seat and then turned back to the rear window. "I hope to see you again."

Franny said nothing. Arnie said, "Night, Keith." As they drove away from the curb, Arnie glanced back at Franny. She was awake, pulling a lock of her hair through her clenched teeth.

"Stop that, can't you? Why do you always do that? You know I hate it."

She stopped. "I know you do. Maybe that's why I do it."

"What's that supposed to mean? Fanny, tell me: Are you on something? Why didn't you go to work?"

She said nothing. Once again her meager supply of words had given out. She thought she might just have enough energy left to get out of the car and get to the bathroom—her need for that was suddenly intense—but nothing much more. But she knew she was out of any words to say to Arnie—or this Keith.

Her eyes fixed on the strange play of lights on the windshield, she saw Arnie's profile out of the edge of her left eye. His face, to her sight, was full of holes, one at his cheek where a pad of flesh ought to be, and another directly under his eye, a shadowy pit. The bones underneath showed in his face, at his forehead where his hair barely covered his skull, light, fluffy graying hair, about to give out. She remembered the number of times she'd looked at his face and thought that his bones were his brains and so she was able to see his brains when she looked at his head. She believed it hurt him to think: *the way the bones showed. Thinking pushed a face and head into shapes like this so you could tell it was going on there, from the outside.* She thought his skull seemed to be made of the same hard, useful stuff as his horn-rimmed glasses.

Franny put her head back and closed her eyes. Under her lids she saw, or dreamed she saw, a long window, lit from behind with Klieg lights, and silhouetted in it, a black-robed woman. Only her head appeared odd. From under the tight black wimple, crinkled yellow hair sprang out at all angles. In her hands she held a silver baton. Franny watched the nun raise and lower the baton in slow, funereal rhythm up and down, up and down. The pleasure of recognition made Franny smile in her sleep.

By the time the car came down through the Hills and pulled into their driveway, Franny was profoundly asleep. Arnie carried her to the house and put her down on the curved sectional couch. She curled up to fit its contour, a ball of golden hair, a pure, adolescent profile and exhausted woman's body, her breasts freed, pouring out of her jacket as if they had been spilled from a pitcher. Dead to the world, she moved forward gratefully from the crinkle-haired, baton-twirling nun into a depthless black night, lit occasionally by a flash, on and off, of an electric cross. Arnold stood looking at her for a moment. Then he covered her with the white trenchcoat he picked up from the floor behind the couch, turned out all the lights, and went to their bedroom.

Later, she dreams about an avalanche of blood. *There's just so much moving blood you can stand.* She sees in the dream that being alive is bloodless. It is a secret, hidden in veins deep under the skin. When you're well, a small burst of it might show, like a bruise, but in a hurt place the blood sits, it doesn't move. It's held in a container of creamy flesh. *That much,* she thinks in her dream, *I can stand.*

But blood showing is death, her life spilling out onto the bed after Jerryboy, life running out of her every month so that when it's over there is less life to count on. She dreams about swallowing the medicine Charlene gave her to make her period come, and then the wire hanger and the blood everywhere. She dreams about being the nun or the baton-twirler with blood spurting out of the ball end of the baton and out of the circle at the end of the cord. Less and less of her all the time, less to act and breathe with, to smile up at men and to appear in public with. Less life with every lost drop.

She dreams she is in New York at the acting school and Patrick and Mollie and Arnie are standing together in a tight little group in a corner of the room looking at her and telling her about a terrible mistake she has just made, like turning the wrong way on the stage, her back to the audience. She hears loud laughter from the darkness just beyond and realizes all at once that there is a right and a wrong way to turn on stage. She grows deadly pale because she knows they are right. She begins to cry. Arnie explains to Patrick that there is no blood under her make-up.

She sits down on a floor—is it a stage?—seeing questions in the faces around her. Or is she asking those questions before she saw them in their tight little group in the corner? What is she doing here on this floor? Why is she so sure she will fail at whatever they might ask her to do?

Suddenly she woke, drenched in sweat. She sat up, gripping the trenchcoat in her wet hands against her chest, remembering little of her dreams. She didn't know where she was, why it was so dark, why the lighted cross, all that remained of what she thought had been her dream, had gone out.

6

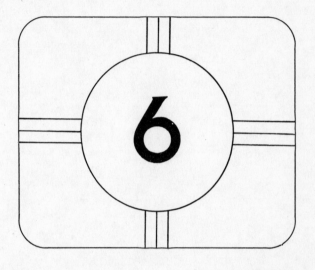

The Parish Visitor

It was Thursday, almost the end of a long week of shooting. Franny had worked four days without interruption. Thursday evening Reuben told her: "The rushes look good, Franny. Want to see them?"

She said no, and went home late and was sick on Friday. Arnie was in New York seeing his agent or someone, she wasn't sure who, so she was alone in the house except for Olivia at the other end. She lay on the couch thinking she'd be alone unless she called someone and said she was lonely and alone and would they come over. Through her head ran the old words and the scene: *Red rover red rover the little boys used to say and then tear across the road and knock me down and my vaccination scab bled all over my leg let Roger come over, they'd all shout.*

But she called no one. *It was Saturday when everybody makes plans,* she thought, *to be with their families or girl friends, or someone.* Saturday was always a long day for her when she wasn't on location or working at the lot. The night, when Arnie was away, was always worse. She walked through the endless house until she found Olivia and told her she could go see her husband who got off at four from the hotel where he worked. Olivia said: "What about your dinner?"

Franny said she didn't need her, she'd make out fine, she'd find something in the refrigerator. Olivia didn't seem to want to go.

"You be all right by yourself, honey?"

"Oh, sure."

"What you do here by yourself?"

"Take a nap, Olivia. Don't worry."

Olivia shook her head. But as it approached three thirty she packed up a supper for her husband and herself, and left. Franny took a pill and lay down on the couch. Nothing happened. She thought maybe another pill would do it. She wanted to sleep through tonight, through Sunday, through that night. After she took it she thought she heard the bell ring. It rang again. Lou, she thought, or maybe even Reuben, who sometimes came by after she'd been sick a day. Or Janet Faith, who had lived next door to Franny when she first came to Hollywood. *It might even be that bastard Brock,* she thought grimly, *who sometimes feels sorry for his behavior on the set* and *says so at the end of a hard week, or maybe Dolores who worries about me a lot.*

She went to the door, unbolted and unlocked it, and opened it to a short woman all in black except for a white fringe around her face, a cross hanging on her chest, and steel-rimmed glasses so thick Franny couldn't make out her eyes through them. *A nun, for god's sake. Is she following me from the school?*

"Are you sure you have the right place?" she asked.

"Yes, miss. I'm Sister Inez, a Parish Visitor. I'm taking the Catholic census of this neighborhood. Are you a Catholic?"

"God, no," Franny said. "Why?"

The Sister wrote something down on a paper she had stuck on a clipboard, and started to walk away. Franny (later she never knew why) suddenly said: "Will you, uh, would you like to come in?"

The Sister stopped, turned around, looked at Franny through glasses like the ends of binoculars, and hesitated. Then she said: "All right. If you want me to."

Franny led her into the parlor.

The Sister's black, floor-length clothing looked odd

against all the white in the parlor. She took off a large, black shawl and folded it carefully over her arm.

Franny said: "Please sit down."

She did, on one of the hard white chairs under the window. She perched on the edge of it and watched warily as Franny stretched out on the couch. The silence grew heavy.

Then the Parish Visitor said: "Is there something I can do for you, miss?"

Franny couldn't think of anything to say, but she wanted to say something so that the Parish Visitor would stay, sitting there on the edge of the chair in the white parlor, like a blackbird in snow.

"Are you the one from the school downtown?" she asked politely, like a little girl making conversation to a grownup.

The Sister looked confused. "No. I don't think so. But the Motherhouse for Parish Visitors is not too far from here."

Franny began to feel the effect of the two Seconals. She said apologetically to the Sister: "I'm a little tired. I hate to go to sleep when I'm alone."

The Sister nodded, as though to indicate that she understood this phenomenon. "Do you want me to stay with you until you fall asleep, miss?"

"Oh yes, I do. Thank you very much." Franny went to the bar at the far end of the room and poured herself a glass of grape juice with gin in it. She took another Seconal from a bottle she kept under the lip of the white bartop, and then stretched out again on the couch. She closed her eyes, waiting for the dark-red film to come over her eyes, *like grape juice, like blood, after I have enough gin and pills, the slow coming on of sleep, not black, not yet, only red and then purple. . . .*

But the black did not come. Franny opened her eyes. The Parish Visitor was sitting there, still bolt upright, her eyes closed, a string of black beads in her hands. She seemed to be talking to herself.

Franny's voice trembled. "What are you *saying?*"

"I'm praying."

"For *me?*" Franny asked in a shocked voice.

"What?"

"Are you saying prayers for me?"

"For the whole world, miss. *In saeculi saeculorum.* For us all. For you too."

Franny shut her eyes. Sleep was just beyond her, across a blood-red chasm she could see with her eyes closed. She thought: *one more pill and some grape-juice gin will do the trick, take me across.* One more pill and it wouldn't matter that Arnie was in New York talking to people who would know how to answer him. She remembered that when that happened his eyes didn't look empty, the way they looked behind his glasses when he looked at her, seeing nothing in her, judging her the way her mother used to do when she looked at her.

Franny went to the bar, and then lay down on the couch. She woke to find the Parish Visitor standing over her, holding her wrist. Franny saw she was wearing a thick plain silver wedding ring. A *nun?* she wondered and then she felt herself falling asleep again. Dark-red blood filled the pits around her eyeballs, and leaked out of the holes of her ears. . . .

The Sister was shaking Franny, pushing at her face, slapping her. Franny muttered in her sleep: "What's a Parish Visitor?" and the Sister said, "Your eyes look strange, miss."

Franny said, "I'm fine. I need to sleep." The Sister pinched Franny's cheeks gently, trying to keep her awake.

"The wedding ring," said Franny flatly, although she had meant to ask a question. She lay still, her eyes shut.

The Sister said: "Bride of Christ, miss. Please sit up and stay awake. Have you taken something?"

"Not a thing," mumbled Franny. "Tired."

"At six o'clock in the evening? You look strange."

"Say the prayers. I'll just sleep a little."

The Parish Visitor turned the beads around in her hand, praying in a low voice.

"Pay for us now and Indy whirl to comb," Franny thought the Parish Visitor said. She felt herself being covered with something, and before she could ask what the words meant she was asleep.

For the rest of the evening, the Parish Visitor sat on the edge of the couch, letting Franny sleep a little and then slapping her awake. She said the rosary twice and then read from a small black book she had taken from her pocket.

At ten, she stood up, putting the rosary and the prayer book into her pocket and throwing the shawl around her shoulders. She said: "I must go, miss. They'll worry about me at the convent where I stay."

Franny heard her, dimly, but could not summon up enough energy to respond, and then fell back into a deep, dreamless sleep.

At midnight she woke to find Olivia there, her brown face having faded into place over the Parish Visitor's white-bread face. Franny said nothing to her about the nun, never told anyone (except Mary Maguire much later) about her coming that night, and was not sure, sometimes, that she had been there at all. But she believed that the Sister, sitting there and praying for her and for all the world with those blind eyes and black beads and the silver Bride-of-Christ wedding ring, had pulled her from the red-running stream of death and nothingness into some saving place. She thought her rescue may have depended on the incantation the Parish Visitor kept saying. She was always to remember her as a person who had words, like Arnie, and she believed that the magic of the words had saved her. Her regret was that the Parish Visitor had gone off to the Motherhouse without telling her what they were, what they meant. She had lost her chance for salvation.

7

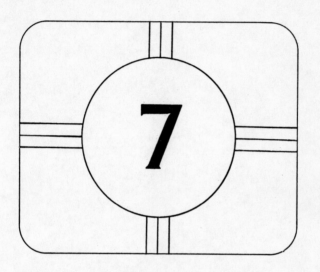

The Missing Person

Two weeks later Franny did not appear on the set for an early-morning call. Reuben waited a day, and then called her house. Olivia said she had not seen Miss Franny in two days. Did she go to New York? She didn't think so. She didn't take any clothes from the house. She hadn't even seen her leave. But Mr. Franklin was due home tomorrow from New York and when he got in she'd have him call. . . .

Arnold Franklin sat in the living room of his wife's house and stared out through the French doors at the banjo-shaped swimming pool. The former owner was a Western cowboy-star who had died of lung cancer in this house. Fanny had bought the house from his estate, and had left everything, furnishings and curiosities, exactly as they were. The swimming pool filled itself from a mound of rocks over which the water cascaded. Now the falls were not running, having ceased when the pool was half full. In the moonlight the whole structure looked to Arnold like an unfinished construction site, black rain water standing in its muddy pit, like the ones he used to see in Brooklyn when he peered through the boards that surrounded an excavation.

The whole house was like this, full of the evidence of elaborate plans which had fallen slowly into shabbiness. A bar with concealed panels opening electrically had suffered a short circuit and now stood, invalided, frozen into a half-shut position. The bar's surface was covered with glasses, bottles, cocktail shakers, and grape juice bottles, mute witness to electrical failure and the triumph of necessity over order.

Most of the upholstered furniture, originally of some delicate white material, was spotted and worn. Marks of the backsides of two generations of motion-picture people were pressed into every chair and sofa cushion. During a party celebrated later in the gossip columns, a glass door of the living room had been struck with a BB shell at eye level: rays of infinitesimal lines, like an imprisoned spider, radiated from the point of contact. Beyond it was the hole of entry, intact: that bullet had proceeded through the door and struck a well-known cowboy star in the left buttock. He had sued the owner of the house, charging his career on horseback had been threatened, and suggesting professional jealousy.

Arnold hoisted himself out of his chair, put his glass down amid the graveyard of drinking paraphernalia on the bar, and went to the bathroom. The plumbing in the larger bathrooms of the house was almost useless. Arnold's own bathroom had a marble tub that filled from a miniature waterfall spurting out of an eroding fake-stone wall, allowing only a trickle of water into the tub and requiring two hours to fill, and a toilet that did not flush. So he had fallen into the habit of using a bathroom in the maids' quarters, the only one in the house that straightforwardly represented its intended function. It had a white-tiled floor, an uncabineted sink, a white tub on clawed, unclean feet, and a working toilet minus the gold-plated flush-handle designed to look like a banjo which adorned the other sluggish (or entirely ineffectual) toilets in the house.

Seated on the toilet in the maid's room, staring at the little octagonal white tiles on the floor, like the ones they used to have in the family bathroom in Brooklyn, Arnold thinks grimly that for the first time all day he knows exactly where he is, maybe for the only time during all his recent Mardi Grasian, grandiose Hollywood nights and days. After a year and a half of life in this mansion he knows he has been defeated by the place. He had come because of Fanny, and because of Hollywood's extravagant promises of ego- and purse-enriching rewards. He now has arrived at the point where he knows what Hollywood and Fanny want of him: his presence, his approval, his appreciation. True, it has paid him well. But he has a disturbing sense of having failed it with his ingratitude. He feels less a beneficiary of this beautiful woman and this city than its captive, a prisoner of too much undigested money and excess possessions, and of the legend that is Franny Fuller, no, Fanny Marker.

So it is now and so it always will be, if I stay here, thought Arnold, walking back to the living room, sinking into his chair and looking out again at the vestigial waterfall. *I'm here, easily located. Fanny's great talent,* he thought, *despite that famous face and body, is for disappearance. I couldn't find her now if I tried. I am furious with her because I know her profound simplicity and still cannot fathom her intentions, her motives, her retreats and tentative, precarious, inexplicable advances. O my frightened shining undernourished symbolic beauty, come back. I have exhausted my energies running you down time and time again, you with your surface magnificence and your unplumbable, subterranean sickness.*

Reaching with his left arm over the top of the couch, he picked up the telephone which was on the end of a long, knotted cord. Inert, too weary to stand up, he put the phone on his knees and, putting his head back to gain some distance from the receiver, he asked the operator for Dempsey Butts's number in Prairie City, Iowa.

Arnold heard the operator give his name and place to someone in Prairie City. There was a long silence at the other end and then the operator broke in to report that Mr. Dempsey Butts was not at this number. Would Mr. Franklin speak to anyone else?

He asked to speak to the Reverend, who sounded polite but uninterested in his problem. "I don't know exactly where my son is tonight," said the Reverend Butts. "If you wait I can look up his last letter."

Arnold waited. The Reverend came back. "He is probably in Florida. He says he was going there for a few weeks. I'll give you the name of the hotel."

Arnold swallowed his pride. "You haven't had any word from . . . Miss Fuller, uh, asking for Mr. Butts or anything, have you?" He hesitated before Fanny's name because he could not think of one that he and the Reverend had in common.

"No, Mr. Franklin, I haven't. Why on earth would she call me?"

Arnold thanked him for his trouble and hung up without explaining about her disappearance. He had called Prairie City because, in other bad times, close to the end of her control, Fanny would talk of her time with Dempsey Butts. Her words were just those: "When I was with Demp," the way a child speaks of being with a governess, or with a grandmother on a vacation. Arnold felt no jealousy of Demp after hearing Fanny tell about their time together. As she spoke he had visions of a vast rural innocence, a bare, windswept prairie on which a boy and a girl, stick figures cartwheeling, somersaulting, wrestling, tumbling like puppies about each other, played on through sunlit days into moon-drenched nights. Dempsey Butts must have been Jack to her Jill, acolyte to her priestess. They had lost themselves, like fairy-tale characters, the athlete and the movie star, in the world's forest, protected only by their glowing faith, their handfuls of bread pellets, and their innocence of the evils of humanity.

Arnold thought of Dempsey as a well-coordinated Kaspar Hauser. Once his plan had been to supersede Dempsey's adolescent place with Fanny, to represent maturity to her, to serve her as guide and mentor, to evoke from her responses beyond the powers of her boyish first husband. He had never met Butts but his view of him, he felt sure, was accurate. Only in recent months had Arnold begun to lose faith in the feasibility of his plan.

The line to Florida was busy. It was half an hour before he could get through, and then he could tell by the blurred sound of Demp's voice that he had awakened him. As he asked his questions he prepared himself for the weight of Dempsey's concern, so that when the inevitable answer came—no, he had heard nothing at all from her—he knew what was going on in young Hansel's mind. He flooded Arnold with questions, Arnold turned them away, professing his complete ignorance of Fanny's motives. On the muffled edge of Dempsey's voice he could hear his doubts. He sounded like a man who had sold the family concern and cannot help questioning the capacity of the new owner to handle all the details of so complex a business.

"If I hear from her I'll call you, Mr. Franklin," said Dempsey, sounding deeply respectful but full of unnamable doubts. "I don't think I will, though. She wouldn't know where I was."

Arnold remembered that once before, the first month after their return to California, Fanny had thought of something she wanted and couldn't find. "Demp will know where it is," she said and insisted on tracking him on the telephone from one possible stop to another. He didn't have the energy to remind the quarterback of this occasion. The weariness in Dempsey's voice seemed to have traveled the long-distance line to him. He thanked him, told him he was sorry to have awakened him, and hung up. Only afterward did he become aware of Dempsey's last sentence, like a mechanical playback comprehended some time after it is spoken: "She'll be back, Mr. Franklin. Don't worry. And . . . take care."

Take care. Of whom? Fanny Marker? It's too late. She's beyond my care, friend quarterback, and beyond yours. Anyone's. I've got to take care of me, to get out or I will go down with her. In this mad airless space in which she lives, no one can find his way.

Now she is off again to some uncharted hermitage. None of us can find her, and who knows if she wants to be found?

For Demp, the night was shot. He shared a room with two vacationing teammates who were awakened by the sound of the telephone. Grumbling, and while he was still talking to Arnold Franklin, they went back to sleep. He decided his bed light would disturb them, so he crept out of the room, pulled on his slacks and sweatshirt in the bathroom, and, gently manipulating the door and the lock behind him, went down to the lobby.

It was deserted except for a night clerk behind the counter under the RESERVATIONS sign who was reading *True Stories*. Demp sat in a cube-shaped chair at the far end of the room, put his bare feet on a hassock, fixed his eyes on a distant chandelier shaped like a wagon wheel, and gave himself up to a daydream about Franny. There would be a long search by all the others, and then he would be the one to find her. Like the youngest son in the fairy tale, he would once again be granted her hand. . . .

The next morning, from the desk of the airline office in the hotel, he called Arnold Franklin to say he'd be in Los Angeles by noon.

Reuben went to the airport to meet Dempsey Butts at Arnold Franklin's request. The well-built, lithe football player was not hard to spot as he came down the steps from the plane. Walking toward him across the hot airfield, Reuben thought of Dempsey Butts in one role only, the former husband of the woman he loved hopelessly. He saw his own love for Franny Fuller as chivalric, nobly silent, adoring. In his mind Dempsey Butts and Franny, Arnold Franklin and Franny, assumed the postures of frozen statues, like those in circus tableaus. Franny stands, white and shining. Around her, the men kneel in the classic attitudes of religious art.

In his fantasy Reuben was never one of the kneeling men.

Instead he was ordering costumes or arranging lights to enhance her beauty or, oddly, holding her in his arms in the posture of a male pietà, a compassionate, grieving, solacing father to a suffering child, a faithful parent, after the surrogates had departed the scene, succoring her in her extremities of suspicion, self-distrust, and despair. His fantasy was never disturbed by the absurdity of its concept, or by her ignorance of his secret passion. She hardly knew he was there. In his daydream, a mode of extrasensory communication existed between them. When she needed him, she would know where to direct her summons, and he, mystically, would unerringly find her.

Reuben expected Butts to be full of eager energy for the search. He was surprised by his diffidence, his boyish uncertainty, his willingness to follow whatever directions were issued to him. His greeting of Reuben was reserved, and then he withdrew into himself as they drove to Fullerton. He was silent during the trip, allowing Reuben the private leisure for further elaboration of his fantasy.

Arnold was on the telephone in the living room when they arrived. Olivia showed them in. Arnold, a drink in one hand, walked about the enormous room talking animatedly to someone in New York, as it turned out. Privately, Reuben thought this was not the proper demeanor for an occasion of such gravity.

"Not before the weekend," Arnold was saying as they came in.

"Any news?" asked Reuben as Arnold circled back to the phone table and hung up.

"What? Oh no. That was about something else."

Reuben stared at Arnold Franklin, unable to believe that he could be concerned in any matter at this moment except the whereabouts of Franny. For six days he himself had been absorbed in the search. He had achieved a new, almost haloed vision of her. He acknowledged to himself now that he had never before been quite so happy, so single-mindedly in pursuit of an ideal, so knightly in his self-image. He was worried about her, certainly, but even more worried about finding her. To whom would she return when they found her? Not to him, surely. But in the interim, while they waited and searched, she was, somehow, his—partly his.

The three men pulled their chairs closer to the coffee table. Arnold refilled his own glass. Dempsey took a long squirt of seltzer water and some ice, a choice that made him seem still more boyish to the others. Reuben said he wanted nothing. Absurd as it seemed even to him, he had been eating and drinking very little this week, as if to preserve himself in a pure, ascetic state if he should be called upon to act. In his lovesick eyes, he, Dempsey Butts, and Arnold Franklin were now trysting Arthurians about to embark on a search for the Holy Grail . . . *oh crap*.

Dempsey listened carefully as Arnold Franklin "filled him in"—he had asked to be told all the details of Franny's disappearance and the places they had looked thus far. Arnold left out all reference to his personal disillusion and weariness with her. This omission succeeded only in raising, in Reuben's mind, doubts of Arnold's innocence in the matter.

Dempsey was not deceived. He had lived with Franny long enough to know that blame for her disappearance could not easily be assigned, especially not fastened on any man with whom she might live. As for Arnold, his deletions were part of the defense he was building, the shifting and reassignment of motives and blame, his preparations for ultimate departure. *Witness for the defense deponeth. . . .*

Arnold began a long narrative, full of dead ends, dumps explored, leads to nothing, as well as a minute history of previous escapes and disappearances.

"Ever since I married Fanny, I've been through this sort of thing, regularly," said Arnold. "Any suggestions, Demp?"

"About where she might be, do you mean, Mr. Franklin?" Dempsey almost said "sir," but stopped himself in time.

"Arnold, for god's sake, Dempsey." He sounded weary.

At this moment, Dempsey's respectful air seemed hard to bear. It made him feel old.

"Well, I remember a place in North Hollywood, I think it was, where . . . where she used to go when she was low. This was some time ago, of course." Dempsey's reticence had grown in proportion to Arnold's outpourings. He found he couldn't add "when I first met her."

"Maybe she's been there recently. She likes familiar places," he said.

Rubin was on his feet. Arnold stood up more slowly.

"Well, let's go," he said.

Dempsey was tired, disheartened by having had to listen to Arnold Franklin's story about his past with the woman he had loved.

Unexpectedly, even to himself, he said: "Do me a favor, Mr. Franklin."

"Sure, what?" Arnold was searching in a hall closet for a jacket, but he was aware of Dempsey Butts's low, strained-sounding sentence through the muddle of tweeds and furs.

"Don't keep calling her Fanny."

As they drove through the streets, it turned out that Dempsey had only a dim idea of where the place was. For a time he could not remember its name. Suddenly it came to him. He brought it out in a voice that rang with triumph, as if this memory might be a giant step toward finding her: "*Castellano's* it was called!"

Arnold drove Franny's red convertible up and down what seemed to him to be the same streets, without finding Castellano's. They had decided to give up when Dempsey saw a familiar corner.

"That's where it is, I think."

A large neon sign extended on a wire arm from the building front announced the name of the place: Pico's.

"Name's different, but I'm almost sure that's it."

Arnold parked the car. They crossed the street and entered Pico's in single file. Arnold and Reuben went to the bar which occupied the entire length of the place. It was shaped like a horseshoe, and the plastic top of each stool was a molded Western saddle. Arnold inspected a stool, bending over to look at the stirrups as though it were not possible to believe in their existence. Disgustedly he climbed into the saddle and ordered a Guiness Stout. Reuben refused to mount. He stood awkwardly beside Arnold. The bartender said they didn't have anything like that. Arnold settled for an anonymous brand of Mexican beer. Reuben asked for root beer.

Dempsey had paused at the door. He looked hard into the dark interior. Searching for the outlines of Castellano's, no, Pico's, he wondered: *Wasn't there another place called El Chico near here?* But the changes in the place disturbed him. Far in the back, where Franny had been that time, her head down in her beery sorrow, there were no tables. Instead, booths made of yellow plastic, decorated with purple Mexican figures sleeping under their sombreros, had been installed. Bright candle-shaped lanterns lit each booth. All the dimness of the old place was gone, there were no dark corners, everything was new, cheesy, overbright. *Franny would never come here,* he thought. *Franny would go to a place full of shadows.*

Dempsey came up to Arnold and Reuben at the bar. "She wouldn't be here. It's all new, all changed."

"Ask the bartender," said Arnold.

"No. He wouldn't know. He never saw her. It was a fellow at the back of the place who waited on her. He isn't here now, that I can see. There's no one back there."

"Well, ask anyway."

Dempsey said to the bartender, bringing out the words so slowly that he irritated Arnold: "Have you seen a girl, uh, a blond woman here recently . . . a . . . a very attractive blond woman . . . ?"

The bartender threw back his head and roared with laughter.

"I see a blond dame in here about every ten minutes these

days. What was she wearing? A flower in her teeth or somethin' that I'd remember?"

Dempsey turned to Arnold. "What was she wearing, Mr. Franklin?"

"How the hell would I know?"

They finished their drinks in silence. At the other end of the horseshoe bar a young couple, both dressed in white men's shirts, were holding hands in the bar, absorbed in each other. Dempsey watched them, thinking, *how nice.* Then he saw that both of them were men, one with very long hair and heavy lipstick, and the other with a Marine haircut and blue anchors tattooed on the back of his hand. The Marine, suddenly aware that Dempsey was looking at him, waved to him. Then his expression changed.

"Hey. I know you. You're Demp Butts, the football player."

Dempsey smiled at the grinning young man and then looked away. In a crisis of disgust Arnold climbed down out of the saddle-stool and threw some coins on the bar. Reuben pushed his glass from him.

The bartender stared at Dempsey. Then, his voice rough with awe, he said, "Dempsey Butts. *Really?"*

Dempsey said yes, shook the bartender's outstretched damp hand with the sincere, automatic single jerk of his wrist he always used on such occasions, and followed Arnold out of the door. Reuben hit the bar with his fist to get the bartender's hypnotized gaze away from the door.

"You would have recognized this woman," he said hoarsely. "She was very beautiful. Blue eyes, lovely, you know?" He could not bring himself to name her. His adjectives, inadequate as they were, must surely, he thought, evoke an image of Franny Fuller.

"I guess I would remember *her.* But I ain't seen anyone like *that.* No sirree. Sounds like some movie star."

Outside the three men stood close together *(a huddle,* thought Dempsey), trying to decide what to do next.

"There's a place called El Chico . . ." said Dempsey.

"That's this place," said Arnold, sounding annoyed.

"No, this is Pico's," said Reuben patiently. "What about El Chico? Where's that?"

Demp didn't know exactly, he said. Once again they climbed back into the convertible and started to drive slowly through the decrepit, endless city blocks, searching for a bar that, it finally seemed clear, no longer existed.

"From now on, you wait outside," said Arnold to Dempsey. "You create too much of a diversion. They don't listen to what we're asking about."

Arnold and Reuben went into a few places that might once have been El Chico, Dempsey thought. It netted them nothing except a repetition of the Pico experience, unbelieving laughter at their description of Franny, and hasty retreat. During the process Arnold was beginning to feel somewhat vague and loose-jointed from the beers he drank at each stop. Dempsey was growing depressed by the fruitlessness of the search. Reuben was still exalted.

In the fifth bar Arnold wanted to stop and settle there. Demp, who knew they were getting nowhere, was willing. Reuben was adamant: "No. If Mr. Butts says she knows this neighborhood, there's a chance someone around here may have seen her."

Dempsey admired the director's determination, but he was too tired after his flight and his sleepless night to go on.

"Try the Y," he said. "She once said to me that she stayed there when she went away. I remember that. Although I never knew whether she was making it up or not."

"Take the car, Reuben," said Arnold, throwing him the keys. "We'll wait here for you." He ordered two scotches without looking at Dempsey, who made no protest. He was ready for one.

Reuben picked the keys out of the air, aping the gesture of a skilled shortstop, and left. Dempsey and Arnold drank their scotches in silence. By the time the fourth round had arrived they had loosened up and begun to talk to each other, Arnold in the thick-tongued way he did when he had drunk a lot of alcohol, Dempsey with his usual exaggerated hesitancy in the presence of anyone whose intelligence awed him.

Absorbed and drunk, Arnold talked of himself and Fanny. Dempsey broke into his story:

"Why do you always want to call her that?"

Arnold reddened. "It's her real name, isn't it?"

Demp said: "Well yes, I suppose, but, well, not now. And she hated that name."

Arnold nodded and went on with his narrative. When he stopped, Dempsey spoke only of Franny and rarely mentioned himself. Both of them reminisced in low, funereal tones, as though they had come together at a wake.

Arnold: "Beautiful, god, so beautiful. And so stupid. Profoundly, exhaustingly, everlastingly stupid. Couldn't find her way to the end of a simple, declarative sentence. A mind like Swiss cheese."

Dempsey: "Yes, I guess so. But a lot of the time she seemed well, more distracted, by things inside herself that I couldn't know about, couldn't even guess about. So she didn't hear what was said or see much of what was going on around her. Maybe that's what made her seem stupid."

Arnold: "I started out knowing she was sick. But I was idealistic enough to think I could help cure her. Now I know there's no way. If I stay around in this ward I'll catch whatever she has. I've got to get out."

Dempsey: "Once she told me about a dream she had when she was a little girl. She was standing up in church somewhere, Utica, I guess it was, and she looked down and found she had no clothes on. I suppose lots of people dream things like that. Except it was queer. Franny said she felt glad, not embarrassed, that she had nothing on because she hated her junky hand-me-downs her mother made her wear and she knew even then that what she had underneath was really good, and now, standing there nude in church, everybody would know that, and she could feel good, it being all she had that was hers."

Arnold: "God, I must have heard every damn dream she ever had. She told them to me endlessly. I understood most of them. They were obvious. They fitted the whole picture, they were composed according to classic psychoanalytic patterns, fully intelligible and easily interpreted. But in spite of this, she eluded me. I suspect it was because actually she wasn't there at all, not even when she was telling me her dreams. There was nothing . . ."

Dempsey: "Something would come over her in public. Her face would . . . well, as she smiled and bent her head to the side. Like a magic cloak, something in stories, something that made her shine, put a glow around her. Everyone, even people who didn't know who she was at first, would turn to look at her."

Arnold: "Perhaps. It must have been a cloak like the one Medea sent to Creon's daughter. When she put it on, it consumed her in flames."

Dempsey: "I never heard about that. But I remember I was never unhappy about that glow of hers in public. When I think of it now I remember feeling *big* in it, bigger than usual, lit up by her. Sometimes now I'm ashamed that it was that way. That wasn't what you'd call a noble reason for being with her. I took from her, a lot of times."

Arnold: "Yeah. But gave it all back, I'll bet. In spades."

Dempsey: "I suppose. But that look, that glow, that thing that Franny was . . ."

Arnold: "No one could ever give her all she asked for. Not if every able-bodied man of draft age in the Western Hemisphere marched in platoon formation through her bedroom, his pack loaded with gin laced with grape juice . . ."

Dempsey: "And zwieback. Is she still on that kick?"

Arnold: "And zwieback. And the contents of the U.S. pharmacopoeia."

Dempsey: "I sometimes wish I'd tried . . ."

Arnold: "What?"

Dempsey: "To . . . talk to her more. I'm terrible at that.

When she said nothing, which was most of the time we were together, I'd say very little. Now I think maybe my silence scared her. Maybe she needed to be told over and over about my feelings for her, all the time, and I could never do that easily. Or do it at all, most of the time."

Arnold: "I'll tell you what she needed, chum. She needed you. Me. *All* of you. *All* of me. The whole boy. Nothing less."

Dempsey: "Maybe. Even so, I could have . . ."

Arnold: "Even so, chum, I never will . . ." They spoke at once.

They talked on. Arnold drank more, Demp nursed his drink without any desire to finish it. The bartender wiped glasses with the end of his spotted white apron and began to sweep behind the bar. They paid no attention to these signals. Caught up in their absorbing autobiographies, they never noticed the tense of their revelations and their reminiscences as they talked to themselves and to each other: In their talk, Fanny-Franny had been dead for years.

Assaulting the fiery hill to free the enchanted princess, Reuben Rubin thinks only in the future tense. He drives slowly through dark, deserted streets, parking the flashy car in front of one dingy, late-night bar or restaurant after another, climbing out wearily to talk to the bartender or the proprietor (Moriarity, Pete, Jack, Fats, Ollie, Papa), climbing back in and setting off again slowly. He fantasizes about the possibility that her inviting look might soon rest upon him, the same look he had directed her to give to that clod, Brock Currier. He luxuriates in the thought that he might be the one to find her, to witness the sudden unfolding of her unbearably lovely smile lighting the air between them as she realizes his love, puts her hand in his, fires his whole being with shocks so profound (because of that touch) that he thinks he will never again be immune to any slight motion of hers.

He is incensed at Dempsey Butts and Arnold Franklin: *O*

ye of little faith. To have had her, and let her go, and not to burn now, as he burns, to have her back, to allow themselves to be anesthetized against her pain by drink. . . . Reuben drives her car with great care as though it, too, were holy, or perhaps it is that there is something holy in the air within it. He is wrapped in his vision of her, he is Dante searching for Beatrice, Petrarch trying to find Laura. . . .

Then he remembers that Butts had said: "The Y."

Reuben asks a gas station attendant who is locking up his pumps where the Y is. He gets elaborate directions which, in his enchanted state, he forgets completely when he arrives at "the first light." He cannot remember whether he was told to go left or right there. Wandering in the direction he thinks he was sent, he comes upon the square yellow-brick building by accident, and feels elated at having found it. Only when he sees a handsome, well-groomed Negro in a brown straw hat come down the stairs and turn onto the street, walking with the jaunty, satisfied stride of someone who has just finished exercising, does he realize that this is the wrong Y.

The Negro stares briefly at him and then at the car as he passes. Reuben drops his eyes, ashamed of his grubby clothes in the presence of the immaculate Negro. Without energy to start the car again, Reuben sits, following the Negro's brisk steps as he runs to the corner and, in one nimble motion, leaps aboard a bus that has only half-stopped. The bus lumbers away down the avenue. Reuben reaches up to tighten his gray tie over the open button of his shirt, turns on the ignition, makes a slow U-turn on the empty street, and starts out on the last leg of his quest, to find the women's Y.

Franny Fuller had been missing for more than a week when Arnold Franklin gave up the search and went back to the East Coast. At the end he hadn't been looking too actively. His post had been home, maintaining telephone connection between the house and the searchers in various places in

Southern California. He felt military and efficient, like a central figure in an underground alarm center during a war, yet removed from the action: estranged, objective, impersonal.

Even this peripheral activity had exhausted him. He did no writing. There was little need to do anything on the film he was involved with: shooting had stopped for some retakes. Besides, there were those Two Competent Young Men. . . . He felt he had to leave.

What purpose does all this shoring up, he thought, *this sustaining of Fanny Marker of Utica, serve? Is there any chance that this* angst *she produces in all of us will enrich me, or will I end like a spendthrift wasting his capital? Will I wake some morning and find all my blood has been transfused into her? I believe I am worth saving. I am no longer sure she is, and if she is, that I can save her.*

Franklin's leaving California, if only for a few weeks, as he claimed, was taken by the other searchers as desertion. But he no longer cared. Suddenly he needed an injection of New York. He took the City of Los Angeles east to Chicago and, in the comfort of its lush parlor-car seats, worked on a draft of a new, long poem.

8

The Car

Ira Rorie worked for the State of California. A 4-F because of a childhood bout of rheumatic fever that left his heart uncertain, and because most of the whites with his education had been drafted and then commissioned, he settled into the kind of job Negroes rarely got: He was director of the Los Angeles Department of Mental Health, with "thirty people under me," as he described it. He had his own office, glassed in and square-shaped like a giant ice cube. All around him secretaries and clerks typed, filed, interviewed clients.

At five o'clock when he finished work, he took his brown straw hat down from the coat tree in the corner of his cube, locked the confidential right-hand drawer, and walked through the room full of white assistants, saying goodnight right and left as he went.

Employees made it a point to smile at him because they disliked him, the Negro director of them all, separated from them in his glass cubicle. He was the boss, and this was offensive to them. Ira Rorie was well aware of their dislike so, when the chance arose at the end of a day, he would pat one of them on the head as she bent to shove papers away in a lower drawer or reach for her purse from under her chair. He knew he shouldn't do this; but it was the only concession he made to the feeling about him he sensed in the outer office. This breach of office decorum and racial separation informed them that he knew. Because of their dislike he would outrage their sense of his place in the scheme of things.

Rorie was always the first to leave the office, another prerogative he assumed to himself. This night was Christmas Eve, but he ignored the holiday. It was five exactly when he went through the revolving doors of the building. He walked across the parking lot full of Fords and Chevys until he came to the gas station at the end of the street. In the office of the station he nodded to Alex, who pumped gas on the day shift, and picked up his car keys from a hook over the cash register.

Alex said: "Merry Christmas, sir," and Ira smiled pleasantly at the dark-skinned, elderly attendant.

Ira said: "And to you."

At the back of the service alley was a shack where he kept his car. Walking toward it from the station he always felt the same intense rush of pleasure. He was leaving the office, the daytime source of his strength as a man, and going to the other, his home.

His car, a black 1940 Cadillac, of the kind that is rented for a funeral to bear the principal mourners to the cemetery, jutted so far out of its garage that the door could not be closed over its mammoth bumper. He stood looking at its shining rear end and then, as he always did, gave it a tender pat on its left fender, walked slowly along the sleek flank and opened the driver's door. Settled into the seat he murmured, as he did every evening, "Hiya, Jeanette."

Ira Rorie had named the Cadillac for the movie soprano whom he greatly admired. On the screen she seemed to him slim and aristocratic, with a high, narrow nose and a grand, aloof look, a long, curving, horsy neck and the suggestion of inner warmth, like his car.

"Good ol' Jeanette," he said, sitting low in her on a wicker seat close to the pedals because his legs were short. Delaying to push the starter and pull out the choke, he reviewed all the appurtenances of the mahogany-paneled dashboard, some of them standard, others wired into place by himself. The additions were distinguished by their knobs, which were gold-plated and elegant; the anonymity of their function made them look like the gold trimmings on a bandsman's uniform, bright and gaudy.

"Ol' girl," he murmured, and pulled the ignition knob. Jeanette started with a low, even purr, making no protest, seeming to follow his instruction with pleasure, like a pliant girl being led in a waltz. *My girl,* he thought. He backed her out carefully, turned her in the narrow alley, and started out of Los Angeles through the flat, commonplace lower-middle-class houses. At a traffic light, as he approached the edge of the city and inched his way in the heavy traffic toward Beverly Hills, he took off his brown straw hat and pressed a button on the dashboard. From under it a small drawer moved out, almost at his hand. He took out a black cap and placed it on his head. With its visor of shiny plastic material, it made him look as he might well have been expected to look all the time, like a clean, well-appointed chauffeur on his way back from an errand for his employer. He put the brown straw hat into the drawer, pressed the button again, and watched with pleasure as it slid noiselessly back into its slot.

The long, smooth, black Cadillac, shining in the declining evening sun, left the city and moved into the suburbs, through flat, straight streets on which the houses, behind great front lawns, seemed to have retreated out of sight. Only the cultivated vegetation remained, as if it had taken possession of the area. In its victory all human life and its habitations had disappeared.

Just ahead the road divided. A lush green strip appeared in the wide lane, and the high hedges shielding the invisible homes ("Palatial Homes of the Hollywood Greats" was the way Mary Maguire described the section) moved even farther back from the two roads. Ira Rorie drove his Cadillac so slowly along the right-hand lane that it was almost silent, allowing it only a humming sound, like a soprano pitching her voice low under the high notes of a tenor.

The wheel was specially set into the floor at an angle that did not interfere with the series of small drawers he had built into the space under the dashboard. With a slight motion of his left hand he turned it. The car pulled to the curb, coming to rest comfortably against the green strip. Its motor seemed to settle down into a warm, easy silence. Ira Rorie took off his cap, put it back in the drawer on top of the straw one, and pushed the button to close the drawer.

It was now a little after six o'clock. He got out, unlocked the left rear door, and climbed into the back which no longer contained the conventional seat but instead, two heavy, plush-covered cushions facing each other. Seated on one, he pulled a lever. A table, thin and black, on two aluminum legs, rose from the floor. Ira set a sterno burner on the table, lit it, and then opened his icebox, a square container that fitted neatly beside one cushion. He brought out a covered pan of sliced chicken and boiled potatoes and put it on one burner, filled his coffee pot from a jug of water in the icebox, and put the pot on the other burner. He sliced and buttered two pieces of French bread which he took from a box at the side of the icebox. Reclining somewhat, he placed a small cushion behind his back. He drew the dark shades at the window behind his head and then at all the windows in his car, including the long one at the back. For this he used a metal bar that reached and hooked on to the holes at the bottom of the shades. In his intimate, secluded corner he ate his dinner and read the *Los Angeles Times* by the light of a battery-operated lantern. Hooked to the car's left wall, it sent its small, directed beam upon his paper.

Ira Rorie was home for the night. After dinner he disposed of his paper plate and cup in a chemical system he had installed in the capacious trunk of the car which he could approach from inside the car. He stored away his pot and utensils to be washed at the garage the next day, used the chemical toilet that retracted under one of the seats when not in use, washed his hands and face in a portable basin filled from a water container he stored under the front seat. Then he made his bed by pulling the two cushions together and spreading sheets and blankets over them, even taking the time to cover his back cushion with a pillow case. Fed, washed, toileted, curtained, and locked into Jeanette, he settled down to read in bed. Tonight he planned to study the text for a course in economics he took two nights a week at the Y, the evenings he wasn't studying or working out in the gym and then having a swim and a shower.

He had come upon this home very simply. Settled into his job in Los Angeles, prosperous and alone, he could still find no place to live except in the city's meager and squalid Negro areas. For a while he lived in a room there. But he hated the filth, the smell of defeat and transient hopelessness that emanated from the broken, disfigured floors and walls and the defective plumbing. He had noticed that, although the Negroes he knew lived in this way because they were not permitted entry into better neighborhoods, they often had elaborate, expensive cars—the only feasible way to enjoy what money they had for the short time they were in possession of it.

His problem was somewhat different; he could buy a car outright with the cash he had saved while living in his miserable room. So he walked about the city exploring the used-car lots until he found just what he wanted—a four-year-old Cadillac in good condition. He bought it on the spot, drove it to his rooming house in East Los Angeles, and spent three months outfitting it. When he was finished he paid his rent, thanked his landlady, packed his clothes, his cooking utensils, and bedding, and moved into the Cadillac.

He had solved his housing problem. The Cadillac—"ol' Jeanette, my pretty"—was unchallengeable, parked as she was each night on a different street in some fine suburb of Los Angeles, wonderfully adapted to her environment, raising no constabulary doubts. Sometimes, in good weather, he would drive thirty miles beyond the city, always being careful not to duplicate his resting place more than once or twice in six months, always choosing a secluded, quiet, aristocratic street, with a good tree for shade from the late-evening or early-morning sun. Shrouded by his dark shades, he would sleep serenely in the pure air and regulated quiet of Beverly Hills or Cold Water Canyon, wake in the morning in time to wash, shave, dress, make his bed, have breakfast, and then join the stream of prosperous-looking traffic making its way from the outlying bedroom areas to city offices.

He always remembered to wear his cap and, as he pulled into the shack behind the garage, he stowed it away in its drawer, locked the car, and left the keys on the hook for Alex, his "housekeeper," as he called him. Alex emptied the trash and the water, put ten pounds of ice into the box, refilled the water containers, dusted, vacuumed, did his dishes, and cleaned his toilet. Each week he took Ira's laundry to the nearby Chink, and picked it up and put it into the car. Ira knew Alex thought he was a nut but admired him and, for the regular stipend he was paid each week for his services, agreed not to discuss Ira Rorie's living arrangements with anyone.

For some time these arrangements served him well. True, he was lonely. At times the Y provided him with some companionship. But, despite their high-minded avowals, he distrusted the blank-faced, white, thin-lipped people that he played volleyball with or discussed The Racial Question or Economic Opportunities for the Underprivileged with. These topics were listed on the bulletin board as Youth Fellowship Activities. He liked the word Fellowship but profoundly distrusted the youth. At twenty-seven, frugal, ingenious and content, for the time being, with his lot as he had devised it, Ira Rorie, in his well-furnished, one-room Cadillac named Jeanette, saved his money, and waited for the time when he could drive her down one of the long aisles of cedars that lined the approaches to invisible mansions, park her in one of the three or four garages he was certain those places came equipped with, and spend the night in a ten-foot round bed in the master bedroom. Until then . . .

His comfortable, solitary existence was interrupted in the

winter of 1944. In the fall he had, with the true home-owner's passion, added a number of refinements to Jeanette. He had installed a radio, and a place in the dashboard into which he could plug it. This meant using his battery more than he liked, but since the winter had a number of cold nights, he consoled himself by using his heater at the same time. That cold Christmas Eve, warm and deep into an article on improvements in the design of typewriters in *Science and Mechanics,* he did not, at first, hear the thump against Jeanette's right front fender.

He thought he must have imagined it. Often at first, outside sounds, someone walking by or a passing car, would cause him to look out under the shade, but he soon learned the danger of such a practice. Once a car had slowed down, he thought, at the sight of a light in his car. Now he ignored the sound. A dog maybe—or a drunk servant stumbling home late. But then he heard it again, this time accompanied by a gasp. He could not resist the temptation to move over to the other side of his "living room," put out his reading light, and raise the shade.

Even then he would not have gone out (his caution was born of his knowledge that in the last year or so the local police had taken to patrolling these sections rather frequently) if he had not caught a gleam of yellow, a look, a tilt to the bulky figure, that for some reason made him think it was a woman.

He took his flashlight from its wall shelf and put on his lumberjacket. The nights were chilly and black in December. Outside he could see no one. Only when he walked around to the rear of Jeanette did he see her sitting on the curb behind the car.

Sick? he thought, then immediately, drunk?

No. She was sitting too still.

"Can I be of some assistance to you, miss?" he said in a whisper. His long nights of being alone had made him unaccustomed to the sound of his own voice. He always whispered to Jeanette, so he whispered to the girl on the curb.

"Oh yes. You can be of some assistance. I'm awfully tired—I'm not sure where this is." She, too, was whispering, he supposed in response to him.

"You mean you're lost?"

"No. Yes. Mostly tired."

Ira Rorie stood looking down at her for a few moments. She had yellow hair and a white face *(Christ!)* and heavy, bulky clothes that looked waterlogged in the dark.

"You look wet. Are you wet?"

"I fell in somebody's pool back there."

"How did you get through there? I thought everything was fenced off and padlocked and full of guards."

"I guess it is. I live back there."

"There?"

She waved her arm vaguely to her right and behind her. "Somewhere there."

White, he thought, *and,* from her voice and what he could make out from her pure profile, *beautiful. Blond, like the soprano, Jeanette.*

"What's your name, miss?" he asked, bending over a little and still whispering.

She did not look up to answer but went on staring at the gutter where two Juicy Fruit wrappers, side by side, nestled in a small pool of brown water.

"That depends," she said.

"On what?"

"On who is talking to me. I've got all sorts of names. And addresses. And clothes. And," she added, glancing at the Cadillac beside her, "three cars. But you can call me anything you like. It's bound to be all right."

"Would you care to come inside and dry off? It's cold out here." His whisper became even more tentative. *White. Wet. Beautiful, and young. Jail bait,* he thought. *San Quentin quail.*

She tried to get up and stumbled. One hand under each arm, he pulled her to her feet.

"Where are your shoes?"

She looked down and seemed to have noticed for the first time that she was barefoot.

"No idea. Maybe I lost them in the pool. It was a long walk. Where's your house?"

"Right beside you, miss. Just bend down and step in. Be my guest," he said, grinning. "What's mine is yours."

"This car?"

"This, miss, is not a car. This is an estate, a mansion, a noble edifice name of Jeanette, conceived in Dearborn, Michigan, it is true, but nurtured and cultivated and matured by the hand of her master, her lover, me. Within this great lady resides all that a man of my color needs to be warm, nourished, refreshed, and elevated into the pure air of the white upper classes."

The girl stared at him as he rolled this introduction off his tongue, his eyes shining in the light from the car as he opened the back door. Then she climbed in and sat down on the cushion nearest the door. He had to climb past her to reach the cushion opposite, but he was skilled at this, and managed to pull off his jacket as he did so. She started to struggle with hers.

"Hey, wait. Be careful you don't upset the lamp. Let me help."

Crouching, he moved to her side and helped her take off the soaking wet jacket and pants. Underneath she wore a nightgown. He held up the wet clothes.

"Where'd you get stuff like this? Are you married to a plumber?" Now he could see her face clearly, and it seemed to illuminate her corner of his "living room." In the kerosene lamp's weak, flickering light, her eyes glowed as if she had a high fever, her cheeks seemed on fire, her hair appeared to flame above her face. A real beauty, he thought, wondering who she was and where she belonged: surely not back "there" as she had said, dressed in these filthy clothes.

"No. I buy them. In a workman's supply store in Hollywood." She looked about at Jeanette's interior, touching the surfaces, smiling a little at all the evidences of Ira Rorie's ingenuity as he pointed out his arrangements for living: "This is where I . . ."

"And where do you pee?" she interrupted, as if she had

waited for this point in his catalogue of riches, and could wait no longer. "I haven't peed since noon, I think."

"I'll show you. He introduced her to the toilet stored away under the cushion and then stepped outside while she used it. On the dark street, he felt uneasy at this unaccustomed exposure of himself. Under ordinary conditions he never left Jeanette. He waited. When she did not call him in he began to worry. He knocked on the rear door.

"Come in," she said and laughed. "Be my guest."

He bent down and went in.

"You didn't tell me your name," she said. Watching him struggle with his heavy jacket, she reached over to help him. He was touched, and felt an odd, unaccustomed sympathy.

"Ira. Ira Rorie," he said. "I work for the State of California. And did you tell me yours?"

"No."

"Well? Tell me."

"Don't you know it?"

"No, why should I?"

"What do you think it is." It was not a playful question but a simple declarative statement.

He thought for a moment. "Beauty," he said.

"Like the horse?" She laughed. "That's right. How did you know?" Unable to think of anything to say to her question, he handed her a copy of *Popular Mechanics*. She leafed through it, and put it down. She leaned back against the upholstered side of the car, closed her eyes and fell into a daze, wondering about having a name, *the one your mother calls you because she can't think of any other name and she never wanted you at all by any name anyway. A name that dirty little boys call you and men like Jerryboy give you like Bubbles and then the names you think up for yourself like Laverne and Melinda and the name that Eddie gave me that stuck and Arnie won't ever use because he thinks I don't belong to it. In all these names,* she asked herself, *where am I?*

Ira Rorie moved the lamp to see the clock on the dashboard.

It was midnight. *White,* he thought. *And beautiful. Kee-rist!* He put the chemical toilet back in its container under the seat and sat down.

The girl seemed to be asleep. He shook her gently.

"Whenever you're ready I'll walk you home," he said.

She opened her eyes. "This is a great place you have here, Mr. Rorie. Like . . . like a cave or a bed with everything. I knew a woman in Utica once who had arthritis and couldn't move much. She had a potty built into the middle of her bed."

"Something like that, I guess. Are you ready to go?"

"You want me to go?"

"No . . . but you know, if anybody . . ." *White. Lord God.*

"Nobody sees *you* here, do they?"

"Well no, but you know. I'm black, like Jeanette, and the night. But you shine, like, all over the place. Someone will see you leaving."

"I won't leave, Mr. Rorie, if you let me stay. I don't have any place to go or anything, much, to do. My job, well, I don't like it . . ."

"Waitressing?"

"Something like that. And my husband, well, I'm a drag on him I think . . ."

Married, he thought. *White. Beautiful. The living end, right here.*

"You don't have to go . . ."

". . . So I left to get really tired so I could sleep and forget about Arnie and me and the part . . . the job, I mean."

"Who's Arnie?"

"My husband."

"Yes. Well, did you get really tired?"

"Oh yes, I'm tired now, Mr. Rorie."

"Just Ira is enough."

"Ira."

A week later, with officials at Premium Pictures, Arnold

Franklin, Lou Price, Dolores Jenkins, Olivia, Reuben Rubin, and Dempsey Butts looking for her, Franny was curled up in Jeanette in the shack at the back of the gas station. She read the magazines that Ira brought her each evening *(Popular Mechanics, Vanity Fair, Literary Digest)*, waiting, when she wasn't asleep, for the black man in his brown straw hat and his suit like an undertaker's. She was alone all day (Ira had instructed Alex not to clean the car until further notice) but not lonely, wrapped in the cocoon of Jeanette, like a voluminous fur coat, like a well-fitted-out tent. It was the first time since she had lived in the daze on her mother's bed that she felt safe, secure, and at home. She could talk to Ira Rorie. She did talk to him, during the long evenings they spent together:

"Makes me remember the time that I went with the 4-H girls for two weeks to a place on a lake near Utica. I wasn't in the 4-H, but my mother used to marcel the leader's hair and she told her about me and so they took me. I was twelve I think yes twelve and the scout leader whose name I remember was Scotty sat next to me on the train to Camp To-Pe-Kay because I didn't know the other girls and was scared of them. They talked and laughed together and had places they knew about that they'd all been. I thought they'd all been to the camp lots of times before but it turned out they hadn't, it just sounded that way to me. Well Scotty came over and sat beside me and told me about all the fun we'd have, the overnights and the cookouts and the campfire stew that we'd eat and I was really excited and glad to be going away from Mom and Frenchy Fry I think it was then and have some girls my own age to do things with. We got to the place and it wasn't much. We had tents with floors though and a big tent we called the rec tent and a fireplace outside where we ate weenies and sang songs at night. At the end of the fire at night we all held hands and sang about what good pals we were and how we'd be friends for evermore but I didn't feel I fit that place any better than I did the chesterfield in the front room at home. I couldn't play the games they knew and when we had to go down to the pond to swim I was so scared I would hide in the john so that I didn't have to go in the water. Once Scotty said I had to try it and near the edge I wet my pants. I could smell the pee through the wool tank suit, and I crouched down on the path and wouldn't go any farther.

"And I remember one night a real thin girl with teeth that came out so far they almost covered her bottom lip sat next to me at the campfire and we all lay back on the ground wrapped in blankets and watched the stars and she said you know it's *comfortable* here and I thought about it and it was right, it was one of the few times I can ever remember feeling comfortable anywhere. Warm, easy, with the stars there not so far, and not afraid, and this ugly girl talking to me and I wanted to reach over and touch her and tell her I loved her, buck teeth and all, I really did. But then Scotty got us all on our feet and I never said anything to the girl with the teeth or ever remember having that feeling again oh yes maybe once with Dempsey that first week . . ."

"Dempsey Butts, the football player?"

"Oh . . . yes," said Franny, whispering, realizing she had made a mistake. But Ira did not notice. In this rash of "telling" as the teacher used to call it in kindergarten, he had been waiting his turn. Butts the football player gave him a lead.

"I've always been interested in sports. Specially in a man named John A. Johnson. Ever hear of him?"

"A . . . football player?"

"No. Oh no. A fighter. A great man. The first black man to be champion of the world. Hear how that sounds? CHAMPION OF THE WORLD! Hear it? He was a heavyweight oh about two twenty I would guess and about six feet and a nobody. Just a real determined black guy. At that time around 1910 there was this white champion named James J. Jeffries, beloved of all the country, the papers said, and he'd been champion a lot and retired.

"On this day a great day the Glorious Fourth of July in

1910 he had come out of retirement, two years before, to fight this black man Jack Johnson who the papers said had a yellow streak. This Jim Jeffries was pure white and had a face that looked like it was cut out of stone, handsome and solid. He was thirty-five years old but then the black man with the ugly, bald bullet-head and the fat nose and lips was no chicken, thirty-two I think. So they set up this great fight on this great day in July nineteen hundred and ten. All the newspapers in the country sent reporters to cover that fight and so sure were they that the big white man would beat the scared yellow black man that one sportswriter from San Francisco sent back a report that said he *had* won and the *Record* put out an extra about it. JIM WINS OVER JOHNSON. But it wasn't so. It was just what they *hoped* would happen. Johnson waited until the fourth round and then right in front of all those watching white "World-Famous Gladiators" it says in the books, like Tom Sharkey and Tommy Burns and Bob Fitzsimmons and the greatest one, John L. Sullivan who was a real old guy by then, that black ugly plug who knew he would win that fight, went in and just about killed that pure white guy. I've read everything about that fight. Back in 1910 it was, and to my way of thinking it was the beginning of the end of the picture everyone had and liked of the Big White Hero beating up on the scared yellow-streak ugly black guy . . ."

"And I remember the noontime I had to go see the principal of the school because I hadn't been there in the afternoons for a long time. I'd been going to the movies. I'd get a guy in the office who liked me, I guess, to sign a pass slip and then I'd write my name on it and go out a side door. I'd go to see Pola Negri or Vilma Banky or someone like that. Once I got caught. The principal said I was a truant and could get into a lot of trouble if I went on doing that. I said, all right, I wouldn't do it anymore.

"Then the principal who was fat and wore glasses with no rims and had two pieces of left-over hair across the top of his head came around from behind the desk and put his hands on my shoulders and pushed down hard so that I felt as if I was going down right through the chair and the floor into the gym or something. 'No more truancy, hear?' he said to me.

"I was scared and said, 'Sure, Mr. O'Brien.'

"Then he leaned down and put his face in my hair and bit on it and pulled some out with his teeth. I pushed at him with my knees and he went back against the desk. He looked like he'd lost his breath, gasping like. I didn't care. I had this pain in my head where the hair had come out, and I kicked at his fat belly and he went *gug*, and then I left. I went out the front door on another made-up pass I'd been saving, to see a Ramon Novarro movie I think it was. I knew then there wasn't anything different about people who ran schools or ran anything. One minute they'd be saying official things. Then all of a sudden they'd change and they'd be down on your level doing strange things, secret things that you thought they would not think of, that you'd never thought of.

"So then I had no more trouble about truancy. I went any time I wanted to and got away from all that civics and guff and saw a new picture as soon as it changed twice a week and sometimes over again the next day twice. I would see Mr. O'Brien in the halls and he would look at me with those cow-eyes and stroke his two wet hairs down on his head and suck in his gut, but he never said anything to me again. I think he was scared of me then, the way people get who do something to you that they're ashamed of . . ."

"Oh yes, I remember once when I got stuck in the latrine at the Y. I tried to crawl out the bottom but I couldn't make it. It was cruddy on that floor, full of wet toilet paper and urine. I tried to climb over the top from the seat and I couldn't make that. Then I shouted and finally the director of the Y was passing by and heard me and came in and kept saying: 'All right, all right, young man, don't panic. I'll get you out in just a moment,' and I was quiet. He worked at the door with a wire. The door opened and he saw me. He said: 'You stupid nigger . . .' The director of the Young Men's Christian Association said that."

The talk between them went on in this way. For a week, in the evenings, they told each other about the wounds, the secret sores they had acquired growing up. They resurrected from the bottom of their memories whatever they had not been able to say to anyone before. In the process, prodded into revelation by the agonized force of each other's histories, they found themselves in wonder at their mutual, recollected pain.

"I didn't know I still thought about that," Ira Rorie said more than once. Franny Fuller, who now referred to herself as Beauty, listened, and when he had finished, like the run-on stories that children tell, one stopping and the other picking up the narrative, she would start. Night after night they went on, remembering aloud, listening to each other.

On the fourth night, when it grew very late, they made love. They approached the act as they had their talk. Each took his turn at a display of prowess, entrancing the other with his performance. Ira Rorie acted out of love and pity, feeling more and more deeply for his guest. Franny, who felt she had nothing but her ugly autobiography to give Ira, offered him her acquiescent self. She tendered him evidence of what had been done to her, her acquired experience, what she had been through, her education in the art by the men in upstate New York, by Dempsey, and Arnie.

She felt pleasure at the way Ira's brown skin glistened with sweat as he approached his moment, she enjoyed the roll of his tongue in the pink, avid cave of his mouth and, when it was over, the light sigh and the sleep of content into which he fell. To her it signified the successful execution of her woman's duty. So seldom in her life had she had a chance to know she had rendered good service. Feeling nothing of the curious excitement herself, this alone was enough to give her pleasure.

When he had finished and they lay together, she would

take his hand. Holding it tight, she went on with her unending memories, pouring out to him what she had always before refused to think about since it happened.

"I remember the time I was getting bathed by my mother. There never was very much water in the tub because she hated to use the hot water. She had to pay a lot for it, she said. The tub stood on paws, like claws maybe, not paws, like it was ready to creep around the bathroom if it wanted to. So I was never really sure when she put me in it if it would stand still. My mother liked to wash me hard because she said that was the only way to get clean. Then all the scaly dead skin would come off, the brown fuzz in your belly button and the scum behind your ears and between your toes and in your bottom. She washed me so hard that I hurt and cried. Besides, I think it was cold because we had no heat in the bathroom and so little hot water in that claw-footed scabby tub. When I cried she always got mad.

"But that night something else made her mad earlier, I don't remember what. Her temper was like one river going into another, so she was mad as hell by the time of the bath. I tried to climb out of the tub. She took my hair in one hand and held me tight so my ears ached and with the other she pushed me back and when I cried harder I remember, I'll always remember, she said:

"'I'll fix you. You behave and shut up or you'll go down the drain.'

"Down the drain in a tub, I thought, that will crawl away after I've gone down and I am gone with the scum and the tub will be gone so I can never get back. But not Mom and her ManBoy. They'll still be here.

"I was so scared when she finally let me out of the tub I got sick on the bathroom floor. And the ManBoy who was there then, I don't remember which one it was, laughed, oh yes, I remember now, he was some kind of Canadian, Frenchy Fry, my mother called him, he laughed in his funny broken voice that sounded like a crow cawing and said that all that was left for me to do now was shit on the floor and then he laughed louder and slapped my mother on the backside while she was mopping up my mess, and that made her madder. And I cried on and on.

"Now I hate the sound of water coming in and going out, even in the toilet. Arnie hated it when I didn't flush the toilet. Do you know, I've got to stand up and then stand back before I can flush the thing. And then when I do, I've got to get out of there fast or it all starts over again and I can hear her:

"'I'll fix you. You'll go down the drain with the scum.'"

One night after dinner Franny said: "Do you know about dubbing?"

"No, what is dubbing, Beauty?"

"For sixteen weeks I worked on a picture called *The Deafening Silence*. Ever hear of it?" For a moment that night Franny forgot that she had not told Ira about her occupation.

"No, never heard of it. Didn't know you worked in pictures."

"Well . . . well, this once I did. *The Deafening Silence* was a sweet name for that stinker because after we'd started it they made a lot of changes and wrote in a scene with me singing to this orphan boy that nobody in the story knew couldn't hear. Then they liked the way that bit came out so all through that tearjerker I was supposed to sing to him, and then later to some tramp friend of his who turned out to be the *hero* for god's sake, I forget how *that* happened. So well, after we'd been shooting a few days it was decided that my voice wasn't right for the songs or that I flatted too much or something. So they decided they would dub Janet Faith's voice in for mine. She's a girl at Premium who never makes pictures or at least you never see her in pictures but her voice can do anything. She sounds like people think *you* would sound if you were singing. Time comes for those scenes, and you get all dressed and made up and they do your hair, and they arrange the lighting on you, and then before they start shooting they brush you up again, and then Reuben calls for cameras and you make yourself go out there—and you *mouth* those words. Nothing, *nothing* comes out of you. They don't even let you sing the song while they're shooting so that it will seem right to you at the time because then, they say, the cords in your neck stand out too much or you breathe too hard or your gums and tongue show too much or some damn thing like that. The longer you do this, like those ventriloquists they had in vaudeville if the dummy is taken away from them, the worse it gets. Nothing comes out, you get to feel, because nothing is in there to come out. You could be dubbed by anyone who wants to speak through your mouth and you can't do anything to stop them. You know what it makes me think of? Of feeling awfully sick and leaning over and thinking now you're going to puke and nothing comes. *Nothing*. Nothing even to be sick with, nothing inside to come out. No voice, no song, everything gone. The deafening silence of Fanny Marker who lost her voice."

For the first time in all the nights of confession Ira Rorie felt confused.

"Who is Fanny Marker?"

Franny hesitated. Then she said: "Oh, I forgot. That's my name."

He wanted her to stay, he had begun to be used to sharing the space in Jeanette, he was over his first fears of her whiteness, and he loved making love to her. So the end of their time together, a matter of his irritation and her stubbornness, came as a blow to him. On the seventh day of her life in Jeanette, on the eve of the New Year, he got ready to go for his evening at the Y.

"Come on, Beauty. We need a bath. You and me both. To celebrate the New Year."

He had been to the Y two days before but Franny had said then that she was too tired to go with him.

"Come on. Your Y is right near the one I go to."

She said nothing.

He put his jacket on and, crouching, moved toward the door.

"Coming?"

"No, not this time."

He couldn't make her come. He left in a fury, slamming the door. He was angry because he had a passion for personal cleanliness (He'd been called a dirty nigger too many times and once had overheard two white boys in the locker room at the pool say that all niggers stank. "You can smell them come into the room," one of them said.) and could not bear the increasingly heavy effluvium in the car. He had relished its fresh, clean, newly painted odor, compounded of gasoline fumes and the camphor flakes he used in the crevices of the bed-seat cushions. But now he was conscious that the air in the car had become fetid. He blamed it on his unwashed companion.

When he came back at ten o'clock, exercised and scrubbed, shining with health, soap, and the natural gleam of his brown skin, she was gone. He made no effort to find her in the night. But he mourned her loss the more since all his anger had disappeared in the workout gym and the long walk back to the parking place where he had left Jeanette and Beauty. He had returned full of forgiveness. Long after her musty sour smell had left the car, and after he had discovered, from a magazine picture, who Beauty-Fanny Marker really was, he thought with longing of her occupation of Jeanette. He had loved that white girl, for all her lack of hygiene. He treasured the note she left under the lamp. It said:

> Dear Ira: I am moving on. I liked it very much in Jeanette. You were very good to me. It was kind of you to have me.

First she had signed it FANNY MARKER. Then she scratched that out and wrote BEAUTY. The note was folded. On the outside, in a flash of memory about someone else rare to her, she wrote:

> For JACK JOHNSON

9

Return

Alone, every evening like clockwork, Dolores had two whiskey sours before dinner. It took her almost as long to make the drinks as to drink them, but she enjoyed the process. It was a positive action against the inertia that inhabited her daily life. Since the extended absence of her mother she had been able to introduce a new order into her life. But systemization of things, while it satisfied something in her, intensified her loneliness. Another person's presence, which might disrupt the strict regimen one laid down for onself, she thought, made one feel irritated, it was true, but also alive.

Approaching thirty, Dolores Jenkins was a large-boned, intelligent, somewhat hearty, comradely kind of woman who chain-smoked, pulling hard upon the cigarette and inhaling as though she wanted to feel the smoke deep in her abdomen. Her features remained good, but became somewhat bolder; she had the kind of face that, as it took on flesh, looked overemphatic on the screen. Having surrendered all claim to a career in pictures, she became capable, efficient, pleasant, and a very good friend to those who knew her. She kept a list of their birthdays (and those of her nieces and nephews in Alabama) and anniversaries, and a reserve stack of appropriate cards to send. Composed by the poets at Hallmark, the sentiments were accurate records of her true feelings. She cared about the health, happiness, longevity, and marital bliss of everyone she knew, especially after she felt she had lost her own chances for some of these things.

Accustomed by now to the thought that marriage and success were not a possibility in her life, this evening she discovered that the remaining gifts of fortune would soon elude her. She had spent the long, rainy New Year's Day with Reuben, Louis Fleischer's secretary, and two studio people reviewing the places everyone had already looked for Franny Fuller. They made plans for tomorrow, the final day of searching in the more unlikely hideouts—good hotels and resorts. The search had been hampered by the necessary secrecy that had surrounded it, broken down yesterday when Mary Maguire had become curious about the long holdup on the Fuller-Currier picture and came to visit the lot.

"That snoop," said Charlene when she saw her and then, in an especially embittered mood, Charlene had given her the whole story. Clearly too good and too big to confine to her column, Mary had arranged with her editor for more space and then discovered her story on the front page with a big byline. The wire services picked it up and by now FF DISAPPEARS was on the front page of every paper in the country.

Dolores's morning had begun at seven when she reported, unnecessarily she was sure, for work, and did nothing. She spent the afternoon in strategy conference about the whereabouts of Franny and then, tired by the long and pointless day, she had come back to her apartment, to her two whiskey sours, while hot water ran into the tub. For her this was, like smoking, one of life's major delights. She sank into the steaming water, scented and softened by a bath oil she was fond of, with a sigh of pure pleasure.

Lying back in the water, and exploring her own flesh the way women do when they are alone and nude, Dolores discovered the lump in her remaining breast. After the first intense shock she found she was saying to herself: *Of course it is small, no bigger than a pea. I am fine otherwise. They will cut it away, a small white scar, that's all.* And then, like the second tremor of an earthquake, a lesser shock because one has already been warned by the first, she accustomed herself to the idea of the lump's fatality. Amazed at the rapidity of this accommodation she lay without moving in the bath, still savoring its warmth, the odors that rose around her. *Think about not thinking. Be the perfect stand-in if ever you were. Can I be the same now as I was before I found it? Am I on the way, this moment, to becoming a corpse? And have I already accepted it? Is my life on the thin edge when, just a few moments ago, it seemed assured, guaranteed?*

Dolores climbed out of the tub, watching her footing carefully, and then smiling at her concern. Drying and powdering herself with a kind of extraordinary compassion, she thought, she felt like a devoted mother caring for her mortally ill child. She chose a robe from her closet, the one Franny had given her. *Poor lost Franny and her presents. And now her poor doomed stand-in.* She put it on, feeling clean, warm, soft, and on this side of death again. *How was it possible that this well-being could be threatened by a pea of a lump? Impossible.*

Then, all at once, as she lit a cigarette she was flooded, almost overcome, by the immensity of a new realization: *not to be, not to be ever again, in the gulf of timeless time that stretches out, that I am allowed to conceive of, but will not be allowed to live to know. Cut off, not in the unimaginable future, but soon. Now. Dear God, I will not think of it now.*

Dolores stood in front of her window, looking down at the street, smelling the sweet, live odor of baking bread, her fist pushed into her mouth, her teeth clenched down on her knuckles, like a small boy holding back his screams. *I will not be dead. I will not be quiet and wait for it. I will scream and cry, everywhere, for everyone to hear. I won't stand still for this indignity to me. I will not allow the rest of the world to go on without me. I will be heard! Oh yes. Write a Letter to the Editor: I would like to protest, to take issue with, a lump in my . . ."*

The scream that came from her, in revolt against the

decree she had just received was heard by no one. Traffic passing on the street drowned her out. She thinks: *Perhaps I am not screaming at all, just acting a scream which will later be dubbed in, so that the real thing is lost or never existed.*

It was not a scream that sounded in her ears, but the telephone. It took a few seconds for her to realize this and to make the adjustment, to change the name of the sound from scream to phone ringing. When she reached the phone her heart was pounding with fright, *because of the noise? or has it been beating so furiously ever since the discovery of the pea?*

"Yes?"

"This is Franny."

"Franny? *Franny!* Where are you?"

There was a pause and then Dolores heard: "Can I come there?"

"Of course. But where are you?" This was the natural question of a weary searching-party participant who had covered every conceivable place in the past week. "Do you want me to come and meet you?"

"No. I'll come there." She hung up before Dolores could say anything more.

Dolores dressed rapidly in slacks and a peasant blouse, thinking selectively about each article of clothing she put on, using total absorption to hold off the possibility of relapse into the abyss. Scrupulously she chose the color of the shoes she would wear, entirely involved in the act of accumulating matching articles of clothing.

She put on the coffee pot, measuring four cups of water and four level tablespoons of coffee with the exactitude of a diabetic approaching his dinner. Then she thought she might straighten up the parlor a bit and, when this decision was made, she felt restored. In the simple acts of housekeeping she had, temporarily, lost her terror. The voice of the lost Franny Fuller had stilled the fearful pounding of blood in her ears. She found herself singing:

I'd like to get you
On a slow boat to China

singing the lines over and over as if they were the only lines she knew, or as if they contained some significance that only repetition could establish.

"Slow boat to China," she was singing when Franny rang the doorbell. Dolores almost pulled her through the door in her delight at seeing her. Once inside she hugged her, her cheek to Franny's, and found that her clothes were damp.

"Where in God's name have you been, Franny? Down a well?"

Franny laughed, her old, familiar, frank, charming child's laugh, instant and gay, so that the beguiling dimple shot into view, like a signal flag from a ship at sea hoisted to greet those on land.

"It's raining out."

"But before that . . . all this time?"

"In a car. A huge Cadillac with a john and a kerosene lamp and copies of *Literary Digest.*"

"By *yourself?*"

"No."

This was all she would say at first. They sat on the sofa and talked in the confidential way of the dressing room, Franny still in her damp work clothes which she did not want to take off.

Franny seemed interested in the saga of the search for her and paid attention to each detail, querying Dolores about who did *what:* "Did Demp really come from Florida?" She kicked off the slippers that Ira Rorie had lent her and revealed her dirty, sockless feet which she quickly drew up under her. Dolores ignored them, knowing better than to mention a bath to her. She offered her a cigarette. Franny said no thank you in her polite half-whisper. Dolores remembered too late that she did not smoke: for Franny cigarettes were too complex a pleasure, like driving a car. She could never manage the simultaneous possession of the pack, the matches, the ashtray, and all the little procedures of lighting, flicking, drawing, and blowing.

"Where was this car, Franny?"

"Everywhere."

Fantasy, thought Dolores. *She's not back yet.*

"I mean," Franny went on, "he parked it everywhere, a different place every night."

"He *who?"*

"A man. Very, very nice. Negro. The car was a Cadillac. Huge. Black too. And, oh yes, I forgot, named for Jeanette McDonald." Franny was speaking very earnestly now.

Off again. We won't work next week if she's like this.

But Franny seemed well in other respects, calm, interested, open. Dolores asked her if she was hungry and she said yes she was famished. They brought a snack to eat from the coffee table, a mixture of refrigerator findings so miscellaneous and ill-matched that it suited Franny perfectly. She ate a little of each thing: chocolate icebox cookies, maraschino cherries in their syrup, hot-dog relish, herring, and pickled beets in a tangle of raw onions. Franny elaborated on her story, giving details about the meals she and the black man had cooked in the car and the things they had kept in their icebox. Dolores, convinced that each new contribution to the fantasy of the Car dangerously established its reality for Franny, tried to change the subject. She moved boldly into an idea she had been thinking about for a long time.

"Do you know very much about psychiatrists, Franny?"

"Sure. Arnie has one. And Reuben."

"I have a friend—a stand-in for Delphine Lacy—whose father-in-law is one. He's a great fellow. If you would talk to him you might not . . . have these spells."

"Do you mean going off, Dolores? I *want* not to have them."

"And these . . . these dreams . . ."

"What dreams do you mean?"

"Oh, like the black car and all."

Franny stared at Dolores, her smile gone, her eyes almost blank with surprise. The room seemed to grow warm with her consternation.

"Oh Dolores, was that a dream? Oh *no*. Was it, do you mean, like . . . a daze? Was it *really* only a dream?"

Dolores, moved by the beautiful child's plea, lit another cigarette and thought: *And Fate's insult to me, the mortal outrage growing in my breast, is that a dream too?*

10

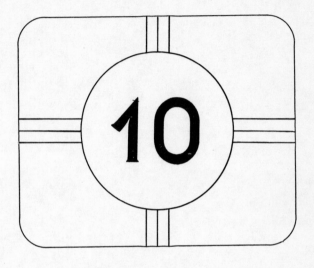

The Silent Star

The war had ended. Servicemen, too long exiled from their familiar and comfortable American world, cleared their footlockers and sea chests, discarding, with some regret, the glossy images pasted inside, photographs that had sustained them through long empty evenings. They returned, not to Betty Grable and Franny Fuller, but to their homely, more immediately gratifying wives and girlfriends.

Sugar, butter, and shoes reappeared in profusion in stores, minus the tag describing how many ration coupons were required for their purchase. Los Angeles was crowded with new cars, suddenly burst from the crop of Detroit factories like released prisoners. One saw their elated owners at the wheel, driving proudly into the suburbs. New things supplanted patriotism in the population. During the six years of the war, civilians had, secretly, felt unjustly deprived of the pride of purchase.

Hollywood welcomed back the drafted heroes, rewarding them with extravagant films starring the queens of Technicolor. Three theaters in the picture capital showed glittering extravaganzas with seductive names: *Cobra Woman, The Gayest Bachelor,* and *Diamond Horseshoe.* Their leading ladies were advertised to possess flaming passions and million-dollar legs. The restraint of the war years, in which curvaceous (a word Mary Maguire made current) stars were compacted into couturier-designed service uniforms, was over. Hollywood was in its proper business; the whole country was ready once more to relax into garish foolishness, the luscious world of colored glamour, the sounds of roaring, overpopulated musical spectacles.

Willis Lord had avoided all contact with the war. He smiled when his friend Delphine wrote to ask if he would like to celebrate the Japanese surrender together. His war had been fought, and lost, fifteen years before. This new, national victory meant little to him. But yes, certainly, he wrote to her, come at the usual time on Friday, the usual day. "We will celebrate together, whatever you wish," he said.

Delphine arrived with provisions for dinner, bags full of the meat and butter so long rationed to civilians. They talked in their customary vein, of their dead friends, their failed comrades from the old days, the few acquaintances who had died in airplane crashes on their way to entertain the troops, or in combat, the deterioration in the quality of movies since the coming of sound. Delphine did not mention that her recent picture had been nominated for an Academy Award and that the Studio had assured her just this morning that she was likely to be named best actress for her role in it. Exhausting her prepared list of suitably dolorous subjects, Delphine fell silent.

It was then that she thought of one other matter, the news of Franny Fuller's disappearance from Hollywood and her suspension by Premium Pictures. Delphine said that, of course, she knew only what she read in the papers. But she elaborated with some details she had overheard on the set, about poor Franny Fuller's failed marriage to a poet who had just won the Pulitzer Prize.

"Who, exactly," Willis asked, "is Franny Fuller?"

"A girl with little talent and a face and figure now very much admired," Delphine said. She filled her glass, thinking that if she drank more there would be less for Willis. "She is strange, makes a practice of disappearing so that she can't be found by the Studio. Her last picture had to be suspended entirely because it would have cost too much to reshoot with another star."

Willis smiled, his small, drunken smile that she recognized at once. "Do they know where she goes? Or why she disappears?" His questions were further evidence of his state; rarely did he ask for more details of her stories of doomed persons.

"If anyone does, I do not know about it."

"How old is Franny Fuller?"

"Quite young, I should think. Or at least, very young to *us*. She once sent me a fan letter. It said something childlike: 'I want to thank you for being such a wonderful actress.' Some small, sweet sentence like that. I was very touched."

"I would be too," said Lord. "My fan mail stopped some time ago." The glass of wine slipped through his fingers, landed against his almost full plate. Amber liquid flooded the creamed chicken.

"I *am* sorry. Careless of me. Perhaps I've had too much. I'll lie down for a bit," he said. "In the other room."

With exaggerated care Willis walked through the stuccoed arch that separated the kitchen from the living room. He sat down gingerly in the exact middle of the couch. Delphine followed him.

"Do that, my dear. Rest a bit while I straighten up. Then we'll talk some more. Although not too much more . . ."

She almost said, ". . . because I have an early call," but she stopped in time. It would not have mattered, she saw, as she pulled a mohair afghan over him. He was asleep, his hands folded on his chest in a touching gesture of drunken obedience or perhaps, she thought, of saintly resignation. She patted his bald spot and said to his sleeping head: "Goodnight, my Lord."

Delphine had sold her famous old mansion and now lived elegantly in a vast apartment at the top of the Laurel Grove Hotel on Santa Monica Boulevard, not far from the ocean. Her housekeeper was a discreet, elderly Finnish lady who also served as her masseuse. In her frugal French way, Delphine worked hard and saved rigorously, wasting little time or money on Hollywood's frenetic social life, taking vacations abroad between pictures abroad. She answered none of her fan mail herself, turning over all but her lightweight foreign letters to studio secretaries who sent out typed replies over her forged signature. Sometimes, to the more caloric correspondents, they enclosed a glossy photograph with her signature in a white replica on the black edge of her gown. She made no public appearances, posed for no advertisements, and would not be interviewed by magazine editors or presidents of her fan clubs.

She thought of her work, and the place in which she lived, as a long but temporary apprenticeship to the life she planned to live, when, in one stroke, she would put motion pictures behind her, leave the apartment, the lot, and the city, and go to Paris. In Hollywood she felt in hiding, not only from fans who were both men and women, but from the people who worked with her in pictures and from those executives who wanted to extend their authority into friendships with their women stars.

Paris was her spiritual home. The day after retakes on a picture were finished, she would pack and be gone on the City of Los Angeles to New York where she would sail aboard the *Ile de France*. On the high seas, she spent her time alone in her stateroom, reading, and eating lightly from the elegant and elaborate display of dishes the infatuated chef sent to her. It was a time of purification, a conscious shedding of artifice, publicity, hyperpyrexia, and the flagrant, exaggerated sexuality of the American screen, all of which she thoroughly despised.

By the time the ship had landed in Le Havre, Delphine Lacy, beloved of vast audiences in America and abroad, symbol to them of barely suppressed sexual passion and intelligent, radiant beauty, felt renewed, refreshed. She retrieved her luggage, had it stowed in the trunk of a limousine she had ordered in advance in New York, and settled back in its darkened interior for the drive to Sèvres, and her reunion with the enduring love of her mature life, the French aristocrat and couturier, Alicia Desroches.

Delphine had been abroad two months. Willis Lord's loneliness, even after the softening effects of gin, began to trouble him. He played out unending games of solitaire, setting up an elaborate three-personed population for his card table. The man at his left bought the pack for fifty-two dollars from him. The man across from him bet against the player. Then he proceeded into the game, hoping always that he would not be able to win, disheartened if success seemed imminent. To work it out inhibited his playing further games that morning, or afternoon, interfering with his assigned day's work which was striving to win at solitaire, betting, competing against "the house" or the ghostly occupants of his table. All the time he was turning up cards, peering down nearsightedly to see them, matching red to black, and shifting piles from one declining number to another, he hoped for failure. Almost always, he lost.

On one of his infrequent walks to the grocery store (the liquor store delivered what he required three times a week) he saw on the rack a magazine with a highly colored photograph of Franny Fuller on the cover. He stood staring at the smiling face. Then, in a rare gesture of extravagance, he paid twenty-five cents for the magazine, called *Silver Screen,* and took it home with him.

Most of that day he sat in his easy chair, staring alternately at an unfinished game of solitaire and at the face of Franny Fuller, at her white chiffon evening gown falling from her beautiful shoulders, at her incredibly narrow waist and luxuriant hips, all photographed in primary colors.

Toward evening he felt himself moving, out of the chair and toward the opposite wall where there was a movie camera on a tripod set up and directed at him, in his easy chair.

"Other profile," he said to himself, cranking the handle of the camera and peering into the eyepiece. He turned his face to the left, entering easily into his old habit of watching himself as he performed every small act of his days and nights, a saving voyeurism that gave him distance from his urge toward self-destruction. It kept him company. When he woke in the morning he turned in bed and smiled at the camera now moved to a corner of his bedroom, its tripartite legs spread out over his wicker hassock, behind it a knickered, capped cameraman who looked very much like him as a young man. In the silence of his first motions: getting out of bed, putting on his slippers, raising the shade at the window, moving into the bathroom, he could hear a director instructing him on the next step. The wonderful sound of direction over silent motion—the way in the old days the director would guide the actors without disturbing the progress of the quiet scene—spurred Willis into living through his day.

"Go to the kitchen now, slowly, don't rush it. Now over to the icebox, take out the eggs. With your right hand, so you don't interfere with the camera. The butter, then the eggs. Now turn to the left, smile a little at the prospect, walk, not so fast, not too fast, to the range."

Willis would act as he was instructed to, knowing that the camera was recording the grace and precision of his every move. This day, and every other day in his life, was being filmed, edited, the film spliced, pieced, canned, and shelved, for his eternity.

Silence had not come upon him gradually. So great was his anger at sound that he lost the desire to speak to anyone for a period after his retirement, as though to do so would betray the validity of his hatred of talkies. He had his telephone removed, and when the tubes in his Stromberg-Carlson burned out he never replaced them.

Once his voice was silenced he decided on further withdrawals. He found his nearsightedness increasing. Through a blur he saw the familiar objects on his nightstand, his kitchen table, his reading stands and desk. But he decided, perhaps because he felt the eye of the camera upon him, not to have glasses made. In his retreat, using the invested returns of his once-lavish salary (he had won the battle with

MGM over his canceled contract), the cameras grinding away and following him from room to room, Willis Lord resigned himself to living in the satisfying past, the edges of the distant landscape softened by gin, his circle of friends narrowed to Delphine.

But she was in Europe. He felt his loneliness even more keenly when he knew she was not in the city. The camera zoomed in upon him, too close, too constant. He heard the director's commanding voice, urging him out of his chair, but he had not drunk enough, or perhaps it was that he had drunk too much? to obey him. It was dusk. He told the cameraman he was going to take a walk, he scooped some change from the top of his bureau, put on his wide-brimmed felt hat and the brown officer's coat he had worn in *Their Marvelous Night,* and went to look for a street corner that contained a telephone booth. At the door to his house he turned and instructed the cameraman that he would be back shortly. "That's all for now," he said. The director raised his megaphone and shouted through it, "Cut!" The camera fell silent, and he was free to make his telephone call unobserved.

The four glass sides of the telephone booth opened him to the silent street. Yet, without the camera on him he felt quite safe. He lifted the directory to within a few inches of his face and found the name of an old acquaintance who, Delphine had informed him, had risen from assistant director on one of Willis's pictures to producer.

"Tony," Willis said when the ringing stopped and he could hear the receiver raised. "This is Willis Lord. Do you remember me?"

"One moment, sir," a voice said. "I will call Mr. Partridge."

Then he heard, "Willis! How wonderful! How are you? *Where* are you? What can I do for you?"

There was a silence. Willis could not remember, for a moment, why he had made the call.

"Are you still there, Willis?"

"Yes, I'm here. Do you by any chance . . . do you know of a new actress in Hollywood named Franny Fuller. Or perhaps it is *Frances* Fuller . . . ?"

"Sure thing. Who doesn't. Not so new, though. She's with Premium, or was, last I knew. She's had some trouble, I've heard."

"I'd like to have her telephone number."

"Yes. Sure thing. Wait up, I'll see if I have it here."

He heard her say she would come. She was indefinite about the time on Thursday, but she would be there. She would ask someone to drive her over. Of course she remembered him. She had seen and loved all his pictures.

Thursday he waited from nine thirty in the morning on. He fixed a little salad lunch. When she had not appeared by dinnertime, and after he had played out twenty-four games of solitaire without, happily, winning once, he converted the lunch into *hors d'oeuvres* for a dinner he had in mind to serve. By nine in the evening he was very drunk because he had eaten none of the food he had prepared, clinging to his superstition that she would come if only he left the spaghetti and garlic bread untouched.

At midnight he was still on the couch, groggy with gin, the camera recording the fact that he was seated erect and therefore in readiness to go to the door when the bell rang. Just after midnight he thought he heard someone at the door. He rose abruptly, upsetting his glass over the failed card game on the coffee table. But Franny Fuller was already in the room.

He stared at her, unable to say anything. She looked magnificent, dressed as she was in a long white chiffon dress, pleated about her bosom and falling off her magnificent shoulders, a wide, abandoned expanse of flesh and material. After he had greeted her: "How do you do, Miss Fuller," he went on staring at her. She seemed so familiar, as though he had seen her before, many times: that dress, that glowing yellow hair, that seductive, uplifted face. For the first time, since the day he had seen Delphine Lacy on the set of *Passion Flowers,* he felt a surge of warmth in his chest. He dug his hands into the pockets of his smoking jacket, realizing that the heat came from his groin, and hoping the swelling was well covered by the folds of his robe.

"Sit down, sit down, won't you? I'm so glad you could come." His tongue, tied to the top of his mouth for so long, had suddenly, like the member in his crotch, become freed. He could not stop babbling. "Over here, right here. This is a better chair."

He swept a jacket from the recliner to the floor and ushered her, holding her elbow as though it was in danger of breaking, onto it. He watched, fascinated, as she sank down, her body undulating to accommodate the tightness of her long draped dress. Every move of this beautiful girl was sumptuous. He was enchanted.

Franny Fuller looked at him, he thought, with pleasure. She said nothing, and he admired her silence, her way of suggesting interest without uttering a stream of stupidities to match his own. He offered her a drink. She shook her head. "Some food? I could heat it up in no time," he said. She waved her hand as though to indicate that she was fine, she wanted nothing.

He sat beside her on the hassock, almost at her chiffon-swathed knees and then, for no reason he was ever after able to understand, he began to pour out to her, for hours it seemed to him, all the frustrations and resentments of his life since his fame had deserted him. She listened gravely, shaking her head often, as if to let him know she understood the agony of his present existence as well as the glories of his past. Now and then she smiled, telling him, he thought, that she recognized the tragic truth of his statements but making no attempts at interpretation. He moved back to the couch and went on talking:

"You thought I was dead, did you say, when I called?

That's what I thought you said." With a sideward motion of her head she seemed to be denying it. "Yes, I know I heard you: 'Willis Lord? I thought he was dead.'

"Well, he, that is, I, am not dead, although sometimes it seems so, even to me. I have been at it a long time, dying that is. I have a long jump on the embalming process, my doctor tells me." He laughed as he told her about the hardening of his liver the doctor had referred to, waving his empty glass at Franny Fuller to show her what he meant. She smiled at him.

He could not stop. "You may think I am talkative but I am not usually. I swallow words or else I bury them. Dampen and put out sounds. I live in a soundless well most of the time. No, not a well, because I hear no echoes. My residence is a hollow set, all front, no rooms or closets or plumbing, just doors that open onto space. There is no content to my words, to myself, for that matter.

"Would you care to play a game of gin? Double solitaire, perhaps?" When she said nothing but continued to smile gently at him, he swept the damp cards from the coffee table onto the floor, and went on:

"Have you seen those coloring books in the drugstores, those paint books for children? Sonja Henie, Queen of the Ice, Coloring Book, and the Betty Grable Coloring Book? On every page is a new costume with the figure of the silent Star hovering behind it in black and white, waiting for the thick wax color of the crayon to be applied. I am the coloring-book hero of the twenties, in hard-and-fast black-and-white lines. I wait for some child-God to bestow Technicolor sound on me. But realize this, Miss Fuller, I did not *fade* to this state. I never lost color in my rage at Fate: I was always, like the Star in the book, in black-and-white. The way you see me now.

"The only difference is that ordinarily I am silent. I can't think what has come over me. It must be your beauty that has untied my tongue. . . ." She smiled as though to acknowledge his compliment, but he waved her smile aside: "Have you thought what the next step is, away from color, turned into black-and-white? Disappearance. Not being there at all. I am waiting patiently for that to happen. But my friend Delphine Lacy—you must know of her—tells me you have practiced this art. I have asked you here because I think we may be very much alike. Lost in the ruins of Hollywood lots, and needing . . ."

He did not finish. Overcome by his unaccustomed talkativeness and the gin, his eyes closed and his head fell to his shoulder. He was in a deep, unhearing sleep, enveloped in the familiar blackness of his drunken nightly despair, and did not know whether she left at once or stayed on watching him as he slept. He never heard the door, and when he awoke the next morning, cold, stiff and very thirsty, she was not there. The room smelled of spilled wine and garlic. Beside the recliner was a full glass of red wine he remembered pouring for her and his own empty one. Had she answered him, and did he not remember?

All day he tried to remember what she had said to him. He sat on the couch, sipping slowly at his glass of gin, looking at the seat he was sure she had occupied, seeing her there almost as clearly in the growing dusk of the living room as he had the night before. By midnight his eyes had closed, his head had fallen back against the couch. But his vision of her was still strong. Just before he slid into his nightly oblivion he thought: *She will come back, she will. . . . Now she has a place to escape to. . . .*

Willis Lord was to live two years longer. Even without the weekly visits of Delphine Lacy, who was killed in an automobile accident in France just before she was due to return to the United States from her three months' holiday, he was never again to be lonely. He had Franny Fuller often, on the chair opposite him. They talked at length or, more accurately, he talked and she listened to him, with her charming, soft smile directed at him. Knowing her aversion to being seen by strangers, he had ordered the camera in the corner to be still in her presence.

Edna-Mae, Dempsey Butts's second wife, said: "Did you know an actor named Willis Lord when you were in Hollywood?" She moved the *Des Moines Register* away from her face and looked at her husband.

Dempsey looked up from *Newsweek.* He was reading a piece about the Green Bay Packers. "No, I don't think so. Why?"

"Nothing. Only I see in Walter Winchell that he died."

"I got to know very few people there in those days."

Edna-Mae smiled coyly. "Just the beautiful ones, huh?" She was a sturdy blond woman from Ames whom he had known briefly in his college days and met again when he went back to coach for Iowa State.

Dempsey looked at her a moment. "Yes," he said. "Just one beautiful one."

The funeral director, a slender, white-haired man in a black suit and shined black shoes, shook hands with Billie-Jo Jenkins.

"Everything will be very nice, don't worry about anything, Mrs. Jenkins. We do our best for our customers."

Billie-Jo mumbled: "For the price, you should."

"What was that?"

"Nothing. Thank you." Her eyes filled with tears at the prospect of a pinched and lonely old age: *the money these people took from you in your sorrow.* She pulled on her white cotton gloves against the heat of the noonday street, set her lips firmly together, and left the funeral parlor. As she walked toward her apartment she said aloud to herself, her voice low and angry: "Robbers."

Mrs. Fanny Marker tried many times, without success, to contact her daughter after she realized who Franny Fuller was. Franny would not talk to her or respond to letters sent to the studio. Mrs. Fanny Marker settled for fame by association.

She took a copy of *Silver Screen* to her customer whose head was encased in a large metal bubble. Knowing she could not be heard over the electric din within it, she opened the magazine at an article headlined in bold black letters, IS FF IN LOVE AGAIN? and pointed to it. The customer under the dryer blinked her thanks.

Fanny had already read the story and was prepared to call it to the attention of captive readers in her shop. She had not seen or heard from her daughter in twenty-five years, but that was okay with her. She got much mileage out of the kid during manicures and while fastening white pin curls to the pink scalps of elderly women. In the stories to her customers her daughter was pure, beautiful, and devoted to her. "My dear husband died very young," she told them, "and I had to be both parents to her." The ladies loved the stories.

Arnold Franklin spent the early part of the spring evening at McGinty's on Second Avenue. Painted shamrocks lined the mirror over the bar and the convivial customers seemed to know each other. Arnold did not join in the joking, but listened and had a satisfying number of scotches and lemon, relishing his feeling of virtue at not eating dinner.

He walked home through the cool streets. He was not in the least sleepy. The smell of washed gutters and bus exhaust was as pleasant as McGinty's sawdust and beery air. He enjoyed the feel of the polished knob at his front door as he opened it, went in, and then bolted and locked it behind him.

He put on a lounging robe and stood at an open window, taking deep breaths of the acrid, beloved New York air. Ready at last to work, he sat at his desk, took a pad of yellow paper from the drawer, filled his fountain pen, and settled his velvet high-backed chair closer to the flat surface of the polished desk. At ease, comfortable, alone, he began to write:

He: deluded, drowning, barely able to make his escape. . . .
She: beautiful, lost. . . .

It was eleven in the morning. Mary Maguire had cleaned her desk and was about to start work on a new book. Putting off the difficult moment of the first sentence, she picked up the last sheets of old manuscript she was about to drop into her trash basket and read:

I remember seeing those shiny ads in magazines with the whole family in them, the boy in a white shirt and a home-knitted woolly sweater ready for school with his Mickey Mouse lunchbox and the girl with a bow in her hair and a white middy blouse and the mother in a gingham robe and her face full of healthy-looking make-up and a short neat brunette haircut and the father, like God the father, shaved and smiling and full of life insurance and his hair just cut ten minutes ago and his eyes shiny from a great night's sleep on a new firm mattress. You look at this family on shiny magazine paper sitting in their shiny yellow kitchen and out of the window in the background you can see a shiny green swing set for the little children and a plastic blue pool and they're all inside eating breakfast things like orange juice for the teeth and cream and eggs and strawberries or some such damn thing and this family looks *holy* and then you know they're the same family you see in other ads about praying in church on Sunday and you feel . . . out of it, like, out of the world, out of the race of people really because they must be the real ones. They're in all the magazines and a million people must recognize themselves in them.

How do I get into those pictures? Is real life like that?

Mary Maguire had not been able to use all this in *The Fabulous Franny Fuller*. Crumbling the page, she sat thinking of the Golden Girl who had put those foolish questions to her, wondering where she was now, how she was. She thought about others like her whose rise to stardom she had reported on, who were now somewhere beyond the limelight. Some had resisted aging until it was too late to grow old gracefully. Some had retired rich, grateful for their privacy and their unlimited acreage in Nevada. Some had traveled down into inevitable obscurity. She tried to recall all the descending trails, but she found herself coming back to the girl on the page in her hand.

Until that moment, and throughout the years of her successful column jammed with the best recorded gossip of her time, Mary Maguire had remained unmoved by her subject matter. Now, on this hot July noon in Hollywood, on the eve of the decade of the fifties in which the Capital of the Stars declined into a provincial city, she was stopped, overwhelmed by the realization of her long, hard passivity before the spectacle of human need. Her familial duties past, she had circled her journalistic subjects like a buzzard, watching them, writing about them, waiting for more, avid for the rest of the story. . . .

Tears gathered in her eyes and rolled down her face. *Have I cried since my mother's funeral?* she wondered. Now her profound sorrow astounded her. Tears flowed faster, her throat closed as though an interior flood had started at the back of her mouth. She put her head down, her ear against the bank of keys on her typewriter. Pity overcame her, she felt drowned in it, reducing her, for once, to the troubled, fearful, uncertain, and mourning creature of her columns.

After a few minutes she raised her head, wiped her face dry, pulled her chair to the table, rolled a blank sheet of paper into her typewriter and began to write:

> Honey Moon is a beautiful young starlet, returned from the obscurity that followed her brief ap-

> pearance as a child star. She has a thrilling voice, and the whole world is before her. She lives in a gorgeous home in Beverly Hills, a mansion that once belonged to Delphine Lacy. But it was not always this way for Honey. Quite the opposite.
>
> She was born in Peoria. Her mother . . .

A year later, realizing that at last she had lost patience with the disappearances and reappearances of Franny Fuller, and believing that her readers were bored by her unending and unexplained acts, Mary Maguire wrote her last item about FF:

> *This reporter gives up. Studio officials will say only that she has broken her contract. Her Ex is in New York, reportedly. At Premium no one knows anything about her whereabouts. So what else is new? Phone at the Dolores Jenkins (once her stand-in-friend) residence is no longer connected. Last night at Romanoff's I asked Brock Currier if he knew where FF was. He laughed and said: "Not me." Later spotted him at the bar with young and beautiful Honey Moon on his arm. . . .*

And Franny Fuller, she of many names for no person, she of mythic, yes, epic body and face, she who obsesses the nostalgic dreams of poets, athletes, and historians, who lives in the fantasies of old actors and young Arthurians, in the imaginations of painters and photographers, in the gossipy, yellowing files of newspaper morgues: What of her? What really became of her?

Let me tell you: She lingers in the umbra between celluloid eternity and the accident of mortality, caught and hung up like an escaping prisoner on the barbed wire of his enclosure. In her, the intimations of immortality are strong. She moves toward them, and then retreats, perched precariously on the swing of the unbearable present, and destined, like everyone else, for the final take on the shores of darkness.